BLACK MAGIC SERIES

BLOODSTONE'S JINX

MAHOGANY AND SAGE

Black Magic Series: Bloodstone's Jinx

© 2020 Mahogany and Sage

Published by Aces Destiny

CONTENT WARNING- THIS BOOK INCLUDES GRAPHIC SEXUAL DESCRIPTIONS AND LANGUAGE THAT SOME READERS MAY FIND DISTURBING. MAY NOT BE SUITABLE FOR YOUNG OR IMMATURE PERSONS. READER DISCRETION IS ADVISED.

To the 3 loves of my life: My Children. Just like in everything, I do it all for you. Y'all are my inspirations and reasons to go on another day.

-Mahogany

To my family, thank you for your love and patience. The creation of this work represents the adventures I have daily, and I'm honored to share this portion with you.

-Sage

A special THANK YOU to Bianca at B. Edits!

PROLOGUE

"IT WAS the 3rd of September.... That day I'll always remember..." played loudly in the backdrop as I rode down the old dirt road heading to our family's plot. It had been many years since I, Anika Howell, saw country dirt, large oak trees, and wild blackberries growing like weeds everywhere. It was fitting that *Papa Was A Rolling Stone* was on the radio. Almost like a sign. It was only September 1st and my daddy had died days before. I heard people say he was a rolling stone, but I couldn't have been sure. I hardly ever came home; this visit was well overdue. Everyone in the family car seemed to nod their head to the tune as the Temptations continued to sing, "mama I'm depending on you, to tell me the truth." I looked across at my mama, who wiped a single solitary tear from her eye. She had a look of relief mixed with the look of grief on her face, like mismatched socks and it scared me. I was more scared of the conversation she wanted to have with me after the services. I had knots in my stomach knowing it would be the same old speech about, coming home. I had no idea the magnitude this day would bring. As the song lingered on, the car slowly drove down the winding dirt road to daddy's final resting place. An eerie low sounding howl was heard in the distance and in that moment, it solidified what was to come.

Papa was a rolling stone
Wherever he laid his hat was his home
And when he died, all he left us was alone...

EBONY

"PEARL EARRINGS, check. Movado watch, check. Valentino heels and bag, check." Every day is the same for me. I absolutely cannot leave the house without looking perfect. Being one of three blacks and the only female attorney in our firm, it was imperative that I'm always on my A-game. However, the bags under my eyes gave away my secret. I hadn't had a decent night's sleep since my 35th birthday, 3 weeks ago. Every night, without fail, I had been having the strangest dreams. In the dreams, there are bright colors and beautiful landscapes. Some dreams are dark and smokey and of an evil presence. But they all end the same. Me, in the center of a circle of people crying, some laughing, some speaking in a language I'd never heard. And they all turn to me saying, "It's my time." Time for what, I have no idea. I talked to my therapist about it, and she chalked it up to me overworking myself and needing a break. *Really, Karen? Easy for your lily-white ass to say.* Ebony Gregory has no time for breaks and because she didn't seem to get it, I was reluctant to tell her that my dreams were spilling over into my waking hours.

Last week, when I was getting out of the tub, I swear there was someone right outside the door. I didn't see anyone, you know, but I felt them there. Cooking dinner earlier this week, after cutting up my cabbage, I turned to drop my Roger Wood sausage in the grease but when I turned back, my knife was gone. Last night, I was rolling my hair for bed and watching my little cousin's newest *Tik Tok* she sent doing the latest dance challenge online. In the background, there was a reflection in the mirror. I know I smoke a little weed here and there and love my nightly glass of Jameson, but I wasn't imagining what I saw. I played it over and over, just to make sure I wasn't losing my mind, but each time, there was her face looking back at me in the mirror. "Wheeewww," I said to myself, shaking it off. I needed to get to the office ASAP.

Today was the big day, the day I have been working so long and hard for. Today, before all the press and media of Atlanta, Georgia I will be named the 1st African American partner at Lieberman, Schwartz and Howard Law Firm. *This is it bitch.* I affirmed to myself. *You did it! Let's show LSH how much they need you and rock this press conference.* After I was satisfied with my look, I locked my front door and headed to the elevators of my high rise. I've been trying to beat him to the parking garage every day but some days like today, I'm not quick enough.

"Hello Ebony."

His deep baritone always made me mush inside.

"Hello Montel," I said pressing the button for the garage, not looking his way.

Montel was a detective with the Atlanta Police Department. Single, tall, handsome and made no qualms about how he felt about me. Yet, I would always find an excuse not to go out with him. I made the mistake of sleeping with him the night of my birthday. I was home alone as usual and drunk as a skunk. It was my 35th birthday and I had nothing to do or no one to hang out with, so why not? He and I were downstairs at the same time grabbing our UberEATS.

My driver, after looking at my license to verify my identity says, "Oh, it's your birthday. Happy Birthday, Miss Gregory."

Montel cocks his head to the side and says "Well, Happy Birthday Miss. Gregory," mockingly. We shared a chuckle, then an elevator, then the bed. And ever since then, I've been avoiding him like COVID-19. We silently rode down together and of course, his Dodge Ram was parked next to my Audi Q7.

"Look, I don't know what to say to you anymore. I ask you out hundreds of times only to get turned down. Then you take my soul one night and avoid me the next. What kind of game are you playing Ebony?"

Damn, so he does see when I go the other way when he appears. Maybe I should give him a chance. My therapist says it's time for me to start dating again. "No, Montel. I'm not playing games with you. And I apologize if that's how it's coming off. I really just do work a lot. But all of that's gonna change."

Montel raised his eyebrow. "Change?" I laughed at his confusion.

"I tell you what, watch the 12-midday news on WSBTV today and you'll understand. Then meet me for drinks at the W around 2. Is that okay with you, Mr. Officer?" I asked walking seductively towards him.

Montel licked those juicy lips that I so enjoyed riding,

leaned in close and said, "It's Detective and I'll see you soon." He winked at me, jumped in his truck and sped off.

I was damn near hyperventilating by the time I strapped myself in. *Did I really just ask Montel out?* "Okay, Ebony. I see you out here flourishing." I hyped myself up in my visor mirror. I noticed that my lipstick was smudged, so I reached in my bag to freshen up. That's when I heard her voice. A voice I'll never forget and had not heard in what seemed like forever. "It is time." I looked up and in the mirror was the same reflection I saw in the *Tik Tok* video that night. Staring back at me was Leola Gregory, my dead mother of 15 years.

I was in my junior year at *South Carolina State* when I was called out of my chemistry class. I knew it couldn't be good if my grandmother had made the drive from Ravenwood to Orangeburg. My mama was dead. I felt like I was floating out my body. I watched the school Chaplin pick me up when my knees gave way. I saw my grandmother wiping my tears. It was surreal. I remember the car ride home. My uncle Thad and Aunt Estelle were in the car along with my cousin Anika. They drove Grandma Louise up to come collect me. No one spoke. Aside from Grandma crying out, "Lawd, why you take my baby?" or "Why Lawd, why?" not a single word was spoken. It wasn't until we reached grandma's house that I learned how my mother died. In true low country fashion, the house and yard were occupied with about 50 people to start the week long *sit-up*. It's a tradition from years past. It started during the plague when people were falsely proclaimed dead but would miraculously wake up. So, it came to be that whenever someone passed, you would *sit up* with the body. Which was usually kept in the front room of the home.

There weren't too many black funeral parlors, so the

family would usually do the dressing and burial. This tradition has turned into a week-long event, where all day and night people are at your house up until the day of the funeral. They would come to cook or bring food. Clean and take care of the children. Little mundane things to allow the family to properly plan the funeral. At night it becomes a crab crack, with tables filled with crab, oysters, shrimp, potatoes, corn and eggs. Coolers were full of wine, whiskey, and moonshine and a big, bright beautiful bonfire to keep you warm.

My aunt and grandmother followed me into my bedroom as I was just about to put my things away. My aunt Estelle is a peculiar woman. I know she loves me, but beyond that, there was nothing. She wasn't mean or mistreated me the small number of times that we did cross paths, but she was never really warm to me. She didn't go out her way to get to know me but more than that, she would never let me get too close to Anika. I don't have any siblings, so I loved whenever Nika, which was her childhood nickname, was around. It was almost like if we were having too much fun, Aunt Estelle would swoop in and take her away. Grandma Louise, who we called Grandma Lou for short sat next to me on my bed, but my aunt spoke first.

"Ebony, Mama and I want you to know that we are here for you and just because..." she paused, but I couldn't tell if she was choked up with grief or disgust. "Because my sister is gone, we don't want you to think you are alone in this world."

My chest became tight for the 100th time that day and I didn't even try to stop the tears from falling.

"What happened? Why is my mama dead?" I asked, looking back and forth between the two of them.

My grandmother began to wail, she was going to be of no use.

"Leola was found in Toogadoo this morning. It appears that she drowned."

Drowned? That didn't make sense. My mama was the one who taught me how to swim.

"That doesn't make sense, Aunt Estelle. My mama knew how..."

"There were rocks in her pockets and bricks tied to her ankles." Aunt Estelle interrupted. I stood straight up when she said that. "Fuck you! My mama would never kill herself. She would never leave me."

My aunt was unphased by my outburst and did something she had never done in my 20 years. She wrapped her arms around me and held me and I cried. I cried until there were no more tears left and my voice was gone. How could she do this to me? How could she leave me like this? Leola Gregory might not have been perfect, but she was all I had. From as far back as I can remember, it was always she and I. I never knew my father and whenever I asked about him, either the subject was changed or if I pushed too hard, she became upset. We moved a lot, but we always ended up back at Grandma's house. I never went without. I may not have had the latest in fashion, but I was always neat and clean.

Mama was what I like to call a dreamer. One of the smartest people I know. My grandparents worked hard to send her and Aunt Estelle to college. While they both graduated, Aunt Estelle went on to be successful in her field as a Nurse Practitioner. My mama, God my mama. Nothing was ever enough. This woman had a degree in Political Science, people say my grandfather would boast that his little LeeLee was going to be a Lawyer. Part of the reason I am an attorney today. But not my Mama. She did one semester at the College of Charleston School of Law before she dropped out to go to South Africa to fight apartheid.

After two years in Africa, things got a little blurry. I know she went to live with my Aunt Estelle and Uncle Thad for a little while to help her out with her new baby, my cousin Anika. But that didn't last too long because she soon found herself pregnant with me and back at Grandma's. And ever since then, she was like a tumbleweed. Going any which way the wind would take her. But never without me by her side. After I composed myself, I sat on the bed next to Grandma silently. The memory slowly faded with me being unable to move, unable to cry, only able to breathe. Just like now. Only this time I can speak.

"Leola Gregory, what the hell are you doing in my back seat?"

ANIKA

I TRIED my best to stretch my calves and ankles as I listened to the soloist belt out *Amazing Grace*. It was one of daddy's favorite church hymns. The low country humidity had me sweating in places I didn't need wetter. The gnats were annoying and there were audible cries and moans as people watched daddy's casket lower into his grave. I was a daddy's girl at heart. He was the first man I ever loved, maybe the only man I ever loved. When I got news of his passing, I instantly felt my insides turn. I never knew daddy was sick. He always seemed to be so strong and healthy, his aging never caught up to him.

I used to tease him and say he might be an undercover vampire, but he would get livid and yell, "Anni! That's devil's talk! I'm a man's man and this is PURE genes!" He was the only one who called me Anni. Everyone else called me Nika, except my mama who didn't believe in using any other names besides the ones written on the birth certificate. My thoughts were interrupted as mama tugged on my arm and sternly whispered,

"What are you smiling at?! And of all places at your

father's burial. Have Mercy Anika!" I didn't realize I was smiling, and I definitely didn't notice the eyes of the guests staring at the now dumbfounded look on my face.

"Sorry mama, I'm not trying to be insensitive, it's just...."

"Stop it, Anika!"

Estelle warned without missing a beat to dab at another solitary tear that fell. I slowly looked around the gravesite to see if I recognized any of the faces. I was a stranger amongst my own kinfolk. They knew me but I hadn't the slightest idea of who these people were. I wasn't even sure if everyone present was family, besides Grandma Lou, who hugged mama, Granny Cary and Uncle Bernard. They stood still and stoic as statues with cold eyes that seemed to pierce right through me. I felt a cool chilly breeze whip my hair and turned around frantically looking for the source. It seemed to generate from the back area of the family plot where a chain link fence separated the dearly departed from the wood line.

I'm not sure how much time passed before I realized the crowd was dispersing. The entire funeral and burial service was a blur. Daddy was gone. I stood staring at the mound of dirt and collage of flowers piled on top of his grave. Mama was holding court with some of the ladies from the community hall and paid me no mind as I strolled slowly towards Granny Cary and Uncle Bernard. I hadn't seen them in years. My mother called my dad's side of the family, backward wild animals and I thought it was because of how playful and carefree daddy had been. I wondered if my daddy was adopted because Uncle Bernard never seemed to have a smile or any light-heartedness about him. Granny was the same and she was nothing like my other grandmother, Grandma Lou.

I plastered a smile on my face and said, "I'm doing okay,

just trying to stay strong for mama." As I stepped closer to the pair. There was a heavy silence as the two looked back and forth at each other puzzled. I noticed the exchange and too eagerly offered an assurance.

"No, it's fiiiiiiine! Mama is doing okay, and everyone knows how close me and daddy are, um... er.... was and- " my granny cut me off.

"Child shhhh, we didn't know you heard us."

My Uncle Bernard had a constipated look on his face as he tilted his head at me as if he was trying to read something deeper in my face.

"Granny Cary, how could I not hear you? I clearly heard you ask Uncle Bernard if I was able to handle it all," I said solemnly.

Again, the two exchanged glances and shared what looked like a secret. Uncle Bernard's eyes widened, and my granny's eyes bore a hole into my forehead. It was creeping me out. Why were they acting as if I didn't hear them speaking about me like I wasn't present and within earshot? I had always had good hearing and maybe they weren't as close to me as I originally thought, but I had heard their voices loud and clear.

Everyone knew I had moved away to DC and was working as a veterinarian and ASL interpreter part-time. Maybe they thought that I had a hearing loss from big city life or being away made me aloof and out of touch also. But before I could inquire any further, I felt the air stiffen as my mother's voice said,

"Bernard... Mother Howell," as she gave a polite bow.

Uncle Bernard gave a quick head nod of acknowledgment while my granny stood stone still without blinking. I

wasn't even sure she was breathing. There were only 2 women on planet earth that could put Estelle Howell in check, and it was her mother and her now former mother-in-law, granny or Mother Howell as she called her. My mother looked uncomfortable as she quickly hugged me to her side and rubbed my arms as if she thought I was cold. My mother was not the nurturing type, so this made me feel awkward.

After a moment of silence, my mother said, "I hope the service was to your liking. I tried to keep things... appropriate and simple... Thaddeus will truly be missed." Uncle Bernard let out an agitated grunt while granny Cary still stood unmoving. I was pretty sure by this point I had not seen her take a breath or even blink. Uncle Bernard then let out what sounded like an inaudible low whine and I looked up and said,

"Are you leaving already? Please don't go!!! Are you coming to the house? I just want to..."

"Anika! Don't be a pest!" Estelle chided as she turned to face me.

"So, you *can* hear us," granny said with a bit of enthusiasm in her voice which surprised everyone.

She winked at Uncle Bernard whose face still had that annoyed look. My mother moved her eyes between the 3 of us flabbergasted because clearly, she thought these people were rude as they had not uttered one word since arriving.

She spun on her heels to walk back to the family car and yelled,

"Let's go, Anika, the family car is waiting."

I responded, "Go ahead mama, I want to pay my respects to the rest of the family here."

Her footsteps slowed but never stopped as she eventually

entered the family car and placed her face in her hands. I turned back to get some answers from granny Cary and Uncle Bernard, but I was shocked to be standing alone. Where had they gone so swiftly and stealthily?

I gingerly tip-toed in my heels over to the connected black headstones that had matching flame emblems on top of each. *Twin Flames,* I said wistfully as I looked at my brother's grave markers. Amir and Aron were twins who died on a mysterious yet tragic camping trip. It happened on their 21st birthday and was reported as a grisly crime scene. An animal attack was what the papers reported, unlike the members of the community who had their own suspicions. I remember my father coming home covered in blood with a look of horror on his face.

"'Stelle Baby... the boys.... the boys... are...'" daddy's voice quivered while trying to finish the sentence.

My mother went into a rage and charged him with her fists balled up beating on his chest.

"HOW COULD YOU?!! HOW COULD YOU?!! THOSE POOR BABIES!!" She wailed.

As I knelt down, I blew kisses to each grave marker and told the twins how much I missed them, and I was sorry for not coming back to visit sooner. I told them to find daddy so they could all be together and to hold on to each other like he taught us. I stood and looked around at the other graves, some were so old that the names were difficult to read due to the age of the stone.

At the very end of the plot, next to a beautiful weeping willow tree was a pink-colored headstone that belonged to my Aunt Leola. She also died tragically years ago, close to the time the twins passed away. This wasn't her family's gravesite, but my daddy had insisted she be buried here. My mother reluctantly agreed after much debating. As I stared at her grave, it was then that I realized that I had not seen my cousin Ebony at all during the service. I felt that cool breeze hit my face again as I thought of her and heard another eerie howl in the distance.

EBONY

TRAFFIC WAS heavy and in true form on the way to the office. I was trying to beat the press and be in the hair and makeup chair in the next 15 minutes. Just as quickly as she appeared, my mama disappeared. I pulled my blunt out to take a few pulls on the way in and calm my nerves. By the time I got to my floor, to my ceiling glassed corner office, my stylist Ashley, affectionately known as Ash was waiting for me.

"About damn time!" She exclaimed. Sniffing me, she added, "I hope you saved me some."

I smiled and pointed to my purse. I put a towel under my door as she lit up. Ash was making small talk as she prepared me for the press conference.

"One Stop goumen yo epi yo dwe sa w ap destine yo dwe," I looked up in the mirror to see if Ash had heard it too. She didn't stop talking. Then I heard it again, "One Stop goumen yo epi yo dwe sa w ap destine yo dwe," I jerked my head this time, causing her to burn the nape of my neck.

"Ebony, girl! What is wrong with you?" she asked, rubbing ice on the burn.

But I didn't feel the heat from the burn, nor the coolness of the ice. It was the same feeling I had when I found out my mother had died. I was floating above myself, watching myself.

"Ebony? Ebony?"

I was staring straight ahead in the mirror at my reflection. Ash moved closer, slightly frightened.

"Ebony, are you having a seizure?"

The whole time I'm watching myself trying to will myself to speak. Finally, I was able to.

"Si li vle di ke yo dwe, li dwe fè."

Ash took a few steps back, "Eb, you're scaring me."

I turned around to face her and repeated myself, "Si li vle di ke yo dwe, li dwe fè."

"I'm going to get some help," my friend said, frantically putting our spliff out and spraying lavender lilac air freshener.

As soon as the fragrance whiffed to my nostrils, it snapped me back to reality.

"Girl, you gonna pass the blunt or what? I gotta be on set in 10 minutes,"

Ash looked at me like I was an alien.

"What?" I asked her.

"WHAT??? Girl, what the hell is going on with you? You were spaced out and then you started speaking another language. Like, what the fuck, friend?"

I cocked my head and let out a deep laugh, she was fucking with me. But the frightened look on her face, made me think she may be right. But it was when she was giving my hair a final spray of oil sheen and spun me around in my chair to see the final product that I believed her. Again, perched on my Italian Leather Sofa, was my mama.

I had 3 missed calls from Grandma Lou by the time I was able to look at my phone again. I would have to call her back after all of the hoopla died down. She knew today was my big day, so she must have been calling to wish me luck. When I reached the conference room, it was filled with all the firm partners and media. Stanley Lieberman was at the podium singing my praise, as I silently took deep breaths rehearsing my speech in my head.

"So, at this time I would like to introduce the newest partner of Liberman, Schwartz, and Howard; Miss. Ebony Gregory."

There was applause as I approached the podium. Mr. Liberman shook my hand and stepped aside. I looked down at my phone and there were 3 more missed calls from Grandma Lou. I made a mental note to call her as soon as I was done but what was most shocking, in the back, in the far left corner was Montel. I gave him a *how did you know?* smirk. He returned it with his *because I know everything smirk.* I smiled and began.

"1st I would like to thank my partners and colleagues for the opportunity to grow with the firm. LSH has been a cornerstone in Atlanta for over 45 years and I look forward to adding to its diversity and advancement into the future."

All of a sudden, I felt it again, I was beginning to leave my body. *No, no, not now.* I begged myself. But it was too late. I watched me stand stoic. The flashing lights of the cameras didn't phase me. My partners looked at each other puzzled, Montel was slowly walking to the front towards me. A reporter from WSBTV was calling my name to ask me a question.

"Miss. Gregory, what are your plans for the future of LSH?"

But I didn't hear them. All I heard in my ear was, "One Stop goumen yo epi yo dwe sa w ap destine yo dwe," over and over coming from the right of me. Before I collapsed and everything went black, the last thing I saw was my mother, but she wasn't alone; with her stood my Uncle Thad.

By the time I came to, I was in my office again, lying on my couch. And at the end of the couch was Montel. I attempted to stand but he hurried to my side to stop me.

"No, lie down and rest."

I was still groggy, but not too out of it to remember what was supposed to happen today. And not too groggy to remember what I saw.

"What happened?" I asked Montel.

He looked at me sympathetically. "You don't remember?"

I shook my head no. He reached in his pocket and pulled out his phone and pulled up YouTube. I immediately became nauseous. I saw myself go to the podium and start to speak, then freeze up. It wasn't more than 45 seconds. But I was staring off into space, a reporter even asked a question to which I gave no response. Then before the video ends, I turn to my right, expressionless, and say something in a language I've never heard or learned before and then pass out.

"Uggghhh," I groaned in embarrassment.

It already had 4,595 views and was growing. Montel told me how he carried me to my office and that the press conference ended. My partners then told him that I was to take 2 weeks off before coming back and to be medically cleared. "Medically cleared?!" I repeated. There's nothing wrong with me!

"Oh, one last thing. Your Grandmother has been calling

nonstop. Maybe she saw the press conference and is worried about you. You should call her back."

"No," I said, propping myself up. "She was calling before I even went on. I'll call her now."

I grabbed my phone and dialed Grandma Lou. The phone rang once before she answered.

"Eb'nee, gal I bun da call you all day," she said in our familiar native tongue of Gullah-Geechee.

"I'm sorry Grandma, it's been a long day. You can't even begin to imagine."

"You need fuh come home."

Here we go. Grandma was always trying to get me to come visit. I would fly her to Atlanta a few times a year to visit, but I very rarely made my appearance in Ravenwood.

"Grandma, I can't right now. I just made partner. I have too much-"

"Ya Uncle Thad dead!" She said it so matter of factly I almost didn't believe her.

"Wait, what are you saying?"

"Ya uncle dead and he done bun bury."

"ALREADY BURIED?!" I yelled back.

Grandma continued, in the same even tone.

"Yea, his mammy and brother insisted. You know 'Stelle is beside herself and Nika could use you."

It was all so much.

"I don't think I'll be able to get a flight that quick to make it home Grandma, but I'll get there as soon as I can." I ended the call with I love you and sat back on the couch in disbelief. In a stark difference to my Aunt Estelle, my Uncle Thad was always kind to me. He would take Nika and I to his mother's whenever they were in town, and we would have the time of our lives, but those times were few and far in between. Now he was gone. I knew exactly how Nika felt.

"What happened? Did someone pass away?" Montel asked. I filled him in as I looked for a flight to Charleston. There were none until the next day.

"Shit," I said out loud. "I'll just have to wait."

"No, I 'll drive you up now." Montel offered.

I looked at him crazy. *Sir, I just invited you for drinks, now you think we're on road trips level?*

"Umm, you don't have to do that."

"I know I don't, I want to," he retorted.

"But what about work?"

Montel chuckled, "I'm the Lead Detective. I'll be just fine." It was settled, Montel was going to take me home to Ravenwood. As I packed up my office to try to sneak out with my last bit of dignity, I checked myself in the mirror. And once again leering back at me was Leola Gregory and Thaddeus Howell.

ANIKA

I FELT my eyelids get heavy as I lay in the guest room of my parent's house. It was a full day after daddy's funeral and I had decided to stay home with mama for several weeks. We never had that talk she mentioned in the family car and anytime I would bring it up, something in her body language got spooked. I assumed it was grief and didn't press the issue. I turned my head to the end table as my eyes focused on the cup of herbal tea my mama made. With my eyes, I traced the floral and dotted designs on the side. I continued until I dozed off quietly and entered into the realm of dreams. I saw myself as a little girl laying in bed with daddy tucking me in.

"Daddy, tell me a bedtime stowyyy, peeeeeaaaase!" I said with my little tongue sticking out between the space where my two front teeth were missing. I was 7 years old, and bedtime was one of me and daddy's favorite pastimes. He loved checking my room to be sure I was safe from monsters and goblins as I recalled, but the best part was his stories. This man could take any story and put a spin on it.

"Okay, Anni.... you know the story they teach in school called Little Red Riding Hood, here is the REAL story..."

Thaddeus said. My little 7 year old eyes widened and my smile matched.

"Once upon a time in a beautiful forest lived a family of wolves. There was a huge daddy wolf, a beautiful mama, and 5 baby wolves. They were a happy wolf family who liked to run through the forest, hunt wild rabbits, and play nibble the tail."

"Daddy," 7 year old me said, "What is nibble the tail?" I giggled.

"Oh Anni, it's like playing tag, you chase after someone and instead of saying you're it, you nibble their tail like this," he playfully tried to nibble my thighs through the comforter.

I yelped in excitement knowing at any moment my mother would come in and shut this story-party down. He continued, "Then one day a woman, not a little girl, came into the woods looking for a rare object. She was called *Red* because of all the bloodshed that followed her wherever she went. You see Anni, Red was a hunter and her favorite thing to hunt was the wolf. She had heard about this amazing and special pack of wolves in the forest, and she wanted to see what was so unique about them. So, she laid a trap and she waited for days until one day, one of the baby wolves got captured and then slaughtered." Thad said in a somber tone. 7-year-old Anika had tears in her eyes as she asked, "Did the bad Yady Wed slaughtered the baby wolf and daddy, what is slaughtered?"

Thad held Anni's hand and said, "Red took this curved silver knife with a jagged edge and cut out the heart of the baby wolf."

7-year-old Anni gasped and hid her face under the covers.

"You see, Red had learned that it was easier to catch a

little wolf instead of a big one, and she would take the heart and eat it," he said.

"ANIKA! LIGHTS OUT! ANIKA! ANIKA!"

Upon hearing my name for the 4th time, I realized someone was calling me in real-time.

"ANIKA! Wake up, honey! You were crying in your sleep."

I jumped out of the bed as my mother yelped. "Sorry, mama! I was having a crazy dream."

My mother looked at me skeptically.

"Do you remember those stories daddy used to tell me as a kid, you know how he would change up all the scenes to make the animals look like the victims or heroes?" I said with a chuckle.

My mother sucked her teeth. "Your father was a delirious man at times. I told him those stories would give you nightmares and now look, years later they still affect you," she whined as she tugged on the straps of her robe.

"No mama it wasn't like that at all. Remember the story of *Little Red Riding Hood*, except the wolves were being terrorized by Red the head hunter and-" Estelle interrupted with a wave of her hand.

"My God Anika, STOP! You really believe that a white woman named Red went into the woods and killed a bunch of wolves? That was just a story honey, your daddy would tell you to get you to go to bed," she exclaimed.

I felt differently. Daddy told me that Red was a colonizer who was intent on learning the secret ways of the wolves for cultural appropriation because white society believed the power of transformation and purity was attainable for them. I stared at my mother defiantly as she shook her head and left the room. Maybe me talking about daddy this way was making her more upset than I realized.

I took the last few sips of my tea, walked over to the window and looked out at the sky. Staring at the moon was another one of me and daddy's favorite things to do. He had taught me all the phases of the moon so looking up I knew it was a first gibbous. Within the next day or so it would be a full moon. Something about looking up at that orb in the sky made me feel animated and regal, yet primal and uneasy.

I quietly crept back to the bed and laid down thinking about Red and the wolves. Mama was right. I knew the story of *Little Red Riding Hood* and that poor little white girl was about to be wolf food. I exhaled heavily and rested my eyes. Slowly I began to drift to that transitional space between deep sleep and being woke. I felt like I floated out of my room right outside the house, where two pairs of eyes both yellow were staring at the window where I just stood.

"The young wolf is ready. Her instincts are developing, and she may have the gift of change. We need to prepare."

I then heard a low-sounding growl come from one of the large creatures with yellow eyes. The other creature fell on its side and whimpered, showing an act of submission while licking the paws of the first creature.

"She heard the true voice of the wolf. We weren't using words, nor did we open our mouths to speak, yet she heard us loud and clear. You think he told her?" Was the message interpreted from the animal whine.

The first creature bared its teeth and in a husky-sounding voice said, "We must let the Spirit of the Lycaon and Anubis guide her if it's her destiny. Come let us go, these woods haven't been safe since the hunters returned."

And in an instant, the two creatures sprinted through the darkness leaving only the sounds of a wolf's cry, the tell-tale howl. I slowly drifted back inside to my bed and smiled. I immediately believed I was dreaming because there were no wolves in Ravenwood. Also, because at night, I remember daddy was always able to make me giggle uncontrollably as he showed me how to howl at the moon.

"See Anni, it goes like this.... aaaaaooooooo, aaaaaoooooooooo!" Thad would belt out in a solid tenor. I would attempt to mimic my father but my howls always sounded like a wounded puppy instead. The tea my mother had given me containing the dark blue and purple petals, was working its own magic as my breathing slowed and got heavy. As I continued to drift into a heavier slumber, I unknowingly let out a soft melodic, "Aaaaaooooooooo!"

He's the type of guy that'll say
hey baby let's get away let's go somewhere where
ohh, where I don't care...

MY LOVE for Aretha came from my mother. From as far back as I can remember there was an Aretha song for every emotion she was feeling. Met a new man? *Dr. Feelgood.* The man wasn't around or making her feel not as loved as he used to? *Call me.* When she was in love LOVE? *Natural Woman.* But *Daydreaming* was always my favorite. The thought of my man just saying, "Hey girl, get dressed let's go," and we just ride off and love on each other and just be with each other. I always wanted that love, but I never got it. Honestly, I think I never got it because I never got to see it. Mama would have her different men. If she felt like it was something that was going to grow into something real, she would introduce them to me.

I'm an adult now, so I know she had needs. And I'm quite sure they were met. Mama was always looking for that man that was going to make her feel like she was the most important person in the world. I looked over at Montel as he drove us down the back roads to Ravenwood, South Carolina. I don't know how to feel about him. I didn't know what it felt like to have someone to genuinely want to get to know me. I think that's part of the reason why I'm so afraid to let him in. He's a good enough man. Successful. Single. Homeowner. No children. The man was a fucking unicorn! Yet, I could not find it in myself to make me feel like he was worth a chance. Now he's seen me at my worst. I really don't know what's going on with me. When I called my therapist, she had the audacity to say that I should voluntarily check myself in for a 48-hour hold. She must have lost her damn mind. Montel witnessed all of this and yet still wanted to do anything to make it better for me. Why?

"What you over there thinking about girl?" he startled me out of my daydreaming.

"My uncle. Can't believe he's really gone."

"Were yall close?" he asked, not taking his eyes off the road.

I looked over at Montel behind the wheel of his custom model 2500 Crew Cab Dodge Ram. It was the 1st time I really got to see the ripples in his muscular arms. My eyes led up to his muscular shoulders. As he waited for my answer his jaws clenched and it was the sexiest jaw I'd ever seen. I hadn't been very successful when it came to matters of the heart. No teenaged love because Mama and I never settled long enough to find one, let alone friends.

In college, I went in a virgin, and by the end of my freshman year, I had my 1st sexual experience. It was nothing like the movies. It was sloppy and it was quick, but it was how he acted after that made the whole thing terrible. He was obsessive. We weren't even in a relationship. It was the first and final time that sealed the deal. When he entered me, his eyes rolled in the back of his head. I was flattered, I thought I just had *it*. Then he began to grab the sheets and say my name in my ear over and over. It was what he said, "Ebony, Ebony. Please let me go. Let me go, baby." But when I tried to get away, he pinned me down. Not in a raping way, but not wanting me to get away.

The next few weeks were crazy. He would appear outside of my classes, outside my dorm. The last straw was when he cornered me in the library, blubbering and crying. He kept saying that he was in love with me and couldn't live without me. He said that he had called his mama and told her he'd met his wife and that we were on the way to drive to Birmingham right now to meet her. We literally went on one date, and I only slept with him to get my virginity out the way. After making a scene and trying to drag me from the library, campus security accosted him, he never returned to campus again. Word on the curb, he had a mental breakdown.

It took 4 years before I had sex again. Next time I was in my 1st year of Law School. After Mama dying and the whole debacle in Freshman year, I kind of scathed off sex however, Brandon was worth a chance. He came from a good family in New Orleans and respected that I wanted to wait to have sex. We went down to visit his family at the end of our 2nd semester. It was my 1st time in the city, and I instantly fell in love. The food, the ambiance, everything! And his parents loved me. They knew my history and didn't judge me.

The next day was a visit to his grandmother's or as he called her Grand'Mere's house. As soon as I walked in, I was overcome with darkness. But it was when she saw me that our visit immediately ended. His Grand'Mere looked at me and stopped in her tracks.

"Brandon, get away from her!"

We both were stunned.

"Grand'Mere, what are you talking about?" he said, walking towards her.

"How dare you bring this.. this juju in my house!" She then started to say something in another language that I couldn't understand, but I had already run out of the house before I heard anymore.

When Brandon got back in the car, he saw that I was visibly upset.

"Babe, don't listen to her. You know how old people can get."

I shook my head feverishly.

"No, I don't. Louise Gregory would never treat you like that. I wanna go home."

We returned to his parent's house to gather our things to go back to Charleston.

That night we made love for the 1st and last time. It started slow and sweet but as I began to take control, his eyes became like saucers. I rode him and arched my back so he could feel every inch of my walls. When I looked back down again at him, his eyes were still wide and involuntary tears were falling. He pushed me off him and backed himself as far back in a corner as he could.

"Brandon, what's wrong?" I asked, instinctively pulling the blanket around me.

He was panting and out of breath.

"Li pral pran nanm ou epi kenbe ou pou tout tan."

I looked at him like he had lost his mind. He repeated himself, "Li pral pran nanm ou epi kenbe ou pou tout tan. It's what my Grand'Mere said today, and she was right. I'm sorry Ebony, I can't do this." He gathered his things, left my room, and left my life. I would see him around campus, but whenever he saw me, he would go in the opposite direction. Since then, I hadn't had been in a relationship, until Montel on my birthday. I dedicated my life to my career and my grandmother.

"Did you hear me?" Montel asked, snapping me back to reality.

"I'm sorry, what did you say?"

He chuckled. "Were you and your uncle close?"

I thought about Uncle Thad. He was actually gone. He was a regular in my life, well as much as he possibly could be. Always sweet to me and allowing Nika and me to play together. Now, he was gone but not so much. Again, in true fashion, mama and Uncle Thad were along for the ride. Strangely this time, mama had her head nestled in the crook of Uncle Thad's shoulder while he stroked her hair. I looked at the two of them in the rearview mirror and raised my eyebrows, cutting my eyes. I looked back to Montel, "Yea, we were close."

ANIKA

I FINISHED my zoom chat meeting with my Deaf friends while mama sat on looking at me with a smile on her face.

"I suppose sending you to summer camp all those years paid off. You really are taking this hand language thing seriously?"

I laughed, "it's American Sign Language mama, it's a beautiful language, and I'm glad I learned something useful from camp all those years." It was one of the sporadic times we were able to sit and have a civil conversation without it getting awkward. She rocked back and forth slowly in daddy's black leather recliner while I sat across the room sipping some herbal tea she made.

"You know I put fresh hibiscus petals along with pure honey I got from Mrs. Lillie Bell. That woman has a yard filled with all sorts of heavenly goodness," Estelle bragged.

I took another sip of the tea and inhaled the fresh scent. It did smell divine. After finishing the last drop, I stood up to place my cup in the sink when I felt a wave of nausea hit me.

"Anika baby are you okay?"

I shook my head slightly,

"Yes mama, maybe I got up too fast."

The swirling sensation hit me once more as I leaned against the doorframe for support. "I think I'll go get some fresh air," and with that, I grabbed my keys and headed outside. The sun was shining brightly, and I could hear the sounds of nature all around me. There was something pure about being outdoors that made me feel alive. I strutted to my bone-white Chevy Camaro and started the engine. The roar of the engine was loud like a lion. My Bluetooth automatically connected and the sounds of J. Cole's *Work Out* blasted out the speakers.

I slowly drove out the gravel driveway not missing the silhouette of my mother, Estelle peeking through the Venetian blinds watching me leave. She seemed to be holding up pretty well and since I've been home made a fuss over me while fixing me different flavors of her now famous herbal teas. It wasn't until this morning I felt a wave of sickness.

I drove into our small town and parked at the local library. Across the street was a park with some dilapidated swings and an old rusty sliding board. I took a seat on a wooden perch and just inhaled the fresh country air. There were a couple people out and around, some just milling about and others walking in pairs.

"Good morning."

I nodded to several people that passed me. I was getting the strangest stares. I thought it was because of my daddy's recent passing or maybe people didn't recognize me as I didn't come home often. One lady was in close proximity I said,

"Hey sis, I loooooove that neck candy you have on."

It was a green stone with red spots, and it was wrapped

with gold wire. The lady stopped and subconsciously raised her hand to stroke the pendant as she squinted her eyes at me.

"Why thank you, it's a family heirloom," the stranger admitted.

"Well, it's definitely beautiful, what is it exactly? I'm not familiar with that type of stone."

The stranger promenaded closer to me and I could see her features more clearly. She had the most beautiful chocolate skin I had ever seen. Free of blemishes and her hair was in a messy yet chic curly Afro. It looked like she had set her natural tresses on perm rods to get the desired effect. She was about 5 feet 7 inches and well built. Her teeth were white, and they seemed to sparkle in the sunlight.

"This is called a bloodstone. It's a talisman of good health and long life. It also represents the purity of blood," she explained.

I stared in wonder as I instinctively put forth my hands to touch the gem.

"Anika, you okay?"

I was interrupted from what seemed like a trance by someone calling out to me. I turned around to see Marshella "Shelly" Bishop, an old high school classmate.

"Hey Shelly," I said slightly annoyed. We had a checkered history as I had once caught her having a 3 some with my twin brothers in high school. I tried to yank every crochet braid out of her head once I caught her with her ass in the air, literally.

"Anika, who are you talking to? You were deep in conversation," she said with her brows furrowed.

I turned back around to the stranger with the pendant,

but she was gone. I looked in the other direction, thinking she had taken off but there was no trace of her.

"I was talking to a lady, I didn't catch her name but she was showing me her necklace."

Shelly now raised her eyebrows at me with a look of surprise on her face.

"Ummm, Anika there was no woman there."

I could see some of the other members of the community pointing at me and whispering. I heard them saying, "She might be losing her marbles, she is in deep grief after her daddy died, that family is really cuckoo." I brought my attention back to Shelly.

"Well, *you* must be mistaken, there was a lady here and well you know what, I don't have to explain shit to you!"

I turned on my heels and headed back to my car. I could sense Shelly staring at me walking away while she nodded her head slowly as if she felt sorry for me. I was a little perplexed that the stranger had vanished so quickly. As I hit the unlock remote button for my car, I saw a reflection of myself and the stranger with the jewel right beside me. I jumped and looked to my right but there was no one. I glanced back at the reflection and there she was, standing next to me and smiling. *What the fuck?* I whispered as I tried to make sense of it. I reached out my hand to make contact when I heard a horn blaring at me.

"Getcho ass out the road!"

A woman yelled out of the passenger side window. I then noticed I was in the middle of the street and ran for cover. When I turned to look, I saw a large Dodge Ram truck with a woman who had features that reminded me of my deceased Aunt Leola. "Ebony?" I said confused as the truck cruised by then came to an abrupt stop. It made the car behind it slam on brakes while swerving to avoid a rear-end collision.

"Ebony, is that you?" I said louder when the woman hopped out of the truck and slowly walked towards me.

"Nika?! Niiiiikkkkaaaa!!" Ebony screamed and laughed as she then attempted to run in her Valentino designer heels. We hugged each other like long lost friends and instantly began sobbing. I had no idea why we were crying. We hadn't spoken to each other in years and while she was my little cousin, we never got to spend that much time together. But in that moment, we shared an emotional bond that made us both have a waterwork of tears.

"OMG Eb! You look amazing! You have really grown up!"

I did a quick once over and noticed her fitted jeans were hugging her lower curves and her halter top was doing its best to keep her breasts contained. I could see some remnants of makeup and it looked as if she had bags under her eyes. "Uncle Thad," was all she could muster up before we both broke down crying again. I didn't cry this much at the actual funeral but seeing her level of sad outburst made me even sadder. There was a man who had finally gotten out of the large truck once he pulled over to the side of the road. He was fit and he was fine. I quickly wiped my tears as he caught up to us.

"Um hey," he waved and said in the sexiest voice I had heard in a long time.

I smiled and looked at my cousin who seemed to forget she was in the company of this exquisite specimen.

"Oh shit, my bad. Nika this is Montel, Montel this is Nika," she said as she sniffed and wiped away her tears. We gave each other a brief head nod and said, "Hey."

"Soooooo who exa-" I started to say before she cut me off.

"Unh uh, please it's not like that," she said with a tone of don't even go there. "Besides who was that lady you were talking to in the middle of the street?"

Montel whipped his head towards her almost as fast as I did as he said, "What lady? There were two people? I only saw her." As he lifted his nose to point at me. I swallowed hard as I turned my head back to the street and then my car window to look for the stranger. At this point, I was afraid to acknowledge out loud that there had been a person I was talking to. But so far, Shelly and now Montel seemed to have not seen anyone. How was it that only Ebony and I had witnessed this stranger? I smoothly sidestepped the question.

"I missed you at daddy's funeral. Maybe you two should stop by the house. I'm sure mama would love to see you."

Ebony kinda smirked while saying, "Yea okay girl," as if she was unsure if that was the truth. Mama always told me that her sister Leola and her *seed* were tainted but I never knew what the deal was about that. I rocked on my heels awkwardly.

"Well, I'll be in touch, we just got in from Atlanta and we want to change clothes. I will call you before coming over. I want you to come with me when I go to pay my respects at the burial area."

I gave her a parting hug.

"Okay cool, I'm so happy to see you."

As she sashayed away I wondered what had come over me. I'm usually not that connected to other people, but at this moment it felt natural. I got into my car and drove away. I turned off the radio so I could think out loud and screamed when I saw the bloodstone pendant sitting in my cup holder.

EBONY

SEEING ANIKA OR AS WE, well, everyone except her mother affectionately called her, Nika was the welcome I needed coming back to my old hometown. She was not only my cousin but the closest thing I had to a Best Friend or any friend at all. She looked great too. 3 years older than me, we would often be mistaken for sisters or even twins growing up. I guess those Gregory genes were strong.

"Who was that?" Montel asked after I got settled back in his truck.

"That's my cousin Nika, my Uncle Thad's daughter."

"Damn!"

I looked at all the sights as we drove through town. The old town hall was now moved to a newer building, but the old post office still stood in its same familiar location. The Piggly Wiggly had long moved before I left for college and now sat vacant and for sale. There was a new fire station that looked foreign surrounded by the homes that had been there all my life. As we approached my old elementary and middle school, I got butterflies in my stomach because I knew my grandmother's house was less than a mile away.

"Where are you at?" Montel asked, breaking me out of my silence.

I did not reply, I just sighed. The GPS let him know we had arrived and in true fashion, Louise Gregory was bunked over in her yard pulling weeds. My grandmother had one of the most manicured yards in the neighborhood.

"Ebony Sapphire Gregory, as I live and breathe! Get ovah ya and kiss yo gamma!"

I ran to my grandmother and let her thick arms surround me. In what felt like the 1st time in a long time, I exhaled. It was something about this woman's love that made me feel whole. In everything I did, it was to make her proud. She had just left Atlanta 2 months earlier, but it felt like forever. Grandma pulled back from me and looked over my shoulder.

"Now who is dis ya?" she asked smiling.

In that brief moment of our reunion, I had forgotten that Montel was there. Montel smiled that beautiful smile and extended his hand, but Grandma Lou was not having it. "We hug 'round ya. My name is Louise, everyone calls me Grandma Lou." Over his shoulder, Grandma mouthed to me, "Wow!"

"Hello, Grandma Lou. I'm Montel."

Grandma stepped back. "Well, thank you for getting my baby here safely."

After watching the two of them share a little more small talk, I proceeded into the home of my childhood. It was like walking back in time. The same pictures that adorned the walls remained the same, aside from Nika and my high school and college graduation pictures. On the coffee table was Uncle Thad's obituary. I gazed at his picture before picking it up. It was him in his Postmaster's uniform. He had the same big smile that he always had whenever I saw him.

He seemed to always be happy, even being married to stuffy ole Aunt Estelle.

When I got to my room, I dropped my bags and collapsed on the bed. I finally opened the obituary. It was filled with pictures of him from different stages of his life. From his childhood, when he and Auntie lived in Africa. There were pictures of my dead twin cousins, Nika, and even Grandma Lou. But what was missing was pictures of his mother, his brother, my mother, and myself. I cannot say I was surprised. This obituary screamed Estelle Howell. My cell phone rang, and I couldn't have been happier for the distraction.

"Hey, Nika what's up? Everything okay since we saw you in town?" Nika was silent for a second too long. "Anika?" I used her government.

"I know you wanted to go to Daddy's grave and all but I wanna go see Granny Cary and I don't wanna go alone."

I knew what she was asking. "Say no more, I'm on the way." By the time I had got outside, Montel was stripped down to his wife-beater and was moving large tree branches from the front yard to the back.

"Grandma! Montel didn't come here to work."

He flashed that smile again that made me melt. "I'm not doing anything I don't want to do." Grandma stuck her tongue out at me teasingly. I laughed and rolled my eyes.

"Well, we've got to go make a run with Nika. So, your help is leaving."

"I don't mind staying. Plus, I'm learning a lot about you. You were quite the mischievous little girl, Ebony."

Now I was annoyed.

"Really Grandma Lou," I lamented.

She threw her hands up, "What?"

I shook my head. "I'm headed to Nika's then we're going to visit Miss. Cary." This caused Grandma Lou to pause and look up at me.

"You fuh go to Estelle?"

I didn't look at her as I jumped in her older model Cadillac. Before I could close the door, Grandma Lou grabbed it.

"Don't stay long, hear? Just honk fuh Nika tah come out."

What had gotten into this woman?

"Grandma, what are you saying? I can't go there and not speak. I gotta pay my respects. She's your daughter, for Christ's sake."

"YOU HEAR WAH I SAY?!"

Grandma Lou was not playing with me.

"Okay Grandma, ok."

Louise closed the door and before I pulled off yelled, "Give my 'dolences and lub tah Cary. I een get a chance to get out dey yet." And with that, I was off.

As soon as I entered Aunt Estelle's, I regretted not listening to Grandma Lou. In true form, my aunt was cold. She hugged me, not the warm matronly hug she gave me when my mother passed. It was stiff and forced. I extended my condolences and attempted to tell her how much Uncle Thad meant to me, but she cut me off mid-sentence and asked if I was hungry. I was, so I followed her into the kitchen. Nika was already there eating Auntie's famous homemade sausage and potato salad.

All my life, whenever my presence was allowed to grace the Howell home, lunch would consist of Aunt Estelle's Homemade Sausages and Potato Salad. She even made her own homemade mustard and called it a family secret. Maybe a little too spicy, but I thought it was delicious. Almost always I would have an unexplainable sensation that would travel through my body and a blinding headache that would last for hours. It had been years since I had enjoyed it and it was going to be worth all the side effects. When Nika looked up at me, she looked worn and tired. Hell, she just buried her father. I felt so bad for her. Aunt Estelle, after setting my plate down, gave Nika a mug of tea. She was also known for her homemade herbal teas.

"Drink this Anika," she said setting it down in front of her.

I ate in silence as Nika sipped.

Aunt Estelle was 1st to break the silence. "I understand that you ladies are going to visit Mother Howell this afternoon."

I cleared my throat, the symptoms were kicking in. But it was so damn good. "Umm, yes ma'am. I want to, um... check on her since Uncle Thad's passing," I looked over at Nika. She was pulling at the collar of her shirt and clearing her throat as well.

"Mama, I don't feel to-"

BOOM! Nika's head hit her plate. "Nika!" I attempted to scream. I stood up, but my feet felt like bricks. Right before everything went black, I looked up into Aunt Estelle's smiling face, "What the fuck did you do to us?"

ANIKA

I OPENED my eyes and it seemed like I was in the woods. I stood up and wiped all the leaves and debris off me. I felt an uneasiness that couldn't be described. These woods didn't seem familiar, and it was eerily quiet. A sudden snap of a twig over my left shoulder caused me to jump and go to one knee. I heard muffled voices and I heard what sounded like footsteps headed in my direction. My forehead broke out into a cold sweat and my heart was pounding like the beat of an African drum. It almost felt like someone grabbed my shirt collar and yanked me up and when I looked I recognized the stranger from the park. She had on the same necklace with the bloodstone pendant. However, her face had a matching expression of fear as mine.

"RUN!!! DON'T LET RED CATCH YOU!" She wailed as she pushed me forward.

At the sound of Red, my body went rigid. I turned back to see a milky white young woman wielding a bloodstained silver curved knife in her hand. She pounced on me and stuck the knife in my chest when I suddenly screamed and jumped up.

I knocked over the bedside table and lamp when I noticed I was back in my parent's house in the guest room where I had been staying. I frantically touched my chest to see if there was a wound and I looked around for Red and the stranger who tried to help me. I was ok, I was in one piece. It took my eyes a minute to adjust to the dark room and I had no idea how much time had passed. The last thing I vaguely remember was eating lunch and I think my cousin had come over. "Ebony!" I shrieked as I spun around to head towards the door.

I ran out to the living room where my mother, Estelle, sat rocking in rhythm to the Motown record playing softly in the background. "Mama where is Ebony?" I was still a little foggy about the last few hours.

"Oh baby, Ebony left hours ago. You weren't feeling well so she packed her lunch and went back home while you slept." She said it very calm and calculated.

I searched her face for answers not sure what I was expecting. I mean Ebony and her friend *did* just make the drive from Atlanta and she mentioned they were tired. I know she wanted to go to daddy's gravesite, and I felt like we were supposed to go see Granny Cary, but I was drawing a blank. "Hours? Mama, how long was I sleeping? I don't remember any of that." I said now pursing my lips and looking upward to the ceiling as if I was figuring out a mystery.

Estelle stood from the recliner and tucked a piece of my hair behind my ears before cupping my face. "Anika you are too young to have memory problems. I can give you a ginkgo Biloba pill to boost cognition if you need it. I got the good stuff from the last pharmaceutical rep that came to my office last week. Wait here," she said. She dashed off to her room which left me standing around in the living room still puzzled by the time chunk I couldn't recall.

I roamed through the kitchen and into the dining room where we ate lunch and the only thing that was left on the table was my tea mug. I picked it up and inhaled the remnants which still had a nice floral scent. Mama definitely had the best herbal teas, but there wasn't any evidence that Ebony was even here. As I continued to sniff the remains of my tea, I noticed my iPhone in the corner and picked it up to check my messages and possible missed calls. I attempted to use the facial recognition, but it kept prompting me for the 6 digit passcode. *What the hell?* I said as I felt myself getting annoyed and went back towards the kitchen for better lighting. I held the phone up again and was startled when it rang, and an unknown 678 number flashed across the screen. The time said 8:33 pm and I hesitantly answered on the 3rd ring.

"Ebony, where are you girl? Grandma Lou is getting ready to serve me some red rice, fried fish, and baked macaroni and cheese! I don't think I've ever had food that smelled this good!" A sexy baritone voice said.

"Ebony? Um, you have the wrong number,"

"Ebony... quit playing, it's me, Montel."

I stood frozen realizing that this phone wasn't mine. "Oh hey, Montel, it's me Nika, we met earlier today. I got confused and thought this phone was mine. Wait, is Ebony not home?" Before I could hear his answer, my mother called out to me.

"Anika here you are, take this pill, and oh look, you still have some tea left." She gestured towards the cup. She saw the phone in my hand and said, "Am I interrupting something?" The way she asked didn't seem to cause alarm, but there was an uneasy existence there.

I took the pill and quickly hit the red end button on the phone as I backed towards the counter. I was now breaking into a cold sweat, just like I was when I thought I was in that forest with Red coming to kill me.

Estelle cocked her head to the side, "Is everything alright? You look like... you look like... well you look like hell, Anika. Let me fix you a fresh cup of tea and that should solve it." She came towards me, and I instinctively side-stepped her. Her eyes widened in surprise. "Anika Emerald Howell, I don't know what's gotten into you, but you need to let me help you," she said in a menacing tone.

I opened my mouth to speak when I heard the ring back tone of Erykah Badu's *Danger* signaling that my actual iPhone was ringing. We both froze as Estelle noticed I already had an iPhone in my hand. In a flash, she dashed towards me again when we both heard,

"Pa fè l 'anyen... pa fè l 'anyen."

I had never seen the level of fear that I was witnessing right now on my mother's face. She dropped to her knees and looked around frantically as she searched for the source of the voice. It didn't take me long to recognize the source since the stranger with the bloodstone pendant stood only a few feet away from me.

She said the phrase again which translated in English, "Do no harm to her," and levitated through the house towards the front door.

"Wait!" I yelled, unaware that I was not afraid. I ran to the front door and saw she was gone. *Man, what the fuck?* I huffed as I swung the door open. I looked behind me again and searched the room. Daddy's recliner sat like a huge monument and everything else was diminutive in stature.

I could hear my mother in the kitchen screaming,

"ANIKA! DON'T LET HER GET ME! ANIKA! COME BACK!"

I had too much to process at that moment and fully stepped outside to let the night air clear my senses. I felt the iPhone ring in my hand again and noticed the same 678 number and that brought me back to the realization that this was Ebony's phone. Where the hell was she? I swung my neck around and almost screamed when I saw the rosy pink Cadillac still parked in our yard. I knew it was Grandma Lou's Cadillac, which she earned from being a top *Mary Kay* saleswoman. I assumed this is what Ebony drove when she came to visit hours before.

"Ebony?!" I yelled into the night and got the literal sounds of crickets. I couldn't hear my mother wailing anymore and I never did answer the phone. I could guess it was Montel calling and I didn't want him to get upset or God forbid tell Grandma Lou. Why did my mother tell me Ebony had gone home, but her cellphone and the car she drove were still at our residence? I closed my eyes tight and strained to make myself remember the events of earlier that day. I could only remember seeing Ebony and Montel in town when they first arrived and then the episode with the stranger and the pendant. I also remembered driving home and sitting at the table telling mama excitedly about seeing Ebony. Then all of a sudden I was in the woods with Red the Hunter driving a curved knife into my chest. Nothing was making sense. The way mama was acting and the fact that I felt she was being dishonest with me. And the stranger was in *our* house. What language did she speak and why was I not afraid? Honestly, I felt a sense of relief when she was present. "Ebony?!" I screamed again and felt paralyzing fear when I heard the bushes beside me move.

An enormous grey looking dog peered out from the bushes and stared at me with large yellow eyes.

"Oooohhh Shit!" I gasped as I felt a warm trickle of pee slowly make its way down my thighs. Being a veterinarian, I knew I wasn't afraid of animals, but this dog looked super-sized and poised to attack.

However, the dog timidly crept towards me with its head low to the ground and I noticed the tail alternating between wagging slowly and being between the hind legs. I knew this behavior with canines showed a level of deference and the need for acceptance. I was terrified. I didn't know if I should run back inside or if I should run towards the woods.

I heard the front door slam and the deadbolt clicked as I saw my mother peer through the curtains with the same look of fear on her face she had in the kitchen. Did she see this large dog and locked me outdoors? I quietly panicked.

I turned without a second thought and raced towards the woods. In the corner of my eye, I could see the large grey dog take off in the same direction and I screamed. As I ran through the woods I felt the sticky burrs and leaves slap me across the face while noticing the grey dog running parallel to me. It was trying to cut me off, I thought as I did a spin move I had learned from my twin brothers when we were children playing freeze tag. The dog was able to change directions fluidly and in stride. It inched closer to me and when it howled, I let out a scream of my own. On my second large breath to cry out for help I didn't even notice that my screams had morphed into a matching alto sounding howl that rivaled the large dog. It caused the dog to slow just momentarily and stop when I felt myself collide with something, or rather someone.

"ANIKA! WHAT THE FUCK?! WHERE THE HELL AM I?!"

I had run into Ebony. She looked mystified and bewildered standing haphazardly in the woods. She had twigs and dried mud on her top and she carried her expensive heels in her hands.

"EBONY RUN! A HUMONGOUS DOG IS CHASING ME!" I yelled out of breath as I tried to grab her arm and pull her to safety. She yanked away from me.

"ANIKA! THERE IS NOTHING OUT HERE!"

I stopped and bent over my knee trying to catch my breath. I looked around and didn't see nor hear anything. I then stared at her in awe and wondered how the fuck she got out here in the middle of these woods while she now crossed her arms and peered at me through squinted eyes. Suddenly, at the same time as if on cue we both said, "I have to tell you something!"

EBONY

"Boom-ba ba-Boom. Boom-ba ba-Boom. Boom-ba ba-Boom."

They were the sound of drums. It was the 2nd time I had regained consciousness that night. The first time I regained consciousness, I was looking up and seeing the stars move above me. They were moving too fast, so I knew I was being moved at a rapid pace. My back was exposed to the ground as my shirt had already ruffled around my neck. I couldn't see who was pulling me, but I could hear her talking.

"I knew this day would come. Leola, even from the grave your shit is still stirring."

It was my aunt Estelle. My eyes were so heavy, it was like pulling teeth to try to keep them open. But my ears, they worked perfectly fine.

"I've worked too damn hard to keep Anika away from this. And all Mama did was cottle her and cottle you, Ebony. BUT ENOUGH IS ENOUGH!" She screamed to no one in particular.

I tried so hard to open my mouth to speak but it was like a hag was riding me. The harder I fought to speak, the more difficult it was to pull my lips apart. Aunt Estelle huffed and puffed as she dragged me through the woods. When she was satisfied with her destination, she stopped. I watched my aunt bend over, trying to catch her breath. When she was finally composed, she turned to me. My mind was so angry with my body. My eyes were open, I was looking her dead in her face, yet my body was betraying me.

"Sweet Ebony," she said, laced with venom. "It's not your fault your mother was a waste of human cells and did nothing but curse you but what you won't do, on my watch, is taint my precious baby."

All of a sudden, the hag released my lips. "I don't know what you're talking about," I stuttered. The blood drained from Aunt Estelle's face. She didn't expect me to be able to speak this quickly. She leaned in closer, so close that I thought she was going to kiss me. In an instant, an object came crashing into my head and then the darkness came.

It was the drums that made me regain consciousness the second time that night. Just like in my dreams, I was in the middle of the circle. But unlike my dreams, the people were really there. The jokester, a man dressed in kente cloth, three red stripes of paint down the right side of his face, three red stripes down the left. His laughter was uncontrollable. Yet it wasn't funny. It was almost haunting, almost like the joke was on me. Then there was the Mourner, dressed in black silk with her face completely covered. She rocked back and forth on her heels. In a repetitive motion, so much so that the markings of the movement were etched into the dirt. She wailed and screeched into the night.

There were others in the circle surrounding me. As I stood to my feet, I turned around to take all of them in. At the head, directly under the North Star, was the obvious leader of the group. When I faced her, there was complete silence. The drums stopped. The laughing stopped. The crying stopped. The leader stepped closer to me, and I realized who it was. It was the woman that Nika was talking to when I first got into town. She broke out in song. It was in a language I didn't know, yet I understood every word she was saying. She would sing a line and the group would respond. They all locked arms and began to rock in unison.

Suddenly, I felt a sensation come over my body. My hips were the first to start moving. Once my hips felt the beat in the rhythm of the song, my upper body began to sway. I kicked off my heels. As soon as my feet connected with the earth, I felt like I was in the place I was supposed to be at that moment. The leader looked upon me and smiled. She looked at her group fellowshipping with her and began to speak in her native tongue. But again, I understood her.

"She's ready. It's her time. I can now go."

When she said the last line, the Mourner began to wail again. The Joker began to laugh. And I began to cry. I locked eyes with her, and she nodded at me. I don't know why but I grabbed my shoes, and I took off running. I don't know where I got this burst of energy from, but I was doing some of the fastest running I've ever done in my life. But for some reason, I didn't feel alone. I felt like someone or something else was there with me.

I was running so hard and so fast, I didn't see Nika in front of me and ran hard into her. She was going on and on about some damn dog chasing her, but there was nothing out there. I had to tell her about her mother, and I didn't know how to do it. I looked at her, she was just as dirty and battered as I was. I open my mouth to tell her I have something to tell her. Imagine my surprise when she said the same.

ANIKA

THERE WAS an awkward pause after we both blurted out in chorus our last statement. I held back just a millisecond almost afraid to acknowledge the myriad of weird things that had happened to me on just that day alone. Internally, I was afraid of how my cousin would look at me if I told her even a portion of what I thought I knew or was trying to put together. I was more intrigued by what she had to say, however. I mean, I did just find her in the middle of the woods after my mother claimed she had gone home hours before. What was with all the lies and the clouds of deceit? Had Ebony really been in the woods for hours? Who or better yet what was out here? I held my breath waiting for her to say something and noticed she was hesitant as well.

"Ebony... why the hell are we in the woods? I'm freaking out and I have so many things going through my mind. I just don't know."

We both jumped when the cell phone vibrated in my hands. I was still carrying it from earlier.

"Is that my phone?" Ebony asked as she snatched it from

me. "Montel?! Can you hear me?" Ebony said with a bit of panic in her voice.

One thing about being in Ravenwood was the poor cell tower reception. Being in the woods made it even worse.

"God damnit!"

She cursed as she marched around holding the phone in the air to get a better signal. I was still trying to process the events of earlier and was ready to offer my own explanation. "Anika, I think your Mama did some fucked up shit to us. I'm sorry but I don't know how else to tell you." She looked at me partly in anger and also with shame.

I was frozen only because deep in my heart I was thinking the same thing, but I didn't want to admit it. Yet the signs were clearly there for me to see tonight. But it was so odd. I mean daddy had just died and despite being a hard ass, Mama loved me and would never hurt me. I knew she had ill feelings towards her deceased sister, but I always thought it was the usual sibling rivalry. But if what Ebony was saying was true and what my gut instincts were saying agreed then I had to swallow the fact that my mother was up to no good.

"Nika, I know we haven't been as close as we were as kids but something weird is going on here. We need to get the hell up out these woods! Plus, my good damn heels and clothes are trashed!" She said as she looked around without taking a step forward.

I finally broke my silence. "Eb, are you sure you didn't see a large dog or hear anything in these woods?"

She opened her mouth to say something but held back instead. "All I know is that Auntie Estelle brought me here, left me, and then I ran into you talking about a dog chasing you and shit. I don't know, I just need to get out of here."

She didn't make eye contact with me, and I sensed she was holding back. I looked around again and decided now was not the time to figure out the specifics. It was dark and I was scared, and we needed to get out of these woods. We used Ebony's cell phone flashlight to be a guide as we slowly tiptoed through the underbrush. Ebony cursed silently as she stepped on rocks and twigs as she refused to put her *good* heels back on.

It took about 25 minutes before we reached the clearing and Grandma Lou's pink Cadillac was in view. I looked at the house and the lights were all off except the front porch light. I huffed as I thought, *did she really leave the light on for me after everything that's happened tonight?*

Ebony wasted no time going to the car and jumped in the driver's seat. "I don't know about you, but I can't come back here anymore. My therapist is going to have me committed for sure after I tell her about this bullshit," she said more to herself than me.

I started towards the house and stopped when I heard a howl in the distance. I jumped and made a beeline to the passenger door. "Maybe I should come with you to Grandma Lou's tonight," I said hoping my trembling voice didn't give away any more suspicion from the night.

Ebony sucked her teeth. "Come on, I'm glad you're leaving anyways. Today has been cuh-rae-zee!"

As we drove away I stared out the window and wasn't sure if I saw the glowing yellow eyes in the bushes or not as we made it to the main highway. I had so many questions and so many emotions flowing through me. I realized as we were cruising that I had left my cell and my clothes at my mother's house. I would need to go back tomorrow when I felt the coast was clear. I could sense Ebony glancing at me every few seconds as if she was waiting for me to give her an explanation. I didn't dare look at her. She seemed to be taking this in stride despite her random outbursts of sucking her teeth, cursing, and saying she knew this was a bad idea.

We pulled up to Grandma Lou's and it looked like every light was on in the house. As we reached the front steps, Montel, dressed in some jeans and a semi-dirty wife-beater came bursting through the door.

"Ebony, where the hell have you been?! I've been trying to get in touch with you and-"

"I'm fine!" Ebony cut him off as she pushed past him.

I hesitated a moment as he finally set his eyes on me and said, "Oh so are *you* going to tell me what's going on? After we got disconnected I wasn't sure what to tell Mrs. Louise... I mean Grandma Lou," he self-corrected.

I exhaled slowly. "We um…. we just needed some time to um… just catch up."

I wasn't a good liar, and I could sense that Montel could tell. He shook his head at me slightly disgusted.

"Humph." He turned to follow Ebony.

I exhaled deeply this time and held my head down as I felt a lump in my chest and my throat. I still needed to process the events of the evening, but my thoughts were interrupted,

" Whey hunnuh bun? I bun da look fuh ya tah come b'fo day clean, cause it done got late," Grandma Lou said. She had a look of concern on her face, but she didn't press.

I opened my mouth, but nothing came out.

"Hunnah come ya, run-bout-gal. GranLou gon mek it all right," she hugged me, calling me by her favorite past time, a woman constantly on the go. I felt warmth as a sense of peace swept over me. I've missed the hugs from my grandma, whom I affectionately dubbed GranLou. She looked me in the eyes, "Hush now, keep ya mout tie, hunnah ain't got to ansuh. Ya got da screnff of ya daddy people fa sho, but ya gud luk come from GranLou side," she joked as she tried to get me to calm down.

I let a small smile escape my lips and headed towards the door when I heard, "Aaaaaooooooo" howl again. I froze because it sounded like it was right behind me. GranLou continued walking indoors as if she didn't hear a thing. I debated going behind her, but my curiosity got the best of me, and I went back towards the steps. I quickly scanned the front yard searching for the source of the sound. Was I expecting to see the large grey dog again? A part of me knew that dogs didn't grow that large, not even the largest breeds like Great Danes or St. Bernards. There was a gnawing in my inner core that was screaming, wolf but that was preposterous. I heard the howling again and started towards the sound when Ebony called out, "Anika, who is that?"

EBONY

BEFORE NIKA COULD ANSWER about who was outside, Grandma Lou had already pulled both of us inside the house. Montel left us alone so that she could talk to us in private. We both looked at Grandma Lou, looking at us up and down. I could tell she was fighting something internally and she was losing the battle. It took a few seconds before she was finally able to speak.

"I tried so hard to protect you girls. But I know'd dis ya day would come."

Anika and I looked at each other confused but didn't say anything.

Grandma continued. "Dey is people out dey who wanna put bad mout on ya, do evil to ya, who wan' see ya hurt. And dey not fuh stop at nothing to see it happen."

"Both of us, Grandma Lou?" Nika asked.

She just nodded. My mother may have been the dreamer, but I was always practical.

"Grandma you have to tell us exactly what's going on. What do you mean people want to harm us? Who are these people?" I asked, practically giving her no chance to answer.

Grandma Lou began to wring her hands and look down at her feet. "I know I bun say to you girls all your lives that you real 'ceptional and I meant it. But babies, you really are 'ceptional. Nika, do you feel different 'round certain times of the month? And I'm not talking about ya womanly?" I looked at my cousin to see what her reaction was. Grandma triggered something. "And you Eb'nee. Have you been seeing people that's really not there?" That caused a knot the size of the Rock of Gibraltar to form in my throat. Grandma just nodded. "Mmm hmm, I know, I know. Girls, you're in danger and I'm afraid I can't help you. 'Stelle-"

"Auntie Estelle?"

"Mama?!" Anika exclaimed.

You could see how much it pained Grandma Lou to talk about this.

"Yes," she paused before she continued. "My daughter. But I can't say no more. I won't say no more."

This had to be something serious if it had Louise Gregory mute. I turned to look at Nika and she was silently sobbing. I can only imagine how it made her feel to hear that her mother wanted her dead. I instinctively reached over and grabbed her hand and squeezed it.

"But I can tell you who can help you. Ya Grandmammy Cary, Nika. I suggest you gals go pay her a visit," and without a goodbye or goodnight, Grandma Lou left us at the table and retreated to her room.

"Are you okay, cuz?" I asked Nika, unsure of what else to say.

She shrugged and gave me a half dimpled smile. "As good as anyone who just found out their mother is trying to kill them can be," she replied sarcastically.

I reached over and hugged her tight. "That stuff

Grandma was saying," she mumbled into my shoulder. "I really do feel different. It's like, sometimes I'm outside of my body and I can't control it. Do you see people like she said?"

I pulled back from our embrace. I wasn't sure I was ready to share but her eyes were longing to not be the only one who told the truth. "Yea, I do."

Anika pushed back from the table and stood up. "That's it then. I'm going to take a shower and get in bed with Grandma Lou. You know she don't allow no shacking up in her house, so I know Montel has the guest room," she laughed. "Besides, she looks like she could use a little company tonight." We gave each other a quick peck on the cheek, and she was gone.

I lightly tapped on the guest room door and waited for Montel to reply. "Come on in," his deep baritone voice said. Montel was laying shirtless watching 227.

"I just wanted to come check on you and apologize."

He sat up at that statement. "Apologize? Apologize for what?"

I looked sheepishly at the ground. This nigga really has me giddy. "Nika said you called a few times for me. I'm sorry I missed your calls."

Montel reached for my hand and pulled me next to him. "You have nothing to be sorry about. I wasn't trying to be nosy, but your grandmother isn't exactly a quiet talker. I could kind of hear what's going on."

I instantly begin to deflate.

"It sounds like you've got a lot going on. If you ever wanna talk about it-"

"Can I take you somewhere?" I asked, cutting him off.

Montel smiled, he knew what I was doing. Trying to

change the subject. "I'll go anywhere with you, Ebony Gregory."

Montel must have asked are we there yet? 10 times before I parked the car. When we finally reached our destination at the end of the long dirt road, we ended up at Botany Bay Beach. Famous for its beached dead and alive trees, it was one of my mother's and my favorite place when I was a little girl. After the half-mile walk to the shore using our phones for flashlights, the gasp of admiration that Montel gave was worth it.

"Ebony this place is absolutely breathtaking!"

Montel stripped off his shoes, shorts, and shirt until he was down to his Ralph Lauren boxer briefs. I followed suit until I was down into my matching La 'Pearle bra and panties. I warned him that it wasn't much of a swimming beach and that we needed to be careful where we stepped, but Montel didn't care.

When that warm salty water touched his body he felt rejuvenated. He felt what I felt whenever I came here. I was reborn. Maybe that's why Mama loved to come here so much. She could come here, and all her mistakes and all of her heartbreaks were washed away.

We played a little while longer and then came back to the shore and sat on the beach. No words were spoken when the first bra strap came off my shoulder. He replaced it with a kiss. It remained silent when the second bra strap came down. Montel looked me in my eyes and told me "If I don't have you tonight I think I may just lose my mind. Ever since that night we made love on your birthday, all I do is dream of you. I'm at work, I think of you. I'm at the gym, I think of you. It's like you've got a hold on me, and I can't shake you. But at the same time, I don't think I want to shake you. Am I making sense?"

I didn't answer him. I wanted to feel him. I kissed him hard and prayed that was enough answer from me. When Montel entered me, I thought that I was losing my mind for a second. Instantaneously and simultaneously, I heard the howl of a wolf and the same drums I had heard earlier that night. Were these the dogs Nika's kept talking about? I didn't know and at that moment and I didn't care.

As I was riding Montel and looking down on him, tears were running out of his eyes. I watched him grip the sand like he was trying to hold on. And the more he gripped the harder I fucked. I was turned on by turning him out. I need to have sex more often. And this is exactly the release I needed to prepare me for the day Nika and I had ahead of us with her Granny Cary.

ANIKA

I WOKE up early the next morning noticing the warmth missing next to me. Grandma Lou was an early riser and had left the bed what seems like hours ago to prepare breakfast. I turned over on my back and stared at the old popcorn ceiling. I noticed the brown rings which indicated a leak from the rain and some random cobwebs dotted across. I wondered if Ebony and Montel were up and was surprised when I heard voices outside the window.

I jumped up and took a peek and saw the two of them giggling and trying to tiptoe towards the back door with their shoes in tow. Their legs had sand on them and their clothes looked disheveled. I smiled to myself knowing they would be caught by Grandma Lou the minute the back knob turned and more so knowing they had spent the night out of the house.

I gingerly hopped out of bed and made my way to the kitchen at the same time the wide eyes of the midnight bandits opened the back door.

"Ohhh shit!" Ebony said when she saw Grandma Lou, who was stirring a pot of hot grits. "Whey hunnah churn bun?" Grandma Lou said without taking her eyes from her pot.

"Gran, what's for breakfast?" I tried to interrupt and distract Grandma Lou to give Ebony and Montel a chance to get their bearings. I didn't see the large crooked index finger until it was almost in my face.

"You tryin to distract ole GranLou but I seent em when dey sneak out and I done caught' em tippin back in," she let out a relaxed humph.

Everyone laughed and exhaled once we realized trouble was not at hand. "Hurry back so ya can eat dis ya food!" She yelled over her shoulder. Ebony zoomed past me and widened both eyes which read, *girl whew!* Montel gave an embarrassed nod and smile as he followed. I sat at the large wood table and waited for the food to be done.

"So, I guess ya gon see Cary'n'those today huh? What bout ya mama'nem?"

I froze at the thought of heading back to my mother's. It seemed like a bad nightmare but I knew what had happened was true. I also looked at Grandma Lou and wondered how hard it was for her to have all this information about her girls. What more did she know? I wondered to myself.

"Yes ma'am, it should make for another wonderful adventure," I said as I felt a slight chill come over my body.

After we all ate a hearty country breakfast, I made plans to go into town first so I could pick up some toiletries which would give Ebony and Montel some time together. When I returned we would go visit my Granny Cary.

After pulling off I realized that I needed to go home to retrieve my wallet and decided to just gather all my things. I drove the pink Cadillac as slow as I could to my mother's place. *Would I be protected? Could I summon that stranger that appeared to me not once but twice? Would my mother even be present?* All these thoughts flooded my mind as I pulled into the circular gravel driveway.

I stepped out of the car and everything looked normal but it was eerily quiet. My mother's car was not here so I assumed she was at work and this would be the perfect time for me to enter and grab my things. I reached for the handle and cussed silently because the door was locked. I walked around the side of the house and tried the back window. I hadn't jumped a window since elementary school but it was a skill you never lost.

I squeezed myself through the window and was happy to land on a pile of dirty laundry that was on the floor. I stopped to listen for someone or something and was relieved to feel like I was alone. I slowly explored and came to the kitchen and dining area where my mother had tried to poison me. It was also where the stranger had appeared and had put a fear so strongly on my mother I was baffled. The house now felt empty and I quickly went to my room to gather my phone and suitcase.

I didn't even hear the footsteps behind me but I heard the voice. "Anika, your time has come."

I turned around ready to pounce and was relieved to see the same beautiful stranger. "Who are you?" I asked as I squinted my eyes.

"The bloodstone will protect you. It will lead you on your path. Always keep it near," she said in a melodic voice.

She came towards me and placed a leather necklace with the bloodstone pendant around my neck. I reached both hands to rub the piece.

"But who are you and how did you get in here?"

The beautiful stranger smiled again. "Always keep it near."

As she said this I felt the bloodstone turn warm between my fingers so I tilted my chin down to get a better look at it. I fumbled with it slightly and decided to look in the mirror for any changes and noticed the stranger was gone. I stood there watching the space where she once stood swirl around little particles of dust as the light danced through the blinds. I should've been freaked out that a person or a being was appearing and disappearing but the more I touched the pendant the more at peace I felt.

I grabbed my car keys as I rolled my suitcase out of the house and made a mental note to come back to get my car. I looked around once I made it outside and jumped in Grandma Lou's car and drove away. My battery indicator was red but I still had some juice left. I had 1 missed call from my co-worker Sabrina and 2 text messages from KB. I anxiously clicked the message and it read; *Hey baby.* Right underneath read; *In Downtown Charleston for a show, give me a call so we can link. Sorry about your pops,* with a crying face emoji.

I shook my head in disgust. I didn't reply to him but instead, gave Ebony a call.

"Hey cuz," she said on the first ring.

"Hey, I'm about to pull up, can you be ready in 15?"

"Damn that was fast! Did you rob the store or what?"

My silence made her say my name. I quietly answered, "No, I went to my mother's and-"

"Bitch you did what?!" She shrieked.

I could hear Montel in the background saying, "Is she ok? Do we need to go?"

"Eb calm down, I'll tell you about it when I get back to GranLou's ok?"

"Hurry Up!" She yelled before clicking off the call. I guess that would be equivalent to slamming the phone down if we still used house telephones.

I tried to creep up slowly in the yard but Ebony was at my door before I could park the car. She opened her mouth to speak but was stunned to silence when she saw the pendant on the leather strap around my neck. "Oh my..." she purred as she looked at me bewildered. "Oh, this is gonna be good," she said as she shook her head and helped me with my suitcase.

"Can I shower first and brush my teeth, I will tell you everything on the way to my Granny Cary," I said looking her directly in the eyes. She just stared at me. "I promise," I said as convincingly as possible.

She rolled her eyes and let me walk ahead of her. I passed Montel who seemed to be staring at Ebony hoping to get some information but she gave away nothing.

I was able to complete my hygiene and get dressed without incident while Grandma Lou took the time to entertain Ebony and Montel. I came out to the porch and heard Montel exclaim, "Grandma Lou is gonna take me crab hunting!" he said while everyone laughed.

"No baby it's crabbin," GranLou corrected as she rattled off all the items needed for the trip. I waited until her list was done before asking

"Do you mind taking Montel to my mother's to pick up my car?" I dangled my keys in the air.

Grandma Lou gave me a stern look as her lips pressed into a tight line. I think everyone was holding their breath until Montel spoke up and said, "That's cool with me, that is if Grandma Lou is okay with taking me," he said in a warm tone that seemed to melt the ice around Grandma Lou's face. She nodded her head and tapped her feet still glaring at me and now Ebony as we headed towards her car.

"Make sure ya fill my tank back up and use premium gas ya hear?" she yelled as she took her attention and excitement back to Montel.

We slowly rode away from the house when Ebony blurted out, "Okay bitch, talk!"

As we drove through town I filled her in on everything from the time I arrived, me jumping the window and being face to face with the stranger. I explained what happened with the bloodstone pendant and the instructions I was given. When I was done, Ebony sat back in her seat. "Who is that woman, you think?"

I didn't have any answers and I was relieved she wasn't freaked out either by her episodes of magically appearing and disappearing. Did I just think magic? I mused to myself as the car seemed to propel us to the wooded area where Granny Cary lived. The area had heavy foliage and there was an old rusted mailbox with the red flag up indicating a residence was nearby.

"This looks creepy AF," Ebony said as she sat up in the seat when I turned onto a non-existent road.

It seemed like fog appeared out of nowhere making the drive seem claustrophobic and mysterious. I kept one hand on the steering wheel and the other automatically reached for the pendant which seemed to be throbbing against my chest. The fog was so thick neither of us could see in front of us. Suddenly the pink Cadillac stalled out and cut off. We both shot each other nervous glances. In the distance, I heard a faint howl but didn't react because I didn't want to alarm Ebony.

"Let's get out," I said hoarsely.

Ebony gave me an are you crazy, expression. The more I held on to the bloodstone, the braver I felt. I got out the driver's side and made my way to the passenger side to link arms with Ebony. She was trembling slightly but made no sound at all. I hesitantly took a step when the voice came out again, "the bloodstone will protect you. It will lead you on your path. Always keep it near."

I felt a renewed sense of bravery come over me and yanked Ebony in the direction of the voice. We felt blind, tripping over ourselves, in the foggy clearing for what seemed like several hundred yards and we both jumped when we heard the 'aaaaaooooooo,' I could feel the hairs on the back of my neck rise and Ebony's grip on me got tighter.

I continued to walk in what seemed like a direction I was familiar until instantly the fog dissipated and we were standing in front of Granny Cary's rickety front porch. There with a smug smile on her face stood my Granny Cary and I looked at Ebony.

"See, I knew we were headed in the right direction," I halfway laughed at her. "There is my granny."

She nodded and then pointed with her chin "Yes, but who is that?"

I followed her gaze and gasped when I saw the stranger who had given me the pendant.

"You *can* see her too?" I asked more out of amazement than anything. It was proof that I wasn't hallucinating but it didn't prove how the stranger could come and go into thin air.

Ebony seemed to be locked in an eye war with the

stranger, communicating in some way. Simultaneously Granny Cary came down the steps.

"Your time has come," she said. She looked over at Ebony who was still frozen in the same spot. "She will come when it is her time, but now I need only you." She gently tugged on me as I sauntered past Ebony who didn't seem to notice me or anyone but the stranger at all. "Did you see your uncle on the way in? He was supposed to meet you out by the mailbox," Granny Cary said as we entered the home.

It instantly smelled like sage with remnants of vanilla and lavender. "Granny Cary, who is that woman on your porch?" I asked curiously while I spun around to look at the room I hadn't been in since a little girl. It gave me instant memories of my daddy and I felt a large burn in my throat that threatened tears.

Granny Cary didn't answer but went back to the front door and peered out. "Did you see your Uncle B or not child?" she asked again.

I made my way to the table where there were various items laid out that seemed interesting. There were crystals of various colors, sage, dried flower petals, leather string, and small vials of a light blue liquid. I froze and spun again on my heels when I heard the 'aaaaaooooooooooo' come belting from Granny Cary. I felt my pulse quicken and my temperature rise when she opened the door to let in a large black dog with yellow eyes in the parlor. I fainted when the same dog creature transfigured into that of a man, my Uncle Bernard! The last thing I heard was a scream before everything went dark.

ESTELLE

CLICK-CLACK, *Click-clack* went the keys on the office computer while patients could be heard loudly in the outer lobby of the office. I typed ferociously and in a daze as I attempted to erase the memories of the last few days. My typing skills: 72 wpm excelled as much as my nursing career. Thanks to Mavis Beacon's Typing Program as well as money from my recently deceased husband Thad, who had paid my way through school. Now as a successful Nurse Practitioner with a Doctorate, I had so many other things in mind I wished money and typing could solve. I was so focused on the document I was typing that I didn't notice my assistant in the doorway.

"Dr. Howell?" Shelly said a little louder on the 3rd attempt.

This caused me to jerk my head up. "What do you want Sherryl?" I snapped. The tension between the air was thick enough to slice with a butter knife.

"Ma'am you have someone out in the lobby requesting to see you," Shelly answered a little deflated.

I stood up and huffed past her as she added in a low whisper, "And it's Shelly you bitch."

I sped walked down the decorated corridor of my West Ashley office suite and opened the door to the lobby. The gruffness quickly turned into pleasantries as I cooed.

"Well, if it isn't Mr. Kelly Bridges, the most talented saxophonist in the entire southeast!" I strode towards Kelly and grabbed both his hands while giving him air kisses on both sides of his cheeks.

"Hello Mrs. Howell, you are too kind,"

"Oh stop now.... call me Estelle and come on back to my office," I said leading him back down the hallway I'd just stormed down earlier.

Kelly smiled, showing perfectly white teeth and politely nodded at the other patrons in the lobby. Everyone had stopped what they were doing to stare at the tall, caramel colored handsome stranger. I even heard someone exclaim, "Damn he fine!"

I re-entered my office and pointed to one of the oversized armchairs for him to sit. "So Kelly, what brings you to town?" I subconsciously smoothed my perfectly styled hair into place. Today I was wearing my long tresses into a pulled back bun, Ruby Woo red lipstick, large rhinestone earrings with a matching necklace and short manicured nails in the color Big Apple Red. My lab jacket covered most of my knee length navy blue Versace knit dress and my feet nestled comfortably in a pair of Barocco Patent Leather pumps in the same color. As I fiddled with my hair a little more, Kelly began to speak,

"Estelle, I'm truly sorry for your loss. My sincerest condolences to you and Anika."

I had to catch myself from rolling my eyes at the mention

of my daughter but instead sheepishly batted my long mink eyelashes. "I appreciate you, Kelly. You've always been so kind and such a gentleman. Especially with you being sweet on my little Anika," I said slyly and with a little more sugar in my tone than usual. "Have you spoken to Anika lately?"

Kelly shifted in the large chair to get comfortable. "Well, that's the other reason why I stopped by your office," he cleared his throat and continued. "I've been trying to get in contact with her but she hasn't returned any of my messages. I know she was close to her dad and I wanted to give her some space, but if she is okay please have her reach out to me."

I breathed a sigh of relief, happy to know that the recent events had not come to light. I smiled coyly again as I responded, "Why yes, of course. I will pass that message along to my daughter. How long will you be in town?"

At this Kelly stood up indicating he had completed his main reason for coming by the office. "I will be here for about a week. My band is playing downtown, headlining the Spoleto Arts Festival. This year they want to highlight the achievements and contributions black musicians have had on the arts in the surrounding areas." He leaned over and placed a handbill on my desk and grinned devilishly as he gazed at a picture of a young Anika in a silver-plated frame on my desk. I followed his eyes then stood to distract his view.

"I am so happy to see you still have feelings for my daughter. It's a shame her father isn't around to see what your relationship will blossom into. Maybe I should have you over for dinner before you leave?"

At the sound of this Kelly quickly diverted his eyes to me and gave me a slow once over. I was still a bad mamma jamma to be in my early 60s. The way he stared, I assume he was imagining if this was how graceful Anika would age over the next 2-3 decades.

"Mrs. Howell, I would love that, you know a brother could get down with some country cookin," he laughed and gestured towards my body with a shrug.

As we both walked towards the entryway, it opened again unexpectedly with Shelly in the doorframe.

"Excuse me Dr.-oh I'm sooooo sorry! I didn't realize you brought your guest to your office," Shelly said looking back and forth between the two of us trying to figure out what was going on.

"What is it now?" The icy tone back in my voice.

"You have a meeting scheduled at 1 and the pharmaceutical rep is already here in the break room waiting."

At the sound of this, my mood changed. "YES! Thank you!" I turned to Kelly, "Please excuse me, I have a very important meeting to attend, but my assistant Sherryl here will see you out."

I excused myself and left the two gawking at my back as I slowly made my way to the stairwell. I could faintly hear Kelly invite Shelly to hear his band play at Spoleto. As the stairwell door slammed behind me I mused *country cooking my ass!*

I rushed down the flight of stairs to meet the pharmaceutical rep in the break room. Upon entering, I reached back to lock the door and turned around quickly, "Did you bring what I asked for?" Casually I strolled to the table to see what was in the briefcase the rep had brought.

"Ev'ry ting you requested is in dis case," the voice said with a Creole accent. The rep opened the black case and revealed large sashes of blue wolfbane petals, several 8oz jars of mustard-colored powder, 2 vials of Holy Water, a set of silver bullets, needles, and miniature silver sprinkles that looked like glitter.

I shrieked with delight as I eyed the contents of the case.

"Now dis case is double the normal amount, no?" The rep had a questioning tone.

"Yes, yes whatever you say," I said without removing my eyes from the case. "I can have my assistant drop the cash off near the old bridge next to Ravenwood Creek in less than an hour."

The pharmaceutical rep nodded and unlocked the door to leave but not before turning to me as I was now fingering the items in the case, "Dis ting ya is getting mighty serious, no? Ya may need a root docta to spell and bind for a stronger effect."

I paused for a second then nodded. "You'll have your payment soon enough... until next time."

I closed the case and headed back up the flight of stairs to my office. As I proceeded down the corridor I stopped by the only office with the door wide open, "Sherryl, I need you to make a drop for me before you leave today. Stop by my office, thanks." I retreated before getting a response. Every time she made these *drops,* it included a bonus of cash and the remainder of the day off.

I went to my private office bathroom and drew back the shower curtain. I removed my shoes and carefully stepped into the tub. My hands methodically pressed above the water knob and opened a secret compartment that looked like the matching marble tiles. I grabbed several stacks of crisp Franklins and placed them in a large leather black case and went back to my doorway where Shelly was standing.

"Take this to Ravenwood Creek and wait for the rep to pick up. I expect complete discretion, you understand?"

Shelly nodded as she took hold of the case. "And take the rest of the day." I flung my wrist, dismissing Shelly as she abruptly spun on the balls of her heels.

SHELLY

"SHERRYL. WHO THE FUCK IS SHERRYL?" I said to no one in particular under my breath. Dr. Howell knew my name and she knew it very well. My mother had made me a junior, naming me Marshella after herself. She and Dr. Howell grew up together in our small, sleepy town of Ravenwood. They used to be best friends, even became sorority sisters but something happened between the two of them and they were never the same.

Then there was Aron and Amir. I often wondered what my life would be like if they were still here. Would he and I be married with kids by now? Would his brother be out of our lives? Would Anika stop treating me like shit? Before the twins died that horrid, twisted night, Anika walked up on Amir, Aron, and me but it wasn't what it looked like. Still, almost 15 years later, you couldn't tell Anika any different. But it also didn't help that I was there the night the twins died.

Since then, Dr. Howell has taken an interest in my life. It was common knowledge that the summer of 1993, my father Alexander Bishop was arrested for corruption and brought up on RICO charges. After a lengthy and embarrassing trial my father, the ex-mayor of Ravenwood, was found guilty and sentenced to 27 years with no parole. My mama didn't allow me to go to the trial. Daddy was on bail, and during the 4 years between the arrest and the start of the trial, daddy was home. Then one day, mama came home without him. And my life was never the same.

We were pretty much lepers in our town. No one would dare say anything or cross Mayor Bishop but with daddy gone, me and Mama were fair game. I noticed she started sleeping in later. I was starting my freshman year in high school, so it wasn't like I needed her to get ready for school but it would have been nice.

Then there was the drinking. Mama became a regular at the local juke joint. Dr. Howell or as I called her then, Miss. 'Stelle made it her mission to look out for her soror and her daughter left behind by the disgraced politician.

When mama needed rehab, I lived with the Howells for 90 days and grew closer to Anika and the twins. It was the closest I had to a normal family. Very rarely, Anika's cousin Ebony would come by. I really liked her. She reminded me of myself. But I could always tell Miss. 'Stelle was ready for her to go almost as soon as she got there. I never got that.

Those times the 5 of us would explore the woods and fields of Ravenwood. On one of our adventures, he grabbed my hand. It was innocent enough but still stirred something up in my young loins. Anika and I were 17, they were 15. Ebony was a few years younger than us but it didn't matter. We all got along wonderfully.

Again, whenever Ebony was around Miss. 'Stelle was beside herself. Always lurking in the shadows, watching us. And like clockwork, she'd feed us lunch, Ebony would complain about not feeling well, and their grandmother, never her mother, would pick her up. I could never tell if she was faking or not. Maybe she felt the prying eyes and ominous presence of Miss. 'Stelle and wanted to get the hell out of there. I know I would.

Then there were the times he and I would try to sneak away alone. 13, I still remember. 13 times we were able to get away and be alone for a few moments from our adventuring group. No matter where we went, how far away we thought we got away, his twin would always find us. It was almost as if he had a tracking device on him. Could smell him out. He hated me. Oh, that boy despised me. I never understood why. I had never done anything to him, was always kind and gracious. I think he thought I was taking his brother away from him. Of the 13 times, only 1 time were we able to be successfully alone. So that's why I hold on to that 1 night.

Miss. 'Stelle and Mr. Thad had gone to the city to catch a movie. Anika and his twin were taking some fabric their grandmother had ordered down to her house. That left me and him alone. I was cleaning the dinner dishes when he snuck up behind me. I never even heard him enter the room, he was like a predator stalking his prey. Being a good 7 inches taller than me, he inhaled my hair as he wrapped his arms around me. Some days, if I sit still enough, I can still feel him. I can still smell him. He turned me around and kissed me like I had never been kissed before. We had snuck little pecks here and there, but this was different. I didn't want it to end. He grabbed my hand and led me to the guest room that I had been staying in and laid me on the bed. He was so gentle as if I were glass and he was afraid to break me.

"Do you want me to stop Shells?" he asked.

He was the only person in my life to call me that, and no one has called me Shells since. I shook my head no. And he took my virginity there on that bed, that night. And sadly, that was the last night I would have him... alone.

Mama eventually got better so I went home, but I was still close to Anika and Ebony. Miss. 'Stelle still came to see us and even made sure I had my debut at the Cotillion Ball. My dress was just as fancy as Anika, although strangely Ebony's wasn't. You could tell hers was used and patched together the best Grandma Lou could. But why would Miss. 'Stelle make sure I had a new dress and not her own niece? It didn't matter, even if Ebony felt self-conscious, she didn't show it. She smiled proudly with the rest of us and kept it moving.

The night after the Cotillion, the Howell's threw a big party. The twins escorted two girls, another set of twins, from Edisto Island. They had stayed for an hour and left. Ebony, Grandma Lou, and her mother never came. We were in the backyard drinking beers that they had snuck out of the house. He and I started to walk away from Anika and his twin so we could be alone. We hadn't been together since the night he took my virginity. And that was almost 2 months before.

When we thought we were far enough away from them, he spun me around and pinned me against a tree. His kiss was long, deep, and hard. I don't know if it was the beer that gave me nerve, but I clumsily unbuckled the belt of his tuxedo as he bunched up the heavy fabric of my dress around my waist. What he did shocked me, but not enough to stop him. He turned me around, pressed my face against the tree, and took me from behind.

We rocked in unison, panting and clawing at each other.

And for a split second, I swear it was like he was howling. I didn't know if I was too tight, was I hurting him? He didn't stop. And I loved it. I reached back and dug my nails into his ass, pushing him inside me. I looked up at that full moon and thought, *God I don't want this feeling to end* but it was when I looked back down, that everything changed. I gasped and struggled to pull my dress down.

"Oh no, no, no, don't stop on account of me." It was his brother.

I was prepared for him to tell his brother to scram or get outta here but he didn't. It was like he caved into himself.

"We... we weren't doing anything," my love stuttered.

His brother laughed, "We... weren't doing anything," he mocked him.

I looked up at him in disbelief, why wasn't he defending me? Hell, himself? His twin, obviously drunk, walked up to me and ran his hands through my hair.

"Well, if you weren't doing anything, then you won't mind if I try right, *brother*?" He ran his hand up my dress and started fingering me.

I didn't have time to put my panties and stockings back on so he had easy access.

"Please, don't do that. Leave her alone," my lover lamented, in the weakest voice ever. But the more he pleaded, the more his brother did.

What happened next happened so fast. His brother kicked me in the small of my back causing me to drop to my knees, laughing. When he reached to help me, his twin said between clenched teeth, "I wish you would." And he stopped. He actually listened. "Now let's see how much she really loves you. Pull it out so she can suck it."

Both he and I looked stunned and instantly protested.

But he wasn't hearing it. He pushed my head towards his crotch and my love did as he was commanded. I had never done anything like this before. And from the looks of it, neither had he. But I didn't want to be hit again, so I complied. I felt awful. I looked up and he was looking up at the sky with tears running down his face. What was this hold that his brother had on him?

Then I felt him. I didn't know he was able to move so quickly and efficiently, but his twin was having sex with me while making me perform this act on his brother. Me crying out made him look down.

"YOOOOOOO WHAT ARE YOU DOING?!" He yelled, pulling up his pants.

Before either of us could reply, we heard, "You nasty fucking ungrateful bitch!" It was Anika. She came looking for us and stumbled upon this tragic scene and since that day we have never been the same.

When the twins died, our friendship became more strained. Miss. 'Stelle and I grew much closer. She's become my mentor, a sorority sister, and a second mother. She has her ways and can be quite a bitch, but she's an amazing practitioner. And I'm thankful for her. Anika and I, who knows what will happen to us. But I keep trying. Maybe I'm childish to still be looking for that friendship again.

But these days all I have is Mama, who is trying to figure out how she feels about daddy coming home next year, and Miss 'Stelle. I'd do anything for her. I owe that lady my life. That's why when she asks me to do these drops, I ask no questions. I grabbed my bag and the briefcase she dropped on my desk a few minutes ago and headed to the crik.

ESTELLE

I PARKED in the yard shocked to see Anika's white Camaro missing. I huffed and wondered how in the hell did she get into the house. I used to leave a spare key in the garden bed of my Gardenia's but that was when she was in high school. She must've had another key or gotten one from my mother. As I slowly exited my vehicle I checked my surroundings and felt an instant shiver of anxiety, fear, and relief.

I was no stranger to *the strange* and had spent my life trying to rid this family of its effects. My dearly departed husband initially introduced me to this lifestyle of *the strange*. When I met Thaddeus Howell, I felt an instinctual attraction towards him. It was more lustful before it became love. The problem was everyone else had that same level of attraction towards him as well. The problem within that problem was that Thaddeus had an unspeakable bond of lust and love for my younger sister, Leola. The intimacy was primal and invigorating which meant the physical act of sex was beyond amazing. But since I was the eldest and had a promising future, he chose stability over vanity.

I shook my head of those earlier memories and smiled as I looked down at my briefcase. The strangeness that Thaddeus brought to my life included the likes of creatures, the unknown, and various elements of hoodoo jinxes. I chalked it all up to hoodoo voodoo and made it my mission to keep my family's bloodline as Christian like and pure as possible. I had seen and heard many things over the last 30 years but I refused to allow myself to fully believe that it was acceptable.

I kicked off my heels as soon as I entered the front living area. The house was quiet except for the monotonous ticking of the black ebony wood clock on the wall. It was an African tribal piece we had gotten from a Yoruba Priestess when we stayed there years ago. The legend behind the clock was that it brought protection from the darkness and all that dwelt therein so long as it kept ticking. I never believed the mumbo jumbo but my husband was determined to have it in the first room of the house upon entering. I had a mind to snatch it down and throw it into the fireplace, but right now my mind was on the items in the briefcase.

Before I entered the kitchen, I dropped my keys into the silver decorative bowl that had lemongrass and camphor potpourri and looked around timidly. I didn't want any surprises like the last incident but after dousing myself with a vial of holy water and even taking a small sip for good measure, I felt I was safe enough now in my home. I also lit a clove and cinnamon-scented soy candle as I glanced towards the hallway to Anika's room and felt a tinge of guilt and sadness because I really missed my daughter, but I was continuing my life's mission to keep her as human and as safe as possible.

I knew she inherited the DNA of her father, who had some undesirable traits, but nothing like a little antiserum to keep her from experiencing major changes. For her entire life, I've been suppressing these traits and even those of my niece, Ebony. My sister Leola had no intention of protecting herself or the family. She was so much in love with my husband and bought into his theology of what I called animalistic behavior. Ebony did seem to turn out a little more stable than her mother, but the sight of her always made me angry. I couldn't blame the child, she didn't ask to be here, but she was her mother's daughter.

I shook my head again and focused back on the briefcase. While I was being exposed to the unnatural all those years, I was also learning how to avoid and somewhat dismantle the unknown. I had visited several creole communities over the last 30 years to learn and gather the information I needed to combat what I coined as *the strange.*

Being in the nursing field had its perks as I was able to locate a provider, whom I affectionately dubbed my pharmaceutical rep to supply me with items needed. It was a family that originated from the bayous of Louisiana and so far I'd worked with 3 of their matriarchal figures in exchange for medical services, prescription pills, and now cash. I eventually became well versed in how to create anti-potions, vanquishing creams, and edible deterrents all while staying under the radar from prying ears and eyes.

Since Thaddeus had passed away and both Anika and Ebony were home, I was more frightened that their shared genes would be surfacing. During the time they were away, I'd been practicing my craftwork on my assistant, Shelly. She is the daughter of a good friend and soror of mine who had a history with one or possibly both of the twins. She didn't know it but the community coffee had hints of ground-up wolfsbane and I always had the local minister pray and bless the 5-gallon water jug for the freestanding dispenser before I had it delivered and set up in the employee break room.

Shelly was an interesting character at times, always staring at that old Polaroid picture she kept in her desk of her and the twins the night of their Cotillion. She had used a permanent marker and etched out the face of one of them and I wasn't sure why. She was also present the night the boys died and may have been the last living person they had contact with. So in a way, I had some sympathy for her, but she never seemed to be able to remember or give me all the details of that night.

Shelly had gotten attacked in the woods when the boys died and that immediately piqued my interest. She had bouts of amnesia and was heading down a similar path of self-destruction her mother had been on until I was asked to mentor her. After her incident, she wanted to work in the medical field to save people and I felt she would be a great addition to my staff. She had been my personal assistant for years, no closer to becoming anything medical but she didn't seem to mind.

I know I annoyed her by calling her, Sherryl but as her boss, I had the authority to call her what I wanted. It also kept her focused on my bitchiness that she never had time to really investigate what I'd been doing all these years.

I checked my phone to see if she texted me the confirmation of the drop but saw no alerts. I sat in the wooden chair in the kitchen and massaged my feet while I studied the items I laid out on the table. Now that Anika had left, I needed to be more creative on how to get these items to her and in her system. I could guess that Anika went to stay with my mother, or even more so scary her paternal grandmother, Mother Cary Howell. There was *no way* I was going over there. That woman scared the hell out of me. If she was at my mother's I could deal with her level of wrath but I needed to be extra careful with how I could get these suppressants to both girls.

Over the years my mother, Louise Gregory had never fully agreed with my methods but didn't want to overstep her boundaries. I respected her as my mother and confidante as she kept my secret of me prohibiting these genetic, anatomical, and soul stirring changes in both girls. My sister knew and she was against it, but she had enough skeletons in her closet she'd rather not have exposed. So that kept her lips sealed.

I continued to stare at the items hoping a master plan would develop when my thoughts were interrupted by knocking on my front door. My heart rate quickened and I grabbed the nearest 8-inch steel chef knife. I tiptoed to the door and glanced out the bottom corner of the blinds. I exhaled heavily and swung the door open.

"Mrs. Howell, I hope I'm not bothering you. I tried reaching you at your office but I now know you weren't there. I couldn't get off in time to pick up the prescription for my wife and had hoped you could help me... after hours?"

I gave a fake smile as I hid the large knife behind my back. "Mr. Ramirez! It's such a pleasure, please come in."

He entered my home and quickly nodded his head, "my family sends their heartfelt love for the loss of Mr. Howell."

I kept the fake smile plastered on my face and said as

solemnly as I could, "he was such a great man, thank you so much."

I pointed towards the living room couch and motioned for him to sit down. I pedaled backwards towards the kitchen doorway to keep the knife hidden and was able to put it away as he looked around the room. I went to my purse to locate my prescription pad and came back to see Mr. Ramirez smiling at my family pictures.

"Is Anika still around? I didn't get a chance to speak to her at the funeral,"

"She is around. Her beau is in town so I'm sure she is spending much needed time with him, you know... for....comfort."

Mr. Ramirez's smile left his face.

"You know Mr. Ramirez, you were so instrumental in my daughter choosing veterinary medicine, when I thought she would pursue more modern medicine like her mother," I said while scribbling the information for the prescription as I continued, "between her father encouraging her love of animals and you spreading your poison, my daughter never had the ear space to hear my words of wisdom to choose being a medical doctor, or OB/GYN, or Oncologist, you know?"

I tore the prescription and handed it towards him before pulling it back. Mr. Ramirez turned a little red in the face.

"I'm sorry Dr. Howell, I didn't know you felt so strongly against Anika choosing to be a Vet. I hear she is an amazing doctor."

"An animal doctor doesn't sound *that* amazing to me," I said while still holding tight to the prescription. We had a mini stare off for about 30 seconds before he cleared his throat.

"Dr. Howell? The prescription?"

I conjured up my fake smile again and handed him the script.

Mr. Ramirez was a nice looking man of Latino descent. He was a little short and stocky but muscular in the arms. His accent bore traces of his first language of Spanish and his skin was a tanned olive color. His wife, Mrs. Ramirez had been diagnosed with a Traumatic Brain Injury several years ago after a serious car accident and still had lingering pain as well as cognitive deficits. He had been Anika's mentor in high school and during her early college years and it was he who either cultivated or solidified her love for the animal kingdom. Just when I thought it was her father who had his filthy claws in her, I discovered this man had the same effect.

"Dr. Howell, could you let Anika know I asked about her?" he asked in a bashful voice.

Just then I formulated a plan.

"You know what would be great? Maybe you could offer Anika a part-time job or even a position at your animal clinic so she could stay home close to her dear mother," I purred with a hint of begging. "She needs to be surrounded by the people and things she loves to help her with healing after losing her dad. Could you do that for me, Mr. Ramirez?" I batted my mink lashes more dramatically this time for a bonus effect.

He stuttered a bit while he turned red in the cheeks again for an unknown reason and I attributed it to the fact that I had sprung this massive responsibility on him unex-pectedly. While he fumbled with his words, I wrote down Anika's cell and passed it to him much quicker than I did the prescription. He stared at it for a few moments before nodding his head yes.

As we said our goodbyes I shut the door and clapped my hands in excitement. If Anika was willing to take a position at the local animal clinic, there were many ways to funnel the anti-potions and elixirs to her. I laughed to myself as I heard the simultaneous gong of the wooden clock and chirp on my phone indicating a new text message.

SHELLY

Can I just see you every morning when
I open my eyes
Can I just feel your heart beating beside me
Every night
Can we just feel this way together
Till the end of all time
Can I just spend my life with you

THERE ARE some songs that when you hear them, you can remember what you were doing, what you had on, and what was going on in the world. Eric Benet and Tamia's *Spend My Life* was one of those songs and it was playing in my Mercedes Benz C Class, right now. But my mind was back in that ballroom in 1999 when I and my love managed to dance together at the Cotillion Ball. It was then that I decided that it would be the song that he and I would dance to at our wedding.

But sitting here, in the present day, it never came to fruition. So whenever it came on the radio, I stopped whatever I was doing and reminisced on that night when life was good because just a mere few hours later, it became bad.

Not even Dr. Howell's pharmaceutical rep flashing her headlights would move me until the last note was sung. I don't know who that lady thought she was fooling. Whatever was in these briefcases at these *drops* was not sold in your local pharmacy. Had it not been for the high-tech, ultra-modern time released lock, I would have broken into a few of them years ago. But she pays me well for my discretion, so I mind the business that pays me.

The song ended, so I left 1999 and joined the rest of the world in 2020. I hated meeting this snaggletooth old, bull dagger. Don't get me wrong, I like to dangle in the lady pond every now and then, but never for anything remotely close to her. And she has no qualms about not hiding how she felt about me.

I sighed, opened my door, and swung my legs out of my car. As I walked around to the passenger's side, I heard her whistle.

"Greeed gawd! Ya get mo' and mo' pretty every time I see ya, girl."

I rolled my eyes and didn't even answer. I reached in to grab the briefcase and I knew without looking she was checking me out. I hurriedly grabbed the briefcase and slammed it into her chest.

"Whoa dere. So tuff, dis one. I like it."

Still not speaking, I rolled my eyes and stepped aside for her to deposit her portion of the transaction. She would usually drop a bag or box on my front seat, but she reached in her pocket.

"Here," she said, holding out a small glass vial. It appeared to be empty.

I shook my head furiously. "You must be mistaken, I'm sure this isn't what Dr. Howell sent for."

She smiled that snaggle tooth smile again and I gagged. "You don't know what you speak of girl. Dis ting here is powerful, I suggest you be careful. Wouldn't want any ting tah happen to all... of... this," she dragged out the last part.

I snatched the vial from her and threw it in my purse.

"No need fah be rude, beautiful!" She yelled out to me as I jumped back behind the wheel.

It's time to ask for a raise, I said to myself, as I flipped my visor down to check my face. But what I saw in the reflection was the most beautiful man I'd ever seen in my life. I whipped my head around as he turned his shirtless back to me.

He was casting a crab trap and looking to someone off to the side that I couldn't see, for approval. It was like the world started moving in slow motion. Every ripple and cut in the muscles of his back flexed and shined under the late after-noon sun. Obviously happy with his attempt, he smiled the whitest set of teeth I'd ever seen. I knew he wasn't from Ravenwood, nothing that beautiful ever came out of Raven-wood. Except my... *Get it together girl,* I said to myself.

I watched the rep drive away and gave myself a *gather yourself look* and exited the vehicle. The loud slam of my door did just what I wanted it to do, it got his attention. I smiled and waved as I walked over to him. That's when his counterpart stood. It was none other than Louise Gregory aka Grandma Lou, Dr. Howell's mother. This slowed my pace.

"Dat dey you, Shelly?" Grandma Lou called out.

She was a sweet woman, just like all the other older women in Ravenwood. She was always nice to me, sympathetic to my situation when I was younger. A few times I would go over and play with Ebony alone. But today was not the day I wanted to chit-chat with her. Although, it could work to my advantage because she was in the company of this new mystery man.

"Heeeeyyyyy Grandma Lou!" I said with so much sugary sweetness it would give you a toothache. I plastered on a fake smile and waved.

She wrapped her large soft arms around me and squeezed me tight. Over her shoulder, I was finally able to get a good look at him. And he was something to see. He caught me looking, and he shyly ducked his eyes. *Ahh, a shy one. This is too easy*, I thought to myself. When she pulled me back from her embrace, my syrupy smile was back.

"How you bun gal? I een seen ya in a month a Sunday's!" She exclaimed.

Grandma Lou had to be almost 90 but was getting around well for her age. I could see her lips moving but I didn't hear anything coming out of her mouth. I nodded my head saying, mmm hmm here and there, but I was trying to catch his eye again. And he knew it too. Because he was doing everything in his power to avoid it.

"Wouldn't that be nice? Shelly? Y'ear me?"

Grandma Lou caught me, I wasn't paying attention. She followed my eyes behind her as if she had forgotten he was even there.

"Oh, where is my head? Shelly, this hea' Montel. He be *Eb'nee* friend from Alanna." She put extra emphasis on Ebony and was looking me dead in the eyes when she said it. No shade, no harshness but she wanted me to know to whom he belonged. I smiled.

"Hello, Montel. I'm Marshella, one of Ebony's childhood

friends. But everyone calls me Shelly," I said with my freshly manicured hand extended.

I'm so glad I opted for the sea salt scrub.

"Nice to meet you, Shelly."

Good Gawd, his voice! That was the deepest baritone I had ever heard in my life. I think I may have actually whimpered out loud. I could have died right there of embarrassment.

"Well, are you and yo mama gonna come by for the crab crack later or not? Me and Montel done got more bushels than we bargained fah."

"Uhhh, yes... yes, of course, we'll be there."

"Great!" Grandma Lou's face lit up.

Montel sheepishly smiled as well. We spoke a little more as they loaded their bounty into the bed of his truck. Before they pulled away, Grandma Lou yelled out the window, "You and Marshella don't be late. I can't wait to see yall gals together again! 7 is when we startin' the fire!" She blew me a kiss and I blew one back. Then I slid my Gucci shades down from the top of my head and said out loud, "Fuck them bitches, I'm bout to start a fire of my own."

I SLOWLY OPENED my eyes after feeling the cool liquid drop down my forehead and towards the back of my ear. My vision was blurry but it looked like Granny Cary and Uncle Bernard were standing over me with worried looks on their faces. I saw their lips moving before I processed the sounds of their voices.

"What happened to me?" I was able to choke out while attempting to sit up.

Uncle Bernard gave me a stern look while helping me to sit upright.

"I thought I saw a big dog, yellow eyes, and then a man."

I felt myself sway again threatening to faint on the spot. Granny Cary took another ice cool cloth and placed it behind my neck.

"You had quite the fall, Anika. Take your time getting up."

I tried to get my bearings as I took a deep breath. I saw little red and green dots float in front of my eyes and wondered how hard I had fallen. Did I hit my head? Was I imagining things? I felt deep in my inner core that I saw the large black dog turn into my Uncle Bernard.

I gasped instantly when I heard a barely inaudible whine come from him. He jumped backward, almost falling himself when I trained my eyes on him. I stood up and scattered towards Granny Cary and stopped suddenly when I noticed the items on the table still.

"OMG Ebony!" I shrieked as Granny Cary touched my arm saying, "Lape."

Instantly a warm feeling of calm came upon me and I could've sworn I felt the bloodstone pendant go warm and tingle against my neck.

My eyes darted back and forth between the table and

Uncle Bernard who was now backing up towards the door. The look of hesitation on his face was apparent as Granny Cary said, "Anika, your time has come."

It was the second time I had heard that exact same phrase, except the first time it was from the beautiful stranger. Hearing my Granny Cary utter the same words piqued my interest.

A vicious low sounding growl seemed to vibrate from my Uncle Bernard. It appeared he was communicating with Granny Cary in this unconventional way as she ushered me towards the low wooden table.

"Anika baby, I need to learn you the true family legacy of the Howler's" she started.

I shook my head at her and corrected "You mean *Howell.*"

She pierced me with her dark eyes that seemed to flash a golden hue and stated, "H-O-W-L-E-R... the *true* family legacy." She hauled a large looking leather grimoire that was worn and tattered and had small indentations on the front cover. Two brass latches seemed to keep the book shut and locked tight.

I didn't recognize the strange symbols that were carved into the leather. Instantly, Uncle Bernard boomed with a deep heavy voice,

"THIS IS NOT THE WAY, THIS IS NOT HER PATH, I REFUSE TO ACCEPT, I-" with a sharp hiss and a right air fist from Granny Cary he was silenced.

It looked as if he was gasping for air and no words were able to leave his mouth. She squinted her eyes at him and coldly said, "Lape."

When she released her fists it was like all the oxygen in the room shot into his lungs and he fought to retrieve air.

There was a look of hurt and surprise on his face as he bolted through the back of the house and out the back door. A chorus of eerie howls could be heard in the same direction he took off. My eyes bulged wide like saucers as I looked to Granny Cary for answers.

"See baby, H-O-W-L-E-R," she said with an impish grin.

I couldn't move and I couldn't speak. I wanted to be absolutely sure I was in the right frame of mind before I uttered anything. Before I could, she took the small crystals that were on the table and placed them in what seemed to be randomly on top of the grimoire.

"Let's see we have; Red Jasper, Tigers Eye, my favorite Rose Quartz.... hmmm, the Amazonite, the Amethyst, which was my mother's favorite, and the Moonstone," she said more so to herself than to me. She arranged the stones on the book and each one sat perfectly in the small indentations. There however was one larger indentation in the middle of the book that didn't have a stone.

Granny Cary turned to look at me, "Place the bloodstone there baby."

I didn't move because I wasn't sure if she intended for me to know what she meant.

"Anika, the pendant.... it's the key to the legacy.... place it in the center," she said more trancelike this time.

I reached out slowly and touched the bloodstone gem that I was wearing. The vibrations were feeling strong and it seemed to WANT to join the other stones on top of the leather-bound book. I slowly released the clamp and gently laid the bloodstone in the center of the book.

I screamed initially when I felt the hurricane-like winds and heard the loud howling in all directions. There was a sweet-smelling fog, almost like thick incense that invigorated yet frightened me. I wanted to scream again as I saw the faces of strangers I had never encountered but seemed to look familiar as they all stared and tilted their heads at me. All the while Granny Cary reached out and grabbed my hand saying, "Anika, your time has come."

It was instantly silent and still and the leather book made two clicking noises as the brass holdings flipped open.

I braced myself for something horrible to happen and when it didn't I looked around for danger. There was none. Only Granny Cary and I were surrounded by the sweet thick fog that seemed to swirl in ringlets near our ankles and near the ceiling.

"What is happening? What is going on Granny?"

I had so many thoughts in my head but the aroma around me was so pleasant and it sounded like subliminal voices were dancing around my head chanting "Lape! Lape! Lape!" Granny Cary looked down at the pages that had what looked like gibberish on them and began.

"Howlers come from the Old World and are the most prominent shape-shifting beings. Numerous animal shape-shifters exist. Your grandfather descended from a long line of wolves, the strongest and most threatening of the Were's. They are said to be at the top of the ladder. The Old Wolves ate livestock and the wandering stranger mostly to protect their family and to keep their identity hidden. All classes of Were's are supernatural and have various degrees of how the change can take place. The wolves have 3 levels of hierarchy. Level 1 is Lycanthrope and is a permanent pure bloodline obtained only by birth. Level 2 is MetaMorph and can be achieved in one of two ways, either by a curse or an enchantment. Level 3 is a SkinAbbie which is a degraded aberration of the true wolf form and happens when someone is scratched or bitten."

I looked at my Granny Cary with my mouth wide open. Somehow it felt like everything she was saying resonated in my mind, body, and soul and I began to quickly replay the stories my dad had told me over the years. She continued her lesson.

"My family has quite another history and ancient lineage. My mother's bloodline runs back before Christ and even so far as the Great Stillness which existed before the creation of the first Earthly Garden and its animals that were made to occupy it. Each stone you see represents a Family of Power. Within each family is a lead priestess or mage worker that can engage all kinds of energy with all earth and solar elements to bend what already exists. The BloodStone family was the first to be created and is my heritage. The bloodstone was formed at the crucifixion of Christ as his red blood fell on the dark green earth and turned it into stone. This is why the bloodstone appears as it does and draws its strength from love and sacrifice."

Granny Cary seemed to pause for a moment until she turned to look at me. She nodded her head softly. "This is sufficient for today. Let us rest." The grimoire shut quickly and locked itself as the air began to clear.

I lightly shook my head hoping to get some clarity of what I had just witnessed as I watched Granny Cary carefully place all the crystals into a beautiful pouch. She came towards me and clasped the bloodstone pendant around my neck and gave me a strong hug. "Young Wolf, you *are* ready," she whispered as she stood back to wait on my response.

At that moment it all came racing back to me. The funeral, the howling, the stories daddy told me, the beautiful stranger, the bloodstone pendant, the yellow eyes, and the large dogs which were confirmed to be wolves, my mother acting weird, my love for animals, the transformation of the large black creature to my Uncle Bernard.

"Oh My God?! Is this a dream?! Am I adopted? Am I even human? Young Wolf? Wolf? Am I really a wolf?" I stated as I expectantly waited for the confirmation I had already received. Life had just gotten another category of interesting and I wasn't sure I was ready to embrace any of it at all.

EBONY

WHAT THE FUCK? I thought to myself.

"You shouldn't curse. It doesn't become you," I heard the beautiful stranger say. But her mouth never moved, just like mine didn't. *Is she reading my mind?*

"I am you," she replied, again without speaking.

It was the woman from the fire ceremony in the woods. I didn't know her, yet she looked safe.

"No, I won't hurt you," she chuckled.

Bitch, if you don't stop! I screamed in my head.

She frowned disapprovingly. I couldn't tear my eyes from her. She was about my height, same chocolate complexion. She had the same high cheekbone I had. She was top and bottom-heavy and pudgy in her belly, just like me. Same thick thighs, same almond eyes. We weren't identical but could have easily passed as family.

I tried to move closer but my feet were stuck to the ground. It was like Earth's gravitational pull had a hold of me and she was not releasing her grip.

"Pretty ain't she?" Nika's uncle Bernard or as I grew up calling him Mr. Uncle, startled me.

I couldn't turn my head to him so he stepped around in front of me, blocking the mystery woman.

Mr. Uncle was a peculiar man. In all my years in Ravenwood, he and Miss. Cary lived together in the small little house on the edge of town. He never took a wife or had children, but that didn't stop him from having his fair share of women. Miss. Marshella Bishop, Shelly's mom, dated him for a time after the mayor went to prison. Mr. Uncle was very handsome. Just like my Uncle Thad was, just like the twins were. But his gruff demeanor and bad attitude didn't make him the most popular.

Mr. Uncle had gotten so close to me, we were almost nose to nose. I swear, although I could be wrong, I heard a low growl come from him and he was sniffing me. But not in a threatening way. I wanted to see her again.

"Ok, I'll get out your way."

Wait? Was Mr. Uncle hearing my thoughts too?

Without moving his mouth he answered, "Loud and clear."

Suddenly, as if he heard someone call him or as if were summoned, Mr. Uncle's ears perked up, and he looked toward the house and without an explanation, he turned and went inside.

That left her and I alone. The air was frighteningly still. I didn't hear a bird chirping, a cricket serenading, or a frog croaking. Yet the silence was so loud.

"I've been waiting so long for you," she finally spoke. She was making small strides towards me.

"Me?" My voice had returned.

She smiled sweetly and nodded.

"Bu... but what do you want from me? What's going on with Nika in that house? How can you and Mr. Uncle hear my thoughts?" I bombarded her with questions, as she picked up her pace towards me.

When she finally reached me, she smelled like jasmine, lavender, and mint. She placed her left hand on the crown of my head and her right on my belly. A warmth began to grow in my womb and travel up my body to my head. Then I felt it jump from me to her. The fire-red light traveled down her left arm, through her chest to her right arm. Until the warmth was returned to my womb.

She pulled away, spent, exhausted. Like what just happened took everything out of her. When she finally composed herself, she looked up at me and smiled.

"It's time, you're ready."

I was getting tired of hearing about time, at this point.

"What the fuck is-"

"YOU WILL CONTROL YOUR LANGUAGE IN MY PRESENCE!" Her voice boomed. So much so that it caused the wind to blow and the ground to shake.

The magnetic hold on my legs was released and I was thrown to the ground with a mighty force. With a simple tilt of her chin, she lifted me off the ground. While helping me dust myself off, she said, "Your power is too great and hard to tame. If you can't control your tongue, it will be of no good use to you or anyone in this world."

"I don't understand." I turned to face her.

She gave the same sweet smile for the 3rd time that day. "Soon you will Ebony, soon you will."

I closed my eyes and tilted my head to the sky. I couldn't say anything or think *"this bitch is killing me"* without her knowing. I took a deep breath and blew it out.

"Well, can you at least tell me your name?"

"Ahhhh.... Anika Emerald Howell."

It was Nika. I looked all around for her.

"Where did she go? Did you see which way she went?"

I took a good look at Nika, she looked disheveled.

"No who? The lady who was here before I went inside? So you *did* see her?!" Nika exclaimed, excited at the discovery.

"Yes, I saw and talked to her. And some weird shit happened and Mr. Uncle was there too! Hey, are you ok? What happened to you in there?"

"My Uncle Bernard was here too?"

I looked her up and down again and nodded.

"Are you sure you're ok?" I asked her again, grabbing her by her waist to steady her.

"I don't know anything anymore. I just don't know," she began to cry.

I hugged my cousin and let her weep when on the inside I was just as afraid as she was. I looked up and saw the full moon rising and the sky darkening.

"What time is it?" I asked, looking at my mother's watch on my wrist. It was 6:30. "Shit, it's late. There's no way I've been standing in this yard since 3:00. How did so much time pass?"

I looked over to Nika and she was barely keeping it together. She was in no shape or condition to tell me what happened in that house or to hear about my ordeal. "Come on Nika," I said, grabbing her hand. "Let's go home."

ANIKA

THE RIDE back to Grandma Lou's was a complete blur. I didn't remember any of the drive and was sure there was radio silence in the car between Ebony and me. Of all the emotions I was feeling, I felt an adrenaline rush pulsating through my body and it needed to be released. I vaguely remembered the text KB had sent me and decided that once I gathered my thoughts I would make contact with him.

"Who the hell?" I heard Ebony say when we pulled up into the yard.

There were several cars parked on the grass and a sparse group of people mingling on the porch drinking store brand peach and pineapple can sodas. Montel came from around the side of the house and greeted Ebony with a peck on the cheek.

"Hey, babe! We're hosting a crab crack! We caught so many crabs today. Grandma Lou invited some of your friends and family over also," Montel gushed out as he ushered Ebony towards the house leaving me to saunter a few steps behind.

I recognized some of the older faces from around town and GranLou's church and I nodded while asking how everyone was doing instantly reverting to my low country roots and upbringing. They fanned the gnats with one hand and waved with the other not stopping their conversations at all. I placed one hand on the rail and heard the equivalent of a melodic symphony of a voice call out my name.

I turned around and was staring into the hazel colored eyes of Josh Ramirez.

"Mr. Ramirez, " I uttered almost questioningly as he came closer to me. We hugged briefly as he gave me a quick once over.

"Please, you don't have to be so formal, call me what you used to," he uttered quickly and then corrected when he realized the guests had their eyes on us. "Or you can call me Josh."

I halfway giggled.

"Woooooow. I didn't expect... what are you? Why are you here?"

He mentioned that he ran into Grandma Lou at the grocery store while he was filling a prescription and she insisted he stop by for her family crab crack social. In the midst of her invitation, she let it slip that I was in town still since my dad's funeral and would be happy to see old friends and acquaintances.

As he gave me the rundown of his informal invite, I scanned him from head to toe. He still had on his work uniform, a light blue collared polo shirt, khakis, and some white sneakers. His wedding ring was visible along with a gold Fossil watch. He looked a little aged and worn, his dark curly hair was cut short into a fade and his shoulders were still wide with a little muscle tone apparent. As he talked I stared at his mouth and recognized the small gap in between his top teeth and his lips were a shade of brown that indicated he still smoked. I'm not sure how long I was mesmerized by his lips because I jumped when he reached out to touch my arm.

"AniChela," he euphorically sang in his deep Dominican accent as he looked at me concerned. He had used his favorite pet name for me when I was his intern. It was considered a term of endearment that included part of my name and a term for the chemistry we had once developed and shared.

I felt my entire body tingle and I was afraid he could read my thoughts or at least the expression on my face. I didn't satisfy him with an answer and quickly turned and hopped up the steps and almost ran inside the house.

It was quiet on the inside so I exhaled slowly to gather myself as I went to GranLou's room and plopped on the bed. Seeing Josh had made me remember the good times I had growing up in Ravenwood, the unconventional relationship we shared. He was originally my high school biology teacher, then my mentor but my secret lover the entire time. We never went public considering he was married and could go to jail. I started to recall the first time I had seen him in high school when I heard the bedroom door close. I jumped up frightened out of my wits and was still slightly alarmed when I noticed it was Josh.

"Hey, I'm sorry about back there. I didn't mean to overstep or upset you," he apologized while looking down at his feet before meeting my gaze.

I opened my mouth to accept his apology but I only

panted instead and felt every erogenous zone on my body amp up to 10. When his eyes moved from my face to my shirt, which now broadcasted my hardened nipples he confidently came closer to me and put my face in his hands. He took hold of my face, brought it to his, and gave me the softest whisper of a kiss I haven't felt since leaving Ravenwood.

I didn't know if his lips were actually touching mine because everything felt like minuscule tickles and warm air. His tongue gently then hungrily entered my mouth and I tasted the tell-tale flavor of the peach soda mixed with a minty cool breath mint. I let out a soft cry when he moved his lips and tongue from my mouth to the folds of my neck. My arms instantly went around his neck and I massaged the back of his head. He slid my waist towards him and I felt his dick stabbing me through the rough material of his pants.

We continued to grope each other like high school teens and in one quick motion, he lifted me and pinned me to the door. I could feel the seat of my yoga pants getting filled with warm sticky secretions while we both panted.

"Con su permiso," he requested in a low sexy gruff.

There was a special commodity about this man when he spoke in his native tongue that was sexy as fuck. I nodded my head in agreement but he asked again, "con su permiso," which meant "with your permission."

Usually, this phrase is only uttered when requesting a blessing from a respected elder, but he always used it during our intimate moments to show he respected my body and my choice.

"AniChela, digame'...por favor," he moaned while sucking my tongue "Con su permiso, te necesito, te quiero?"

Telling him *yes,* he lifted my shirt and pulled my swollen DD's out and ferociously started sucking my nipples. He was making me dizzy so I wiggled enough so he could let me down and I could catch my breath. He looked scared as if I was going to change my mind and then pinned me to the door again and kissed me from my lips down my body until he reached the chocolate mound of my yoni.

I didn't notice when or how he yanked my pants down but I felt the cool tingle on my clit when the tip of his tongue swiped across gently a few times. "Ohhh shit," I shouted out loud and realized it had been a while since I'd had anybody lick me down there. He spread open my legs and my yoni lips and licked me so slow that I felt the entire room go into a freeze-frame like a matrix.

I opened my eyes and noticed that everything in the room was frozen in time, even Josh. His eyes were closed and his tongue was sticking out of his mouth while making contact with my clit. I looked at the ceiling fan and the old clock and noticed that each had a blur where there should have been movement.

What the fuck? I mused to myself as I had a familiar feeling of dread come over my body. Except for this time that dread felt like the adrenaline rush, I experienced in the car and it was as if I was injected with super sensations.

I inhaled deeply to regain my composure and instantly jerked my head back as everything suddenly came back into real time. Josh was tongue lashing me something serious and I was a little disappointed when I didn't feel the warmth of his tongue anymore. He released me from being pinned to the door and lifted me up instead and pinned me back again. This time I felt all 8 inches of his hard, fat curved dick doing the pinning.

When he entered me I could feel a slight gush of liquid as we both moaned, "Sssssssss." I orgasmed immediately. "Oh shit," I said in a matter of fact tone, a little too loud to be exact. He had to pause for a minute to catch himself from finishing too soon and then he fucked me against the bedroom door for a few minutes.

For those few minutes, I felt myself floating high into the sky. I soared over the house where all the people were mingling and standing around the bonfire, I soared over the thick forest with scattered streams and could see wildlife roaming freely, I soared into the white and grey tinged clouds which felt like wet cotton candy. When I made it to the stars, I felt the cool stiff air tighten around my body making my nipples extra hard and my yoni super juicy.

I looked around expecting to escalate even higher but I slowly felt myself coming back down as gentle and coordinated as a feather fluttering from the sky. My own moans brought me back into the room as I cried out, "ooooh Jaaaaay! Jaaaaay, damn!" It was the name I used only in private whenever we were being intimate or having a deep conversation.

Josh slowed his pace just enough to carry me to the bed. He laid me down and moved in and out of me so slowly I almost screamed. I was on my 3rd orgasm if I was counting correctly. I opened my eyes and saw him star-gazing into mine. He was so fucking sexy and I realized how much I had missed him. I missed this energy exchange. I needed this release, but at what price?

The more he stared into my eyes and slow-fucked me, the more uneasy I became. This man was making love to me and my body was loving it.

"A.. Ni.. Che.. La," he paced his words on every stroke.

I didn't know if it was his dick or his voice that was making me more wet.

"Jay pleeeeease," I whined wanting him to stop the wonderful feeling of torture but still rocking my pelvis to his rhythm.

What I didn't want to do was make this emotional connection with him. The timing was all wrong and we were in different places in life. I begged some more but it only made him kiss me and turn his strokes more firm and passionate, yet still slow.

"I missed you," he crooned when I looked into his eyes again.

I felt the head of his dick swell and start to pulsate inside me as I opened my mouth, " I... I... I'm cuming," was the shaky cry I let out. I felt his pace quicken.

"AAaahhhh 'Chela!"

We both had firework type orgasmic explosions at the same time. I shivered and jerked like I was a possessed woman even after my orgasm was finished. Josh laid beside me and kissed each of my fingertips until I could regain my composure.

When I was done I felt invigorated and turned on even more. I exhaled loudly, "Whew!" and turned to face him. "That was amazing," I exclaimed with a smile. When I heard the laughter outside my window, I jumped up remembering we were at GranLou's house and not alone. "Oh shit! You better get out of here before someone sees us! This is fucking crazy!" I whispered as I threw his clothes at him.

He took a minute to process what I stated and quickly got dressed. Before he left the room he turned, "it was really good to see you. I'll call you. Your mom gave me your new number," he announced.

At the sound of that, every good sensation I had drained from my body. "My mom? What the hell were you doing talking with her?" I now asked angrily.

Surprised at the sudden change in my tone and attitude he answered, "I was at her house earlier and.." but I cut him off by shaking my head and throwing up my hands.

"Get the fuck out of here! GO!"

He started towards me and paused with fear in his eyes when I growled, "get yo shit and get the fuck out of here Mr. Ramirez!" The hurt and pain on his face were evident but I didn't care. What business did he have with my mother at her house and now he just happened to be invited over here the same day? The coincidence made me feel uncomfortable and I didn't wait for him to retreat.

I grabbed my toiletries and pushed past him as I went to the shower. I let the scalding hot water spray onto my skin as I let the warm salty tears stream down my face. I started to heave and held on to the walls as I broke down crying. I cried for my father, my mother, and my life over these past few days. I cried because I felt vulnerable and allowed Josh to partake of a precious part of me that I had now felt he had taken advantage of. I cried for all the things I had no control over and for the things I didn't understand what was happening.

My chest ached from the heaving I was doing when I heard a soft voice, "Nika, don't cry," It was Ebony. Hearing the concern in her voice made me cry even harder but I knew I had to get it out. I quickly washed all of my hot spots and came out of the shower, my eyes red and puffy. She was sitting on the sink staring at me with her eyes watering as well.

"Remember when we were kids, we used to all squeeze

into that old porcelain bathtub," she said excitedly trying to change the mood. She was great at deflecting, she was like a thermostat being able to shift the temperature of emotions in a room. I

laughed while I wrapped my body in the old hard towel. "Yes and that water used to be dirty as hell too," and we both giggled out loud. I continued to dry my body off and headed back to the bedroom with Ebony close on my heels. Once inside I sat on the bed and began to apply my moisturizing creams to my body.

"Damn this smells good! What's in it?"

She was reaching for the bottle.

"Girl I bought that from the flea market, it has lavender in it which is my favorite scent," As she continued to sniff the contents I asked "Eb, do you believe in magic?"

Her body stiffened but she recovered quickly. "You mean like jinx, hocus pocus or some abracadabra type shit?" she motioned with her hands as if she had a wand.

I shook my head, "no like... magic... like blood magic, potions and crystals... spirits and chanting type magic."

She studied my face for a long while before she made her way towards the door. "I know one thing about magic... you had some magical shit going on in here tonight with Mr. Secret Lover and you're gonna need some *real* magic to keep Grandma Lou from knowing you been fucking in her house, in her room, and in her bed!" she stuck her tongue out and made a hasty retreat.

I threw a small throw pillow at the door missing her, but she opened it again, "For the record, this hoodoo voodoo shit is a lot to think about but yes I believe there is some type of magic out there." She smiled tightly showing a single dimple in her cheek and closed the door quietly. I continued to stare at the door and gulped down the magnitude of her words.

SHELLY

"I ABSOLUTELY WILL NOT!"

Marshella Bishop, Sr. was perched at her vanity, putting a top coat of polish on her perfectly manicured hands. I was in her closet going through 100's of sundresses, trying to find one that was appropriate for Grandma Lou's crab crack.

"You are going and I don't want to hear anything else about it, Mama."

I eyed a light blue and yellow *Diane Von Fürstenberg* halter and pulled it down from mama's revolving rack. I did a 360 in the spacious closet that I spent countless childhood hours in playing dress-up. Before daddy went to prison, Mama and I would fly to New York or LA just to shop. We would have our packages shipped home and spend the rest of the trip sightseeing and catching shows. Those days seemed so long ago.

I tossed the dress on the bed and stood with my arms crossed at my chest behind her. Mama looked up at me in the reflection of the mirror. "Did you forget who the parent was?" She took a sip from her flute of champagne and slid her hand under the UV light to dry her nails.If there was one thing Marshella Bishop was, it's stubborn. Born May 9th under the sign of Taurus, no one was going to make my mama do anything she didn't want to do. But there was one person she had a soft spot for and would cave in every time, me.

"Mama, Grandma Lou invited us and you know we can't say no to her. Plus, both girls are in town and I would love to see them."

Mama looked at me again in the mirror. She didn't understand why I would, as she puts it, torture myself to have a relationship with Anika. But I think most of that apprehension came from her and Dr. Howell's relationship.

"No, she's not going to be there. She's never there." I answered her question about Dr. Howell before she could even ask.

Marshella tossed her head and sighed loudly, "Ok, ok, I'll go. But I'm not staying long. Two hours top, and not a second more."

I squealed and kissed her cheek and ran to my room to get dressed.

To be fair, Ebony and I are associates at the most. We weren't as close as Anika and I was, not in the least. This is what I was telling myself to justify making my move on Montel. But I liked her; she was a loner just like me. And Grandma Lou just said, "Ebony's friend," not boyfriend. So I don't see any harm in seeing where this could go.

Ever since leaving the creek, I haven't been able to stop thinking about Montel. I memorized his license plate number and had my friend at the DMV run them for me.

Montel Turner, 09/25/1979, a Lead Detective with Atlanta
Police Department. That's all I needed her for. The rest I
did myself. He has a Facebook page that he hadn't posted on
in over a year. But I knew that didn't mean shit. He still
could have been active.

Luckily, I was Facebook friends with Ebony. Imagine
my shock when I discovered every pic or post Ebony has
made in the past 4 to 5 months, Montel liked or loved
them. I looked at his post and pics, not one like or love
from her. Hmm, this may work to my advantage. I learned
that he was a lover of British History, which ironically so
was I. He had no children and was never married. He liked
hiking and the outdoors; he was a sneakerhead and was a
huge UGA fan, which really worked in my favor because
that's where my daddy went to college. That was all I
needed.

I took a quick shower and pulled my hair into a tight
ponytail. I threw on my UGA sweatshirt and skinny jeans. I
topped it off with my custom black and red Air Jordan 1's.
When I walked out my room, mama was leaving hers as well.
She frowned in disgust.

"Is that what you're wearing? And you made me wear a
dress?"

I had to think quickly.

"I wanna be comfortable. You know you don't eat crabs,
and I don't want to wear something that I'm going to mess
up. You know?" *Fuck!* I said in my head. Since I was a child,
whenever I lied, I always added you know, at the end.

My mama looked me up and down, "Mmmm hmmm."
She didn't believe me but didn't feel like arguing either. We
walked outside and I locked up the house. I went in the
direction of my car; Mama went towards her Lexus truck.

"Oh, I'm driving," she asserted. "When it's time to leave, I want to be able to leave."

I didn't want to fight her or else she would change her mind. We made small talk on the way to Grandma Lou's, about nothing.

"Mmm mmm," I cleared my throat. It started tickling me suddenly.

"You okay Shelly? here drink this," she said reaching behind her to grab a bottle of water.

I drank it, but the tickle only subsided slightly but I didn't think anything of it. By the time we had gotten to Grandma Lou's, it was so crowded there was barely a place to park.

"See, I told you we shouldn't have come."

I ignored her, checking my lipstick in the visor mirror.

"Alright Mama, let's go," I smiled.

She rolled her eyes. I opened the passenger side door and as soon as my legs made contact with the ground, I felt an electrical charge travel up my spine.

"Whoa," I said falling back into the seat.

"Marshella Jr. are you ok? Do we need to go to the ER?"

The ER was the last place I wanted to be.

"No, no I'm fine Mama."

She was already on my side of the vehicle, looking me up and down.

"Are you sure M.J.?"

Only she called me MJ.

"I'm sure, mama. Just a little light-headed because I haven't eaten all day, you know?"

Mama cut her eyes.

"Come on, let's get this over with."

The backyard was full of people. 90% of them I've

known my whole life. And then there was Montel. I had hit the damn jackpot. He and I had on the same UGA sweat-shirt. *This is too easy*, I thought to myself.

I looked over at mama who was visibly uncomfortable. These people weren't exactly kind to us after daddy's situa-tion. As bad as I wanted to get next to Montel, I wasn't going to leave her there by herself. Who was noticeably absent was Anika and Ebony. I wonder where there were. I wanted to see them too, even if Anika hated me.

"Well, key ya? If it ain't Big and Lil Marshella. I too glad fuh see yall," Grandma Lou said, scooping me and mama in a big embrace.

On her heels was Montel. *Showtime*, I said to myself.

"Sr, your baby met him earlier but dis ya Montel. Eb'nee friend from Alanna."

Mama extended her hand politely.

"You're named Marshella too? You've got to be her big sister, there's no way you're her mother." Montel was laying it on thick.

"Oh stop, you're too much," Mama blushed.

I rolled my eyes to myself. They were talking quietly to one another, mama asking all kinds of intrusive questions. I felt my phone buzz in my pocket. When I pulled it out, the display read, Dr. Estelle Howell. Oh no ma'am, not tonight. I placed it back in my pocket. "Mmm hmm," The itch in my throat was getting worse.

"Did you say something, Shelly?" Montel asked.

I was embarrassed.

"Ummm, no. I think I'm coming down with something. Just a little scratchy throat." Mama looked at me and got really close to my face.

"What's going on with your eyes, they look jaundiced."

I flashed mama a *really nigga* look and turned away. Montel rescued me when he said, "Well, let's go find you something to drink."

As we walked away, both mama and Grandma Lou were staring at me. Mama gave me the *Praise God, she finally found someone look.* Grandma Lou was giving a *what's going on with you?*

Once we were out of earshot of the two women, Montel asked me what I knew about UGA? I smiled and ducked my eyes behind my long lashes. A trick I learned years ago that drives men crazy. He blushed and looked down at his shoes, it worked.

"My dad graduated from UGA. So I'm sort of a fan by default. What about you?" Montel slid the sleeve of the sweatshirt up his left arm so that it wouldn't get wet from the cooler. My mouth began to water looking at the muscles in his arms.

BUZZ, BUZZ! It was my phone again, and yet again it was Dr. Howell. She had to be out of her mind if she thought I was going to do anything work-related again tonight. I ended it, but before I could put it back in my pocket, she called back.

"Do you need to get that?" Montel asked, holding out a cold beer.

I shook my head no. I was afraid to speak because my throat was itching like crazy. I popped the top and took a few gulps of the cold drink. It helped.

"Thanks, Montel. I don't know what's going on with me."

I took a few more sips and surveyed the crowd again. Still, I didn't see the girls. "Where are Anika and Ebony?" I asked.

Montel threw his hands up, "I have no idea. They went inside to get ready after visiting Anika's grandmother today-"

"Miss. Cary?" I asked, interrupting him.

"Yea, I think that's her name."

Shit, I thought. I didn't know much about Miss. Cary, but I knew that Dr. Howell despised her and did her best to keep Anika away from her. Maybe that was what she was calling me for.

"Montel, if you'll excuse me. I think I will return that call." I walked away from the crowd to the front of the house.

SCCCCRRREEECCCCHHHHHHH!!!!

I heard the loudest, high pitch sound ever. I turned in all directions to see where it was coming from. My phone was going off again, I pulled it out. It was Dr. Howell but the sound wouldn't stop.

"Hel... hello... Dr. Howell?" I couldn't hear myself.

"You... to... mama... now!" Dr. Howell's words were coming in sporadically.

I didn't know if it was because of reception or the high pitch sound.

"Dr. Howell, I can't hear you! Something's wrong!" " Shelly... get out now!"

The call disconnected. A lone cloud that was in the sky blocking the full moon moved aside, and my entire body began to pulsate. I tried to call out, I wanted my mama. But no one was paying me any attention. I looked down at my hands, my nails began to grow. They were yellow and curled. I felt my canine teeth extend.

SCCCCRRREEECCCCHHHHHHH!

It was that damn sound again. I felt out of control. I needed the sound to stop so I could make heads or tails of what was happening to me. I was getting light-headed. I felt like I was going to pass out. I dropped to my knees, trying to will myself to stay alert. The last thing I saw before I lost consciousness was Bernard Howell standing over me. And I had to be losing my mind because he went from being himself to a dog.

EBONY

"WHY THE HELL do you keep ducking that girl?"

I asked Nika when she finally stopped her power walk. We were about to join the festivities when she spotted Shelly and her mom walking up. Before we could even step off the porch, she grabbed my hand, pulled me back inside, and we went out the front door.

"Look, I've said 1000 times, I don't like her. I don't trust her and I think she had something to do with my brother's deaths."

Nika had been saying this for years. I didn't believe it. Hell, Aunt Estelle is like her mentor, there's no way she would deal with her if she thought she had anything to do with what happened that night. I took a swig of the moonshine a family member had brought.

"I think you're tripping. It's been too long for you to still feel like this."

Desperately wanting to change the subject, Nika teased,

"Grandma Lou and your man Montel did good today down at the creek," she playfully punched me.

I stretched my eyes at her.

"I know your ass ain't talking. At least I wasn't fucking in my grandmother's bed, nasty! And who was it anyway?"

Nika blushed and looked away.

"Naw buddy, who is it?"

She stopped walking and turned to me.

"Ugh, Mr. Ramirez," she sighed.

"Whhhhaaaattttt?! You still fuck Mr. Ramirez?!"

"Girl, hush," she tried covering my mouth. "Somebody could have heard you!"

I was just busting her balls, I didn't mean any harm. I just wanted to make her feel better.

"If you must know, this is the 1st time we'd even seen each other in years. I was just as surprised.....AHHHHHHH!!"

Nika doubled over, covering her ears. I ran to her side.

"What? What is it?"

Only she couldn't answer me, she was clawing at her ears.

"Make it stop, please make it stop!" she begged.

But I didn't know what she was hearing. "Nika, I don't hear anything."

Luckily, the music from the backyard was drowning out her cries. Then just as suddenly as she started screaming bloody murder, she stopped. By this time, she was sitting in the grass, trying to catch her breath. That's when I noticed the pendant around her neck was glowing.

"Nika, look. Your necklace."

She looked down and grabbed it between her pointer and thumb. The bloodstone pulsated in rhythm with her breathing and my heartbeat.

"There, there it is again. You can't hear it, Ebony?" Nika turned to me and asked.

"Hear what cuz? You're starting to scare me."

"It doesn't hurt anymore though. She said the bloodstone would protect me. I didn't know what she meant, but-"

"No!"

Nika and I looked at each other. The cry came from the other side of the front yard. We walked over and what we saw would haunt our dreams for a very long time.

Our childhood friend Marshella Bishop aka Shelly aka the chic Nika hates but I think is actually kinda cool, was curled up in a fetal position covering her ears similar to how Nika was just a few minutes ago.

What the hell?" I whispered as Shelly twisted and contorted.

When she finally pulled herself to her feet, Nika said something that shocked the hell outta me. "Maybe we should go help her," she said, standing up.

"I think the fuck not!" I answered, snatching her back down in our hiding place. And not a second too soon.

Slowly emerging from the trees was a dark figure. I could tell it was a man from his structure, but it wasn't until he turned in the direction of the streetlight that we saw who it was.

"Oh shit, that's Mr. Uncle!"

He was seemingly unaware of Nika and me so focused on Shelly. He leaned over her and appeared to be talking, but Shelly looked like she was going in and out of consciousness. What happened next was scary and strange.

In a smooth fluid transformation, Mr. Uncle turned into a dog. But not just any dog, a really big dog. Almost like a wolf. That is what scared me. I opened my mouth to scream, but Nika covered my mouth and stifled it before it could escape. The strange part was that Nika wasn't fazed by this at all. She didn't seem afraid, she almost looked like she knew what was happening.

Mr. Uncle circled Shelly's unconscious body, sniffing and nipping at her. Once he was satisfied with her debilitation, he bit into her sneakers and began to drag her into the woods. Nika and I looked at each other, too afraid to speak and be found out.

All of a sudden a cherry red convertible came to a screeching stop in front of the house. Nika and I knew immediately who it was. My Aunt Estelle came flying from the front seat and ran in the direction of the large dog and Shelly.

"You stop right there Bernard!" She was out of breath but determined to stop him.

"What in the world?" I whispered. "She knows that's Mr. Uncle?"

Mr. Uncle growled a low, threatening growl. Never letting his hold on Shelly go. My aunt walked closer toward him, unafraid.

"I said you stop now!"

Mr. Uncle barked and howled, asserting his dominance over the two of them. Aunt Estelle was unphased. She reached into her bra and pulled out a small marble. She held it in her right palm. Then she began to chant in a language I didn't understand, but I had heard a lot growing up. It was Swahili. My mother was fluent and told me she learned when she lived in Africa. Aunt Estelle must have learned too. She chanted and walked closer towards Mr. Uncle and Shelly. Suddenly, the marble began to glow. A bright yellow light emitted from it and shot to the middle of the canine's forehead. Mr. Uncle whimpered, dropped Shelly's leg, and ran off into the woods. Nika and I exchanged another, what the fuck look, still too afraid to speak.

Aunt Estelle ran to Shelly. She looked around to make sure no one had seen or heard them. When she touched Shelly, she growled and bit at her. Shelly had the same mannerisms as Mr. Uncle but from this distance she looked like herself.

"Ohhh you almost got me, Shelly," she laughed. "Looks like I got here right on time." Shelly continued to bite at her not allowing her to get near her. My aunt pulled the marble back out and chanted to cause it to reactivate. Only she didn't direct it at Shelly, she just wanted to distract her to look away. It worked. As soon as it lit up, Shelly was captivated by the light. While she was distracted, we watched as Aunt Estelle pulled out a syringe and plunged it into Shelly's neck. She instantly become incapacitated. My aunt tossed the syringe and grabbed Shelly by her legs and dragged her to her car. We watch her struggle to get her in the front seat and buckle her in. After lifting the roof closed on her convertible, she screeched off the same way she came in. I definitely would be calling our cousin to bring me something good to smoke because this was some trippy shit.

"What the hell is going on Nika? Why weren't you scared when Mr. Uncle turned into a damn dog before our eyes?"

Nika stood there dumbfounded, but not answering me.

"Girl you better talk!"

"Ok, ok! This is all new to me. I was gonna tell you later, but I guess now is as good a time. When I was in Grandma Cary's house, I found out-"

"There yall go!" It was Montel.

I quickly composed myself and plastered on a fake smile.

"Hey Montel, yea it's us,"

He came over and hugged me. He smelled so good. He looked at Nika and I sensed that something was off.

"Y'all alright? Nothing happened at your Grandma Cary's house, right? I know when I was talking to Shelly and mentioned that's where you went-"

"Shelly?" We said in unison.

"Umm, yea. She's been looking for yall all night. Hell, everyone has been looking for y'all. I learned how to crack and eat crabs. Grandma Lou showed me how to take off the dead man and everything."

Nika and I both laughed at that. We made eye contact that read, we'll talk more later.

"So what else has Grandma Lou been telling you?" Nika asked Montel, grabbing his elbow leading him to the backyard.

When they were a few steps ahead of me, I went to the spot I had been eyeing for the last 5 minutes. I watched as it cascaded through the air and saw exactly where it landed. As Nika and Montel turned the corner to go in the backyard, I pocketed the syringe my aunt used on Shelly.

ESTELLE

TURNING up the AC on the lighted front dash of my BMW convertible, I cussed under my breath as sweat trickled down my face. I looked over to the passenger seat at Shelly who was still unconscious. I had gotten to her in a nick of time. Forgetting to give her a dose of her anti-potion this month, I slapped the steering wheel.

"Damn you, Bernard Howell!"

I huffed as I rounded the last curve heading towards my home. I had been taking care of Shelly ever since the accident years ago when the twins had died. The incident flashed back vividly. Thad had insisted the boys spend the weekend in the woods to celebrate turning 21, but mostly to have their coming of age initiation into the World of Were's. Shelly had snuck out to be with them and got caught in the drama which caused her to get scratched by one of the boys. I had already spent most of my married life suppressing the change in my daughter Anika and niece Ebony but Thad was adamant that the boys experience their *true nature*.

"We don't even know what the hell they may turn into.

With your whoring ass putting your filthy dog dick into every creature that moves!"

"Baby calm down! Why do you say you forgive me yet continue to bring up my past mistakes? I thought we were over that hurdle," Thad countered.

The argument continued.

"A wolf is one thing, Thaddeus but a hyena or whatever that tribeswoman was? For one, we don't even KNOW for sure if her lineage is legit to mix with yours—ugh I can't imagine."

I folded my arms while my eyes bore a hole into his forehead. Thad exhaled and tread slowly towards me. He loved me because I was strong and smart, but at times like these, he wished I would just trust his judgment since this was his world, his legacy.

"'Stelle baby, when we brought these boys home as infants we both made an oath to love them, nurture them and let them grow up and experience their truest selves. This is only right. They deserve to not be deprived of their blood heritage. They will be perfectly safe with me and Bernard at their sides."

My memory dissipated as I rode over the bumpiness of the stones that made up the driveway. Shelly had begun to stir just a bit and I wanted to get her inside quickly. I drug her out of the passenger seat and onto a sheet already in the back seat. Rolling Shelly into a burrito, I was able to move her swiftly across the yard, up the few front steps, and into the house. I was breathing like a woman in labor as sweat poured from my forehead as I dragged then placed her onto the couch with a cool cloth over her forehead.

Shelly still had her eyes closed but she was snarling and gnashing her teeth while turning her head from side to side.

Her skin looked like it had random stretch marks running from top to bottom with various dark spots. Her eye sockets and cheeks looked saggy and ashen. Her perfectly manicured nails were replaced with crusty yellow curved daggers.

When Shelly changed, she was still in a humanoid form, having arms and legs, but her mannerisms were those of an animal. It was hard to say which animal because she had only been able to fully change 3 times to my knowledge, with this being the 3rd.

I shook my head and opened my briefcase and took out a vial of holy water and dropped a few droplets into a pot of tea that was already brewing. Inside were small remnants of wolfsbane and some of the silver-coated sprinkles I had just received in my recent package. I took a shot of New Amsterdam to calm my nerves, letting out a hard *aaahhh*, with a scrunched face.

"What happened? Where am..." Shelly breathily spoke as she removed the cool cloth and started to cough.

I lit the clove and cinnamon candle before walking back into the den.

"Hush now and rest. You fell and hit your head. I found you on my way to my mother's and brought you here," I lied handing her the cup of tea loaded with the anti-potions.

"Dr. Howell?" Shelly closed her eyes again trying to shake her head of the fog. She tried sitting up and mumbled something about going to the crab crack and flirting with that sexy detective Montel and a bizarre memory of a large dog growling at her but not attacking. "Why am I here? Why didn't you take me home? Where is my mother?" Shelly shot off a series of questions.

"Shhhhh, you'll make yourself sick child. Here drink

up," I urged pushing the cup towards her mouth. "Your mother.... my soror wanted to stay and mingle a bit longer, I told her I would take care of you. Besides, I can visit my mother tomorrow. I'm not into the big crowd thing you know... germs and virus season, eeek!" I explained trying to be more believable.

Shelly stared at me knowing her mother would never select the option to stay anywhere public when there was an opportunity of escape presented. Yet she drank the tea and appeared to calm down. Shelly rubbed her throat and sucked her teeth when she noticed how dirty her fingers were.

"My polish!!! Oh my God! I just got my nails done! My mani is ruined!" Shelly whined while holding her hands up to the light. In doing so she then noticed small bruises and cuts along her wrists and hands. "What the..." she started to say looking at me with fear before she felt her head get too heavy for her neck. My concoction was working rapidly as Shelly nodded her head and drifted hopefully this time into the dark abyss of sleep.

Early the next morning, I checked on Shelly, who was still in a deep sleep and prayerfully groggy about the previous night. I had to convince her that the crab crack had gotten a little too wild and we both decided to have private drinks and talk about her next work promotion. Which would explain why she woke up at her boss's house. I made a mental note to create a new unimportant position to give to Shelly to help cover this lie. The anti-potion had worked wonders as her skin was back to being flawless and any traces of her change or being in a Were-state had been suppressed in the dark recesses of her mind. When I was satisfied with the additional herbs used to prolong sleep for possibly another 24 hours, I locked Shelly inside Anika's bedroom and took the drive down towards the battery.

Once I arrived, I trekked a few paces down the length of the bike trail. Bernard Howell sat as still as stone, chewing on a piece of sugar cane and spitting out the remnants on the ground next to him.

"What the hell has gotten into you, Bernard?" I demanded stomping towards him.

He growled and produced a vicious sounding bark causing me to jump momentarily before he winked and responded, "Good Morning to you too princess."

I sat at the table and glared furiously at him. "Why would you compromise EVERYTHING like that and in public no less. And at my Mother's house! Are you crazy?" I tried lowering my voice as passerby's hiked in athletic unison stealing glances at us. "This was not the plan Bernard. Where did you get it? Huh? Tell me? Where did you get the whistle?" I questioned as Bernard continued to gnaw on the cane like it was a dental stick.

"The Filimbi? I was able to steal it years ago from our family's stash. Mother didn't have everything spell locked and I swiped it and have been trying to figure out how to use it ever since."

"Well, how the hell does it not work on you?" This time my brows knitted downward. He shrugged his shoulders and turned to face me. "What came in the case this time? Are you keeping YOUR end of our deal?"

I shuddered, not wanting to share what I had. Years ago we both agreed that this bloodline should be kept secret from the town and the younger members of the family. In an earlier time, a personal feud happened between Bernard and

Marshella which caused him to grow angry and bitter, but when Shelly got attacked in the woods he had a newfound interest in Marshella and her daughter. Back then we made a pact that none of the children would ever be able to turn, due to Thad breaking the ancient laws by co-mingling with other species.

Now I was unclear what scheming Bernard was up to. I had caught him using a magical flute called the Filimbi to paralyze and enchant Shelly before trying to drag her body into the woods.

"You know she had fully changed. What were you going to do with her Bernard?"

"You call what she did a change?! That SkinAbbie doesn't deserve the respect of being called anything except a disgrace! An abomination to the true bloodline."

He made reference to the non-respected and lowest tier of Werewolf caused by a scratch or bite.

"Yea, yea, yea shut up Bernard!" I cut him off and rolled my eyes. "I got my same shipment, wolfsbane, silver and holy water. Now that Anika has moved out I can't give her any of my anti-potions. Can you help?"

Bernard looked at me and stopped chewing for just a moment. "She doesn't have the anti-potion in her system anymore? Did she change?"

We both froze and had a look of fear in our eyes. My chest got tight as I struggled to breathe.

"Bernard, I need that family grimoire and I need it soon. Is there any way you can..."

"Not while Mother lives. You know she started to tell Anika the Howler Family History. I tried to protest but Mother was firm. She has all her items spelled so I can't access it. I don't even know WHERE she keeps the grimoire, it usually appears out of thin air when she needs to access it."

I shook my head, feeling a migraine coming on.

"Do your damn job, Bernard! Keep your end of the deal! Get the grimoire!"

With that, I stood up and stomped back to the paved walkway. I recognized the sounds of footsteps crunching in the leaves but when I looked back Bernard was gone. In the spot where he was sitting was the half-chewed-up piece of sugarcane.

I dry swallowed two Imitrex pills before checking my reflection in my handheld compact. I felt like I needed to take a Xanax to calm my nerves for what was next. I took my time driving and let the top down on the BMW convertible as I made my way to the next destination. When I turned the radio on, sounds of Nina Simone's *I put a spell on you* drift through the low country air.

I put a spell on you
'Cause you're mine
You better stop the things you do
I ain't lying
No, I ain't lying
You know I can't stand it....

I SLOWLY TURNED the radio down and crept into the familiar yard. There were remnants of crab shells and cans scattered about the lawn. A few red solo cups and a light puff of smoke still coming off the hot embers of the bonfire that

had long since burned low but not quite been put out decorated the rest of the yard. I saw a very muscle toned built
young man with his shirt off walking around picking up the
items and wondered for a moment who it was.

Mama's pink Cadillac was parked under the large oak
tree and next to it was Anika's White Camaro and a super
sized Dodge truck with Georgia tags. I swallowed the lump
in my throat and stepped out of my car. "Why hello sir. It's
so nice to see America's youth doing community service as
I'm sure it keeps you out of trouble." He stopped and looked
at me quizzically.

"Pardon me, ma'am."

"You know, staying busy with positive tasks keeps you
away from drugs, gangs and being a... hoodlum."

A small smile escaped my lips. He seemed surprised and
a bit put off by this as he stared at me and didn't respond.

"He isn't a hoodlum nor does he do or sell drugs! HE is
LEAD DETECTIVE Aunt 'Stelle!"

The voice was my niece Ebony, who sounded like she
intended for her voice to be cold and menacing but I could
hear traces of nervousness. Her face showed her inquisitive
nature.

"Now what the hell are you doing here?" she exclaimed
with a little more confidence in her voice as the muscled
stranger hugged her for moral support. Before I could
answer, Mama Lou and Anika came out the front door and
looked at me.

I was so happy to see my baby girl but the look of disgust
on her face told me all I needed to know. She did not want to
see me.

"Hey, Mama Lou. I'm not here to cause any trouble. Just
wanted to drop off some of my homemade mustard and tea

for the girls and to say I'm sorry I missed your crab social last night."

GranLou used her hand to push Anika behind her like she was her armor-bearer. She stepped off the porch,

"I sway you fuh stay stirrin up da pot." She said while hugging me.

One thing about my mother, she treated everyone the same no matter what was going on. The warmth of her embrace made me momentarily forget my reasons for coming.

"Mama Lou, I need you to make sure the girls get these items.... put it in their foods or drinks. It's for THEIR safety mama."

I whispered to her as we walked suspiciously to my car. I handed her the small parcel.

I looked up and saw Ebony mean mugging me as she rode off with the muscled stranger in his truck. They cruised out of the driveway and she continued to stare at me unblinking until they were out of sight. I turned my head back to the porch where Anika was still standing, breathing heavy and hard.

"Give dat chile space now, 'Stelle. She gon need her mammy but ya gotta do tings right!" She bowed and stepped back so I could slowly approach Anika.

"Anika? I know you have so many questions and I promise I can explain everything, just please come home or... or... um.... at least come for dinner?" I asked in a high pitch voice hoping my desperation was enough to pull at her heart strings.

Her eyes began to tear.

"It's okay, baby. You don't have to answer me now. Just know the invitation is there."

I backed up and almost sprinted to my car. Once inside, I wiped the light tears that had made their way to the corner of my eyes and kicked up dust as I sped out of the yard. In my rearview mirror, I could still see Anika standing motionless on the porch while my mother waved and fanned away the dust.

ANIKA

I STOOD on the porch willing my hot tears to stay behind my lids as Grandma Lou plodded back towards me.

"Come inside chile. It gon be alright. By da help of da Lawd yessuh."

Her Gullah- Geechee accent thick as she gently touched my arm. I wanted to yell and scream but GranLou didn't deserve any of it.

"What did she want?" I finally asked letting Grandma Lou pull me inside.

"Dat Chile of mine... I don't know where I go wrong. After ya Pop Pop went on ta Glory, 'Stelle try her bes to be the smartest in da room. Maybe I spare da rod too much, but das ya mammy and no matter what, she love ya," Louise tried to explain.

"Grandma, how can someone love me and try to hurt me like you said at the same time? I don't trust her!"

This time I let the tears fall.

"Shhhh, I don't understand all the ways of ya mammy chile, but she has her reasons. Now dat ya gotta figga fuh yaself," she sauntered into the kitchen and placed the small parcel on the counter.

I stared at it and asked, "did she ask you to poison us too?" Almost scared of what the response was going to be.

"No chile, ya mammy does have a concern. There is a ting in the blood of ya daddy people ta make ya sick and with her being docta and all, 'Stelle always been trying to keep ya 'mune system up. I bun drinking her tea and tings, using her ointment fuh years fuh dis ole arthur in my knee ya."

My eyes rolled up towards the ceiling remembering how my mama always made a fuss about me and my siblings taking our elderberry, vitamins and sea moss tinctures. I was led to believe in the existence of a strange medical illness on my daddy's side of the family that dated back generations. We never questioned it as we never got sick. Every month Ebony and I received packages from my mama with her various homemade creations and stayed in great health.

GranLou told Ebony and me before that people wanted to hurt us, with people in my mind being my mother. Plus with Ebony so convinced that we were poisoned, by my mother, I had more questions than answers.

My displaced thoughts were disrupted when I felt my cell buzz in my back pocket. "Hello," I answered with an unwanted grin escaping my lips.

"What's up, baby?" KB crooned into the earpiece.

I sent him a late night text after the crab crack telling him to hit me up and he didn't immediately respond.

"I didn't get your text until late, you know the guys and I had a set to do and when I got back to the room I was spent!" He went on to explain. I could hear the covers shifting on his end of the receiver as I imagined him trying to get more comfortable.

"Well, thanks for calling me back. How was the show?" I started to draw imaginary shapes on the countertop with my finger as I listened to the huskiness in his voice.

"Man, shit was bananas! I ain't never seen so many white chicks drunk and trying to dance some hokey pokey shit to our jazz music!"

We both laughed in unison.

"Yo baby, I'm sorry about ya pops. I wish I could've been there with you, ya know. I have been trying to contact you but I see your Facebook shit dry as hell," he teased.

"Hey, hold up! I know yo almost famous ass ain't on Facebook?!"

I caught myself as GranLou spun around and gave me a stern look.

"I mean, I didn't know you were stalking my Facebook page," I said again this time in a lowered, more lustful tone.

I instantly regretted it because like a moth to a flame, he picked up on my innuendo and said

"Oh, baby I've been stalking and I bet I know what you got that ain't dry."

At the sound of this, I felt electricity surge through my body. It was like something woke a sleeping dragon and I felt hot and bothered all over.

"Boy, hush! So how long are you in town? What are your plans?"

I stood now walking towards the bedroom to gather my purse and phone charger. I stopped dead in my tracks when he said,

"Ya moms didn't tell you? I'll be here for a few days. She invited me to dinner. I'm definitely gonna take her up on that, besides your Grandmother Louise, Mrs. Estelle can burn her ass off!"

He laughed out loud not noticing the silence on my end.

"My mom, when did you see her?" I asked more curiously than annoyed now.

"Oh, when I got into town she had a little shorty she worked with escorting me out and shit but invited me to grub. I told her about my show. Maybe you could come check me out."

I rolled my eyes when he said shorty, it was no one other than that skank Shelly Bishop.

Yea, maybe I should, I said more to myself as I began to formulate a plan.

I told KB to text me his location and I would meet him in under 30 minutes. I then informed Grandma Lou I would be going out as I texted Ebony to tell her the same. Ebony responded to be careful and that she loved me, adding a smiley emoji. She texted back again, saying that she was taking Montel to the Jazz Fest tonight at Spoleto Festival Downtown. I texted her the thumbs up, making sure not to mention KB was in town. I needed to get my plan in motion and having Ebony as my unofficial bodyguard was not on my agenda. She was the younger cousin but she was overprotective and with all the crazy shit going on, she would shit bricks if she knew what I was scheming.

I stopped at the corner gas station to fill up on petro and to clean the dust off my windshield. The day was beautiful and sunny despite all the darkness I had been surrounded by. I still needed to have some deep conversations with Ebony and my Granny Cary but figured I'd get around to it. I felt my phone buzz again in my pocket and I took a few steps away from the gas pump. I looked at the caller ID and saw *DC Metro Vet Clinic* flash across the screen.

"Hey guuuuuuys," I said in a familiar cheerful tone.

It was my work peers and this was our customary greeting to each other. It was also the company greeting we used when owners and their pets entered our clinic.

"Dr. Anika Howell, girl, we have been worried sick about you!" Came the valley voice of Sabrina. She was of mixed heritage, her dad being Latino and her mother White. She had fire red curls but the whitest skin I'd ever seen. She stayed in tanning booths and vacationed down south but it never seemed to help darken her complexion. "Did you get the floral arrangement we sent on behalf of the office?" she asked. I could hear the dogs barking in the background.

"Hey, Bri! Yes, I did thank you, guys! My dad would've loved it." I said remembering the bone-shaped arrangement from the funeral made of red roses. "How is everyone there? How is work?"

I didn't notice the silver-colored Honda Accord pulling up behind my car.

"Girl, ewwww! Don't worry about the dogs and cats of this circus! Spend this much needed time away and get your life together."

She had no idea how much time I had planned on being away. I reluctantly pushed the uneasy, discomforting thoughts away. I already had enough problems right now than to deal with old ones. She promised to stay in contact with me and update me as needed. We exchanged a few more pleasantries before I pressed *end*.

"AniChela," the voice carried gently over the breeze.

I didn't speak, but just bit on my lower lip.

"Please talk to me. What did I do wrong? Help me make it right."

"You know what Mr. Ramirez, maybe I was just having a moment or a bad day but it's not important."

I proceeded towards my car. He looked confused but followed me.

"Okay, but I didn't mean to hurt you. Honestly, I don't even know why you were so upset with me."

I rolled my eyes. "Yea, well it doesn't matter. It is what it is right?" I reached for my door handle but he blocked me.

"AniChela, por favor," he started and I shook my head trying not to let his voice or his familiarity disrupt my state of mind.

"How is your wife?" I asked nonchalantly.

At this, he stammered a bit before answering. "She is ok. I mean she is still ill if that's what you're asking. Anika, where is this coming from?"

I could see I was still hurting his feelings. Since he was still blocking my door, I used my cell to open my Chevy app and pressed the button to auto start my car. The engine roared to life and Mr. Ramirez nodded his head understanding that he was being dismissed.

"Look, I really enjoyed seeing you and being with you. If you plan to stay in town, come by the animal clinic. I could always use some backup." He placed his card in my free hand and walked back to his car.

I smirked and stuffed the card into my sun visor before pulling off.

The Downtown traffic was still the same. Lots of road construction and one lane openings. I decided to park at the local drugstore and walk the few blocks to the Sheraton Hotel where KB was staying. Parking at the hotel was for guests only and I didn't want to feed any meters.

I traipsed in and stopped by the hand sanitizing station allowing the foam to squirt into my hands before I made my way to the elevator. I smiled at an elderly couple who were holding hands and got off on the 10th floor. Once I found the door I was looking for, I knocked gently 2 times. It was our code knock. 2 meaning one for you and one for me. It was a rule we came up with in college for when we wanted to secretly hook up. I shivered again thinking of how my life had been shrouded in secrecy over the years when the door swung open. Standing there in a towel only was KB.

"Kelly Bridges, you haven't changed!" I said as I playfully slapped his bare chest.

He bear-hugged me and lifted me off my feet.

"Nik! Damn you feel so soft and smell so good," he said as he buried his face in my neck. It tickled a bit and I pushed him off me. We stood back to check each other out again and I felt that flame begin to grow. I hungrily licked my lips and went to him quickly as we began to kiss and grope each other. I pushed him onto the bed and started grinding my hips at the bulge growing beneath the towel. His large hands grabbed my breasts then my ass as I leaned forward to allow him to get a better grip. When he touched the pendant dangling from around my neck he yelped.

"Ouch!"

I stopped and came out of what seemed to be a trance I was in and jumped off him quickly.

"No baby, don't stop, I think your necklace shocked me. Could be the static electricity or whatnot from the carpet." He said hoping that would cause me to come back.

"I'm sorry, that was rude." I offered as an apology fixing my hair and while stuffing the pendant into my shirt.

"Baby that ain't rude. Your ass just horny as fuck! Come here let big daddy put that fire out for you," he said in his sexiest of voices.

By now the towel was open and standing as tall as the

Eiffel Tower was his dick pointing almost at me.

I dashed to the open bathroom door and started to splash water on my face. What the hell was going on with me? Even though I had a healthy sexual appetite, I felt like a stronger force took over me and I liked it. I went back out to the room and KB had put on a pair of boxers and was flipping through the channels on the tv.

"So you coming through tonight or what? We play the early show and I have the rest of the day to chill or whatever."

I put my plan into motion.

"Yea, I'll come only if I can get floor seats for me and my cousin and her date."

He looked back at me and nodded, "Okay yeah, that's cool, I can do that."

I continued,

"And I want you to call my mother and tell her dinner is on for tonight." My palms got sweaty at this and he nodded even more feverishly.

"Oh, hell yea! That's what I'm talking bout Nik!" He came over again and gave me another hug and we began to sway together to the inaudible music. He looked me in my eyes and without breaking our gaze asked, "You ready to let me eat that pussy?"

Ebony and Montel looked cute together as they moved in rhythm and chair danced to the sounds of KB & Kompany. The band had been together since they pledged the same fraternity during our undergraduate days and had always played well together.

Looking around the room I noticed we were the only brown faces in a sea of white and light-colored ones. KB gave us a quick shout out before ending his set. Everyone was on their feet when it ended. The house music came on once the band started breaking down and KB came over to where we were standing.

"Hey man this was dope!" Montel said as he stretched out his balled up knuckles to dap up KB.

"Yes, do y'all have a CD or a playlist on Spotify?" Ebony asked in excitement.

I made small talk with some of the band members who I hadn't seen since college until I heard KB, "Yo you ready?"

I gave Ebony and Montel quick hugs goodbye. KB escorted me to my car and watched as I got in.

"I forgot your moms asked me to bring her a bag of ice. Go on ahead and I'll meet you at the house. Bet?"

I nodded nervously and started the trek back to Ravenwood.

I drove up in the yard, noticing how beautiful the flowers were in the garden bed and decorative pots as they danced in the moonlight. I could hear the light classical music and smelled the smothered oxtails coming from the house where my mother stayed. I looked up into the night sky and smiled at how crystal clear the stars shone and how crisp the moon was as I basked in its glow. I could also hear the rap music blasting from KB's car as he started up the long driveway. I waved my arms to signal him to park behind my car and he nodded acknowledgment.

I took one step forward and felt the most excruciating pain of my life. It felt like someone was breaking all of my bones and my skin was burning off my body. My teeth ached like I needed root canals done on every single one, my eyes felt like someone splashed me with lemon juice and hot sauce.

I heard the tearing of fabric and hoped it was my clothes

but noticed it was my skin shredding to pieces. I tried calling out but no words came, just loud whiny sounds as my larynx began to itch uncontrollably. I felt myself curl into a tight ball praying death would finish its work when suddenly I smelled a thousand new scents and heard things that appeared miles away.

I opened my eyes and shook my head and body and noticed my chunky curly afro was now a chocolate mid-coat length of fur. I felt like Mufasa or Simba from *The Lion King* as all that fur spread out in all directions as I shook my head again. I tried to turn around because I saw a brown rope behind me and went around in circles for a few minutes until I got dizzy.

Was that a tail? I thought to myself and then froze. I crept low to the ground and put what used to be my hands, but now two furry paws up against the side of my car and saw a large chocolate brown wolf with yellow eyes staring back at me. I knew it was me because the Bloodstone pendant was around my neck like a fancy collar.

I yelped and started to jump and writhe in an attempt to get back into my regular body. My head shot up as I saw what looked like two large eyes coming up from my rear. I put my head low to the ground again and growled at first, but then recognized the so-called eyes were only headlights.

KB stepped out of the vehicle, looking amused as he whistled at me. "Hey girl... come here girl," he made lip smacking noises while patting his leg.

I growled at him before dashing off into the woods. I turned back and watched him walk up to the front door with a bag of ice. He smiled as he knocked and then fixed his clothes while he waited. When my mother answered the door I heard him say, "Hey, when did you get a dog?"

EBONY

MY MAMA WASN'T LOVED PROPERLY, SO I never really had an in-home example. Pop Pop died before I was born, but I wish I was around to see how he treated Grandma Lou. Then there was my Aunt Estelle and Uncle Thad. When I was allowed over, he was hardly there. It was no secret that philanderer would be a nice way of saying what he was. And no matter how much he embarrassed her, she was not leaving. Add that to every time I sleep with a man, he freaks out and loses his mind. It didn't go unnoticed that Montel was grasping at the sand on the beach like he was trying to hang on for dear life. So it became easy to shrink into school, then work.

Walking on Waterfront Park tonight after that amazing set was exactly what I needed after this eventful week. It didn't hit me until now that Montel was still here with me. I knew for sure he had to get back to work.

"I guess you'll be leaving soon to head back to Atlanta," I said breaking the silence.

The cool breeze coming off of the Atlantic was sending light sprays of salty water in our faces.

Montel sighed, "Yes, I was gonna talk to you about that tonight. I'll be leaving on Sunday. I was going to see if you were heading back with me."

I nodded my head.

"I might as well. It's time to face the music after my press conference fiasco."

Montel looked down at me and smiled. He reached for my hand, it felt nice. We walked the boardwalk listening to the waves crash against the rocks below. That's when I saw her, I knew it was her because I had memorized every crease on her face.

"What the hell?" I whispered.

Montel frowned and looked in the direction I was looking.

"What is it, Ebony? You see someone you know?"

I pointed. He looked again in the same direction.

"I don't see anyone, babe."

He called me babe, I blushed. I didn't want to risk looking crazy, so I brushed it off as maybe I was getting tired. But I knew she was there, I knew because I could still see her.

The ride back to the house was just as strange. When we stopped at the light before we crossed the bridge leaving Downtown, in the car next to me was her. We stopped at a local ice cream parlor to get a couple scoops, she was in the back in the kitchen. Lurking in the open, yet blending in, no one seemed to notice her except me. I excused myself to go to the restroom, I was really going to call Nika. No answer. I called back to back 4 times with the same results. Something wasn't right. I waited for the 4 rings until her voicemail picked up again.

"Hey, girl! Where are you? I've been calling you back to

back, I'm getting worried and why is that bitch following me? I'm seeing her everywhere. Call me, please!"

I ended the call and left the bathroom. When I got back to our booth, I must have had a worried look on my face.

"You sure you're ok, Ebony?" Montel asked, genuinely concerned.

I tried my best to act like everything was ok.

"Yea, yea. I'm just a little tired."

Montel threw some money on the table and stood up to leave.

"Come on then, let's get you home."

He stepped aside so that I could leave the booth and rested his hand on the small of my back, ushering me out. The whole while, she was watching my every move until I left the parlor.

We let the songs of the quiet storm playing on the radio be our entertainment on the drive back to Ravenwood. When we passed Red Top's famous Dodge Store, she was standing in the doorway of the convenience store. Once we reached the train tracks, she was sitting on the caution arm as a freight train went by. Never unlocking eyes with me, she spoke to my mind,

"She's lost, she needs you."

I frowned but quickly recovered. I didn't need Montel thinking I was losing my mind. Who is lost? Who needs me? I asked her telepathically. She just kept on staring at me.

"Who bitch?!" I screamed silently at her.

Suddenly, the caution arm she was sitting on broke away and hit Montel's left side headlight. I jumped out of fear.

"Hey, it's ok, it was probably about to break soon anyway. It could have been worse. I'll have it repaired before we hit the road."

He was oblivious to what was happening. She was upset with me for cursing and she was also gone.

I tried Nika again for what felt like the 1000x. Still, no answer. "Hey, do you mind swinging by my Aunt Estelle's before we go to Grandma Lou?"

Montel screwed up his face.

"This late, why?"

Nigga will you stop asking all these fucking questions? I said to myself.

Instantly feeling a sharp pain in my belly. I immediately doubled over. It was in the same location of the warmth the mystery woman had transferred to me not too many nights ago. She was punishing me for cursing.

"Yo, you ok? Do I need to turn around and take you to the ER?" Montel asked with genuine concern.

I shook my head no, as I attempted to rub the pain out. I didn't see her again until I reached my aunt's street. Perched on a branch that may have fallen from a recent storm, was her. I was going in the right direction. It immediately hit me. *She* was Nika.

Once we reached the house, KB and Aunt Estelle were in the yard. They didn't look happy. Nika's Camaro was parked under the big oak tree, but she was nowhere in sight. Montel barely had the truck in park before I had already opened the door.

"Oh Ebony, thank God!" my aunt said, running to my side. She hugged me, then pulled back slightly, just enough to put maybe a foot of space between the two of us. "Have you seen Anika? Is she with you two?" she rushed out looking over my shoulder to see if her daughter was exiting Montel's truck.

It had to be serious if my aunt was genuinely and internationally embracing me.

"No Auntie. The last time we saw her, she was with him," I offered, pointing at KB.

We all turned and looked at him. KB defensively threw his hands in the air.

"She was right here," he said pointing to the spot he was standing. "I turned from the driver's seat to grab the ice off the back seat floor, when I turned back around, she was gone." We all looked at him like he had two heads.

"What do you mean she was gone?" The detective in Montel kicked in.

I looked at him scanning the perimeter. I'm assuming looking for any drag marks or disturbances.

"I mean she was here, then she wasn't. Then there was a dog that was walking from around her car."

"Oh, here he goes with the dog. How many times have I told you I don't have a damn dog."

Aunt Estelle was beside herself.

"Alright, alright let's just all go inside and calm down so we can think" Montel commanded, taking control of the situation but my feet were planted.

She was back. Sitting on the Camaro was the beautiful stranger. And she was smiling at me.

"You guys go on ahead inside. I'm going to call Grandma Lou. She's expecting me back about now and I don't want to worry her." I pulled out my phone for added effect. When the trio was behind the closed door, I turned back to her. "What do you want from me?" I asked her out loud.

She didn't utter a word verbally or telepathically. She pointed to the right of her into the woods, but I didn't see anything. I sighed out loud. I was over her.

"There's nothing"

She was gone. As usual, my beautiful stranger swooped in and mysteriously left just as fast. I looked back in the direction she was pointing. I still didn't see anything. Then out of nowhere, 2 small yellow orbs appeared just behind the tree line. If all the crazy shit that had been happening didn't happen, I would have been afraid but I was unmoved. Until the orbs began to move towards me.

I started to walk backwards as it got closer until I was stopped by Montel's truck. It was when the orbs cleared the tree line under the bright light of the full moon, that I saw what it was. It must have been KB's mystery dog. I have been deathly afraid of dogs since I was a little girl. I wanted to scream so Montel could rush out, shoot it, and rescue me. But I couldn't, not because I wasn't trying, it was like my vocal cords were frozen.

The dog slowly walked towards me, seemingly just as afraid as me. This was one big ass dog! Then it cocked its head to the side like it recognized me and ran full force at me.

"So this is it, this is how you're gonna take me out, God?"

I looked to the heavens and said. I closed my eyes tight and braced myself for whatever was about to happen. The beast jumped on me and I just knew I was about to die. It was massive because its front paws were on my shoulder, I could feel the weight of it bearing down. Then it licked my face.

It literally took its tongue and slobbered on my chocolate skin. I could feel the heat from its mouth as it happily panted.

So it's not a threat? I thought to myself. I can open my eyes.

Slowly, I opened each lid. A beautiful curly, brown

haired beast with deep yellow eyes stared back at me. It was starting to weigh me down from holding my shoulders. Then I saw it. Her Bloodstone pendant. I knew every curve and crack in it like it was my own.

"Nika?"

As I slid down the truck into unconsciousness, I heard the animal give a sad, mournful bark and growl.

I WAS YELLING and screaming out, "Ebony! Ebony! Wake up!" noticing that all my learned speech patterns were coming out in canine gruffs of barks and whines. I was so happy to see my cousin that I didn't think ahead of what my current transformative state may have done to her state of mind or sanity.

I realized that there was nothing I could do at this point to help her, as I needed help myself. I took off back into the woods as soon as I heard the front door swing open.

"Ebony! Anika!" Came the cries of my mother Estelle.

I ran with a speed I didn't know existed within me. The wind blowing in my face with the leaves and branches swiping across my snout made me wild with euphoria. The large pads on my new canine-like feet absorbed all the shock of each pebble and stone I ran over. I corrected myself mentally and thought, not feet, paws.

My large yellow eyes seemed to have a wider depth perception as I could see from one side of my face to the other without turning my head. And even with all this sprinting, I wasn't even exhausted. My nostrils picked up a familiar scent and I slowed my pace and began furiously sniffing the air, then the ground.

As I made my way down this strong-scented rabbit hole I could feel the bloodstone pendant around my neck throbbing. I couldn't see it, but I could feel the strength of it coupled with the moon's effects and knew something was going on. I halted immediately when I heard then saw the menacing growl ahead of me.

It was the large black wolf and it was bearing its teeth with globs of foam in both back corners of its mouth. The ears were pointed backward and the creature crouched low to the ground poised to attack. Right before it was about to attack, Granny Cary stepped out of the shadows.

"Bernard!" She said sternly without taking her eyes off me.

I tilted my head as if to get a better view of the large wolf she called my Uncle's name, and then I recognized him.

In a familiar, scent-based way. I mean, he didn't look anything like my Uncle Bernard, considering I was staring at a much larger black wolf with a double coat of black fur and razor looking teeth. I then trained my eyes on Granny Cary as she quietly whispered some words and then instantly morphed into a large grey wolf.

I immediately recognized this wolf as the one chasing me in the woods when I first came into town. I barked in a series of short bursts until my brain began to comprehend the sounds as my own native Geechee-English tongue.

"Granny Cary? Uncle Bernard?" I said with expectancy.

The large grey wolf started towards me but I scattered back unsure I could trust them and myself.

"It is okay young wolf. This is your time," she had said the words with such conviction that it gave me courage.

"How is this possible? Are you a wolf, Granny?"

I tried controlling my thoughts. Every sense in my body was on overdrive. I was smelling everything, hearing everything, seeing everything, and feeling everything. My taste-buds were still limited as I had not consumed anything while in my transformed state.

"No Child, I can metamorph into an L2 with an enchantment I learned to whip up myself."

L2? I wondered to myself. *What is that?*

Tired of the small talk Uncle Bernard growled out, "Level 2 Wolf. Didn't you pay attention during your personal history lesson when you last visited?"

I was astonished he could read my thoughts.

"Can all wolves read one another's thoughts?"

Granny Cary let out a slight chuckle.

"No wolf can read thoughts unless they are versed in stone magic from a Family of Power."

"Well, how did-"

I started before being cut off by Uncle Bernard

"It was the most logical question in your puny brain that would come up next," he was still sneering and his ears were still pointed back as if he was waiting to attack. He didn't because Granny Cary gave him a quick growl as she snapped at him and proceeded to walk towards me.

I stood perfectly still as she encircled me and sniffed me

in the manner most canines do when socializing for the first time. I felt my tail wag uncontrollably from side to side with excitement as she gave me permission to do the same to her. When I was done registering her scent I yelped with excitement.

"Oh Granny Cary! It's really you!"

We both jumped and pawed at each other and playfully nipped at each other's necks and ankles. My excitement was suddenly wiped out when I headed to greet my Uncle Bernard. He snapped at me and had his large jaws around my neck quicker than I could move out of harm's way. I cried and yelped desperately when I felt his large canines sink into my skin drawing droplets of blood.

Granny Cary rushed at him with her teeth bearing and chomped down on his hind quarters. He let go of me and began to cry and whine like a newborn pup that was being disciplined by its mother. As he lay on his side with his paws up, his countenance instantly changed from aggressor to victim.

Granny Cary's large grey form hovered over him as her thick saliva dripped onto his dark coat. "Bernard Howler! You know to *NEVER* attack a fellow wolf and especially not a pure blood family member. You have disgraced me tonight. For this, you will be punished!"

While she continued to admonish him, I could feel the bloodstone pendant warming and vibrating against my neck as the small gashes were being healed and the blood drying up. I felt the energy of the moon recharging me and the stone as we stood in the wood clearing.

"You will remain unchanged in your wolf form until the next lunar cycle 30 nights from now." Granny Cary continued.

Uncle Bernard whined loudly and sadly slapped his thick tail against the dirt softly hoping to receive mercy. He continued to lay flat on the earth when Granny Cary trotted back towards me and licked her face.

"Oh young wolf, your Uncle has always been so overprotective and a tad bit jealous. But don't you worry about him. The Howler bloodline continues to flow through you and the pendant will always keep you safe. Come, let us enjoy this night."

I turned again to look at Uncle Bernard who was now shaking the dirt and broken twigs off his body. He looked at me with pain and dark anger in his eyes before he took off in the opposite direction. He let out a long howl which was full of sorrow and I was able to interpret it as;

I have to roam this earth in my truest form, unable to have control over my change. No control is the worst punishment of all.

I felt my heart sync with his lament before another more cheerful howl greeted me,

"Young wolf, catch up!"

I sped off in the direction where Granny Cary ran and was able to catch up with her in record time. We dashed through the familiar woods with ease, at times racing each other to known landmarks. We had run from Ravenwood to as far as Holly Hill, Savannah, and even the outskirts of Myrtle Beach. It seemed so effortless. I was also surprised at how agile Granny Cary was in her wolf state.

When we stopped to take a sip of water from a natural stream, she said, "The night is almost done, we need to get back before the change."

I was having so much fun, I forgot about my real life and responsibility as a human. I went back to lapping the cool water, mesmerized at the sensation the droplets were having on my canine taste buds and how thirsty I appeared. I sat on my hind legs and began to groom myself by licking my chocolate coat and using my paws and nails to scratch and straighten out any knotted fur balls I came across.

I heard Granny Cary laughing. "You are a vain one young wolf," she said as she watched me.

I felt self-conscious then nauseous as I realized I was licking hair and fur. I hacked up a few dry coughs realizing nothing was coming up and then shook my mane again to gain my composure.

"Granny Cary so much has happened so fast. How do I process all of it?"

She looked at me and howled the most beautiful tone at the moon. After 3 howls, my canine ears were tuned in and I heard the song of the wolf.

"Young Wolf... your life is full of grace, mystery, strength, and power... the wolf is a blessing since the dawn of time... this blood must continue with every change of the moon." When she stopped, I joined in with howls of my own. I didn't understand the full meaning of the song, but it resonated with me on a cellular level. It made the essence of my being vibrate in harmony with the bloodstone pendant. The mental clarity that came upon me was as though someone had removed dark curtains from my eyes, unclogged my ears, and opened my voice box to interact in a spiritual realm I never knew existed.

I howled louder and longer until I could hear the ancient howls of my wolf ancestors before me. I saw my dad in his wolf form next to me howling.

"Daddy!" I cried out before I was met with a large cold splash from the stream. I had somehow ended up toppling over into the stream and could only hear the insects and gurgling water in the night air. "What happened? Where is daddy?" I shrieked as I jumped out of the water to shake myself dry.

Granny Cary sat looking at me like a large grey statue. "When you become one with the moon, you have to remain in your wolf state. You young wolf somehow began to mix your signals between being a wolf and a woman." She stood and headed back in the direction of which we came. I followed close behind still confused by her explanation.

We ran silently back to Ravenwood and my mind was filled with split thoughts. My first few hours of being a wolf and my entire life of being a girl and a woman. Granny Cary went with me to Ravenwood Creek where I now sat overwhelmed. The new dawn was approaching and I could feel the same aches and discomfort from when I had initially transformed.

"Granny Cary, will it always hurt?" I moaned as I crumpled to the ground.

Before I could hear her answer, I felt myself entwined in agony while a warm and sweaty sensation came over my body. I heard an audible scream leave my mouth as I felt my human hands grope my neck, touching the pendant simultaneously. I sat up and saw small traces of chocolate-colored fur on my naked body and Granny Cary standing over me in her human form.

"How did you get dressed so fast?! Where did you find clothes?" I asked while trying to cover my body.

She smiled coyly and pointed to a duffle bag she had hidden in the bushes.

"A wolf runs wild, but a woman is always prepared."

SHELLY

THE RIDE HOME WAS AWKWARD. My morning began by being awakened by Miss. 'Stelle at 4:30 am. I was awoken in Anika's bed. I knew that bedroom like the back of my hand. I spent some of the best days of my childhood in the room. I looked down at myself, I was wearing unfamiliar clothes. They had to be hers, they smelled like her. At the edge of the bed was the UGA sweatshirt and skinny jeans I wore the night before, freshly washed. That meant Miss. 'Stelle had undressed and redressed me.

I instinctively crossed my arm across my chest. I took off Anika's clothes and slipped mine back on. I was trying hard to remember what happened the night before that would cause me to end up at Miss. 'Stelle's but I kept drawing a blank. The last thing I recall was getting dressed to go to Grandma Lou's. I shook my head at my discombobulation and picked up the unopened toothbrush she left on top of my freshly washed clothes.

I entered the hallway to grab a face cloth from the closet. It felt crazy being in the 2nd home of my childhood. I knew the house like I knew myself.

"I don't care how much it costs, I need more as soon as possible."

Miss. 'Stelle was speaking in a hushed voice on her cell. Her door was slightly ajar, so I pressed my body as close to the wall as I could so I could hear her.

"Anika fully changed last night, and I barely got to Shelly in time 2 nights ago."

What the fuck? I said in my head. *Changed? It's been 2 days?! What the hell was she talking about?*

I listened more.

"Listen, I don't care what you have to do to get it. I may be too late with Anika, but I can at least try to stop Marshella Jr. from turning into one of those dirty, filthy beasts."

I gasped and covered my mouth, but I was too late. I heard Miss. 'Stelle's footsteps came closer to the door. She swung the door open and pulled me into her plush bedroom.

"I'll call you back," she said without waiting for a reply from the other end and ending the call. "What were you doing sneaking outside my door? What did you hear? Why are you being so sneaky?" she fired the questions at me without giving me a chance to answer.

I immediately had a flashback of when I crawled out the woods the morning after the twins died. She did the same thing, yelled questions at me without giving me a chance to answer. But it was understandable then, her sons were missing and I was about to tell her that they were dead.

Today, however, was different. I wasn't that little girl anymore.

"What did you mean by change, Miss. 'Stelle?"

We both stared at each other, seeing who would break the hold. I won, she was defeated as soon as she stuttered.

"Wha... what do you mean?"

If I had a dick, my balls would have grown 3x in size. I walked closer towards her and her eyes grew wide. She wasn't used to this type of defiance from me. Each step I took towards her, she took the same back. That is until she met the edge of her bed. Standing nose to nose with her, there was nowhere for her to go.

"Dr. Howell, what did you mean change?" I asked her again, my tone more serious.

She looked around and realized there was nowhere to go. Dr. Howell sighed, she knew she was defeated.

"Marshella Jr, I'm trying to save you. I've been trying to save you for over 15 plus years now."

I raised my hands in exasperation, Dr. Howell jumped.

She's scared of me, I thought to myself. I squinted my eyes and turned my head to the side. I leaned in and inhaled her. *Am... am I smelling her fear?* Dr. Howell put her small palms on my chest to push me away, it was only then I realize that I was heaving and panting.

"Ok, ok," she cried in fear. "I'll tell you everything."

I stepped aside and watched Dr. Howell go to the drawer of the massive mahogany desk. She pulled out a tightly rolled cone joint. She extended towards me, I cowered backwards and shook my head no. I didn't trust her.

"Believe me, you're gonna need it, Shelly."

I still was apprehensive to take it from her.

"Look," Dr. Howell said, lighting it and taking a few puffs.

Who would have thought, Dr. Howell likes her some ganja. So did I, that was one of the things that bonded Ebony and me. I grabbed it and we both sat on opposite sides of the edge of her bed.

Dr. Howell began to talk, telling me the whole, horrid

truth. I know she was talking to me, but it was as if I were watching us. Intruding on a private moment. I saw Dr. Howell wringing her hands as she spoke. I was acutely aware of the trickle of sweat trickling down the side of her thin neck. Every few sentences, I would gasp or curse out loud. We passed the joint back and forth until there was no more.

Without stopping her story, Dr. Howell retrieved a box containing her stash and handed it to me to roll another one. By the time she was done, we had smoked 3 joints and had 4 shots apiece of *Tito's*. Also by the time she was done, she'd convinced me to get weekly shots and help her *save* the girls. I was given my 1st shot before we left the house.

Now sitting in this car, it was a hella awkward ride home. We had a plan and I had instructions. My 1st mission was to keep the girls away from any men, in fear of procreating before Dr. Howell could gain control. This would be okay with me. I want nothing more than to sink my fangs, no pun intended, into Montel. The second wouldn't be so easy. Keep the girls away from Miss Cary and Bernard.

I hated Bernard and he scared the fuck out of me. I don't know what my mama saw in him. We pulled into my driveway, and I saw Mama's truck. I know she was beside herself right now.

"Before I forget, here."

I handed Dr. Howell the vial I got from creole bull dagger days before. Dr. Howell formed the 1st genuine smile in the last 12 hrs.

"Yes! That ole wench came through!" she exclaimed, damn near snatching my hand off with the vial.

"What is that?" I asked her, closing the door and talking to her through the downed window.

She gave the most sinister grin and returned to the Miss. 'Stelle I knew.

"Hmm hmmm," she laughed. "This is the final piece of the puzzle that's going to change our lives... forever!"

ANIKA

I LINGERED at the creek watching the sunrise come up. Granny Cary was thoughtful enough to leave me with a faded floral printed mu-mu. I felt refreshed yet exhausted at the same time after spending all night as a wolf. I shook my head in disbelief as I replayed the images in my head. Surprisingly, I couldn't recall all the details as if my human senses weren't keen enough as my canine ones.

I roamed near the muddy water as the fiddler crabs scurried into their makeshift dens in the marshland. The salt-scented air and cool breeze gave me slight chill bumps as my toes felt the crisp creek water.

"Oooh-Ooooo,"

I heard the catcall come from my far left.

"Yo Dib! Ain't ole' girl yo cousin, yo?" Came the scruffy voice.

I whipped my head and saw 3 men headed towards me. I instinctively froze in fear, not having any weapons at my disposal and not feeling safe enough with the pendant as my only means of protection.

"Anika, girl what you doing out here looking like some-body grams?"

The familiar looking one in the middle called out.

"Dibs, that's Anika? Boyyyyy, nooooo!" Said the third guy.

I squinted my eyes and smiled when recognition hit my brain.

"Malik!"

I ran to my cousin and gave him a big hug. I ignored the other two as they laughed at me while splashing mud and water over both of us.

"Man cuzzo, what the hell you got goin on, why you out here so early? And why you got on GranLou house dress man?" Malik said, now hunched over with laughter.

I rolled my eyes at him and swatted at his arm. I felt self-conscious thinking about my previous few hours in my transformed state. I crossed my arms over my chest and wrinkled my nose.

"First off, shut the hell up! Second, I think I make this so-called house dress look sexy, ok?" I retorted trying to shake off my nervous vibes.

His two minions continued laughing harder this time holding onto their sides.

"Shut up Frick and Frack!" I snapped at them not really thinking the incident was that hilarious.

"Man, you remember my boys right? This here is Lil' Wes from the Bottom and this is Tram," he pointed at each one on either side of him.

I looked back at the two guys and shook my head.

"Wait, Lil' Wes as in Westavious? Oh My God, I used to babysit you at summer camp! Wow! You have grown up!"

While I reminisced on this memory he smiled showing his bucked front teeth.

"Cuh, dat been me! I ain't no baby no mo cuh! I'm a man now cuh, know what I mean?"

I halfway smiled at his attempt to flirt and run game and turned to the other one.

"Tram? What kinda name is that?"

He licked his lips and flipped his snapback hat to the side and started to freestyle,

"Them butches call me Tram, but them butches is flam, them butches be lookin for me and don't even know where I am, them butches do it for the gram, when I lay the pipe slam, them butches all say damn!"

I held my hands up and stretched my eyes.

"Ok, I guess you're the rapper of the crew."

I thought he was horrible but who was I to stunt his dream. His heavy Gullah-Geechee accent caused him to pronounce bitches as butches. He sucked his teeth and took off walking with Lil' Wes leaving Malik and I alone.

"Man, cuzzo I'm glad you home! I been meaning to come by and shit but ya boy out ya grinding!"

I looked at him and smirked. "Doing what Malik, you didn't even come to my Dad's funeral."

He shook his head.

"Nah, I don't do the dead. God bless the dead but I don't fucks with no dead."

He said it with such conviction that I believed him. He hadn't changed since I last saw him many years ago at a family dinner or gathering at GranLou's. He was the cousin that knew all the gossip or tea about every and anyone in town.

My mind quickly wondered if he had any idea of the magic that encompassed Ravenwood.

"So why are y'all up here at the crack of dawn?" I wondered aloud as we both stared out at the sun rays lighting up the creek and trees.

"Man shit, we come here to smoke cuzzo. Nobody is out this early and we like to get a start on the day. Tram gets his inspiration out here. I may or may not have a few transactions of business, and Lil' Wes, well he just like to ride out ya know?" He responded as if this was everyday business.

"What about you girl, you out here looking halfway homeless and shit. Damn, cuzzo what's up?"

I hesitated for a moment and then realized I needed a solid plan and alibi for when I went back for my car at my mother's. I had no idea what I was going to say to KB since he practically saw me disappear into the night. And Ebony had seen me in my wolf form, then I left her unconscious outside. I needed a cover and quick.

"Hey, you think you can do me a favor?" I asked hoping he wouldn't press for details. I was mistaken, however.

"Damn, cuzzo you come out the gate asking for shit! I ain't got much on me and we bout to smoke that shit now!"

"No, I don't want... ugh!! I need your phone, I have to make a call."

He cocked his head and pursed his lips to the side before asking,

"You ain't out here ho-ing is you?"

I rolled my eyes and held out my hand for his phone.

"I'm not a ho, Malik! Please let me borrow your phone so I can check on something."

He turned back to look at the water as one of his boys came back towards us.

"Yo! Dibs where the lighter, man?"

My cousin reached into his pocket and pulled out a Bic lighter and tossed it to him. He then reached into the same pocket and withdrew a cracked screen cellphone.

"Why are they calling you Dibs?" I asked while reaching for the phone.

He held it above my head watching me squirm and jump.

"That's my hustle name. Doin It Big!" He said proudly.

I stopped jumping and looked at him. "You're joking right?"

He sucked his teeth and slid his fingers across the screen unlocking the phone. He pretended to ignore me as the thick scent of loud drifted in and out of my nostrils. I coughed slightly and then cleared my throat as he handed me the phone while rolling his eyes.

"Yo ass can't even handle the scent! Man, city life done made you soft cuzzo!"

I shook my head at him and dialed the familiar number waiting for someone to pick up. As I waited I yelled back, "I only smoked with y'all one time and that shit was horrible. You remember that time when you and Ebony-" but I stopped talking when I heard GranLou's voice.

"GranLou it's Anika. Is Ebony there?"

I could feel the tension in the air as she hollered out,

"Greeead gawd gal where you? Ya mammy bout to drive us fool and ya cousin bun roun ya da crack teet and holla all night. Chile been pacing the floor wanting to get in the woods. We almost call the Ol' Buckra but Montel said he would handle it, him being police and all. He been out in dat dark lookin fuh hunnuh half the night. Whey is you chile?"

The guilt that washed over me made me feel small as I

tried to put on my strongest voice to reassure her that I was ok.

"GranLou I'm ok. I just needed some time, maybe the way I left wasn't in good taste. But please, please put Ebony on. I really need to talk to her."

Grandma Lou hesitated again. The next voice I heard was Ebony's. She had to have been standing next to her because she came on the phone quickly.

"Nika! Oh my God! I'm coming for you! Where? How? I saw... oh my God!"

She cried out unable to manage her thoughts or words. It almost sounded like she was in tears. The guilt blanket I already had on only seemed to get heavier.

"I need your help. Please come to the creek and get me."

Before I could get a response I heard GranLou,

"Hello, you still there?"

Ebony had dropped the phone and was already en route.

I mulled around the creek's edge tossing rocks into the glistening water and listening to my cousin and his friends talk as they smoked. They all watched me curiously and I'm sure fabricating a wild version of why I was out here without means of transportation. I heard the engines of 2 vehicles pull up and saw a large truck and a car come near the bottom of the old bridge.

"Oh shit, five-oh!"

One of the guys yelled as they tossed their blunt into the water and took off further down the bank. Malik tried fanning the air as if that was going to clear the scent and began walking towards me with Tram at his side.

I recognized Montel and Ebony as they stepped out of the cars. Montel had gotten out of his truck and still had on the same clothes as the night before from the show. Ebony was driving my Camaro, she came running out of the car with a pair of leggings and a large t-shirt. She had red puffy eyes and her hair looked a mess.

"Nika! Oh My God!" She said as she broke into tears as she hugged me.

Montel reached us and had a look of relief on his face, happy to know that I was alive. The detective nature in him took over as he suspiciously eyed Malik and Tram. I could tell his nostrils had already registered the scent of weed in the air. He looked around and noticed footprints leading from the bushes to the water's edge, then to the side leading up towards the bridge. He saw me shoeless with this old smock on and instinctively his hands went towards his piece in the back of his waist.

"Yo dude chill," I heard Malik say.

I glanced up in time to see Montel aiming his Glock 22 at Malik and Tram as both men had their hands up in the air.

"Put that shit away!" Ebony chastised as she yanked at his shirt super annoyed now, all the while wiping her eyes. "You can't come here in town and act like you're about to shoot up shit like it's the O.K. Corral! My family lives here! These might be my people! Damn!" Ebony shouted as she trained her eyes back on me.

"Eb?" Malik said quizzically as he kept his hands in the air.

Ebony yanked her head suddenly as if she just now noticed the two men. "Malik? I should've known it was your ass out here smoking this shit! I could smell it all the way by the gas station!" Her tone made it hard to tell if that was a compliment or a chastise. She turned back to Montel who seemed confused on whether to keep his weapon pointed or to put it away. "Montel, please! That's my cousin!" Ebony said again, this time with more whine in her voice.

He reholstered his weapon but never took his eyes off them. I reached towards Ebony to hug her on my terms but she stopped me and sternly.

"Oh, get your ass in the car! You got some explaining to do!" She spun around and stormed back to my Camaro.

I tossed Malik his phone who hurriedly showed it to Montel.

"See man, it's just my phone, don't want to turn into no damn hashtag. You know, cause Black Lives Matter and shit," he said trying to sound fake deep and political.

Montel shook his head and slowly walked back a few steps before heading for his truck. He went to the driver's side window of my car and said a few words to Ebony before rubbing his face and head. He got into his truck and left us alone by the bridge.

I got into the car and bit on my bottom lip waiting for the verbal lashing I knew Ebony was waiting to give me.

"You just left me there. You didn't even come back. You didn't let me know you were okay or where you were," she started as tears welled up in her eyes again.

I wasn't used to seeing her this emotional at all. I let her finish before I started.

"Ebony, I'm super sorry. I wish I could give you a better explanation but I can't right now." I then proceeded to tell her everything I could remember from when I left the show downtown, to arriving at my mother's house, the Wolf transformation, and my interaction with my Granny Cary and Uncle Bernard. I left out the details about being the actual wolf. One because I couldn't remember everything and two it felt personal, and I still needed to process those parts myself. When I was done, she was turned against the door in the driver's seat looking at me with eyes wide.

"If I didn't see you myself, I would've sworn your ass was smoking that shit Malik had," she said. "And to be clear, that big ass dog was you? Cause I saw your pendant."

I nodded my head wondering how this became such a normalized conversation. I looked in my backseat and saw my purse and shredded clothing tossed into a pile. My cell phone was in the cup holder and as I stared at it, it vibrated.

"Sorry, I couldn't figure out your passcode so your phone may be disabled," Ebony said, not looking sorry at all.

I typed in my 6 digit code and noticed I had almost 57 missed calls and almost double the number of text messages, mostly from Ebony and my mother, Estelle. My phone buzzed again, indicating I had a Facebook friend request. I clicked the notification and smirked when I saw it.

"What is it?"

"Not what, but who you mean?" I turned the phone around to face her.

"Malik DoinItBig Gregory, is he fucking serious?" Ebony said as she shook her head. "Why does he have that childish ghetto shit as his Facebook name, no wonder I couldn't find his ass on here!"

I laughed as I told her how I ran into *Dibs* and his boys this morning, which led to me finishing my story of Granny Cary and I transforming back to our human forms near the creek. We sat in my car for nearly 2 hours talking about the recent events and trying to piece together all the weird shit that had been happening.

As we got ready to pull out she said "Nika, I may have to go back to Georgia. I need some time to work out all this crazy shit in my head, I need to see my therapist something serious and I gotta fix this thing with my new job." Her words hit me like a Mack truck. I forgot we both had personal obligations and lives that existed outside of the new ones we were currently exposed to in Ravenwood.

While I had already made a long-term commitment to avoid my unspoken troubles in D.C. and stay in town on a month-to-month basis, I never fully thought about the plans Ebony needed to make for herself. As we rode through town back to Grandma Lou's, I looked out the passenger side window and I felt the tears begin to form and spill from my eyes.

ESTELLE

NOTHING COULD DAMPEN the mood I was in. Despite all the recent events, including my daughter completing her first transformation, Bernard being stuck in lycanthrope mode and Shelly being filled in on the entire magical happenings, there was still a sense of hope in the air. I was on my hands and knees during the midday sun, gently pruning the garden flowers. I designated space for various plants and herbs that doubled in toxicity and danger aside from their beauty.

In one section I grew daturas, also known as moon flowers. Its leaves gave off a hallucinogenic effect that could cause fevers and respiratory distress. Next to them were brightly colored pink poppies. In the front of the garden bed were the salvias. In small singular clay pots placed strategically between the rose bushes and gardenias were the jimsonweeds, both flowers when steeped in tea could cause intense visions.

I hummed a cheerful melody to myself as my fingers prodded the dark cold earth. The hairs on my arm raised and my heart skipped a beat when a low, creepy growl come from behind. Without turning my head I said, "Too bad I didn't save my chicken bones as a treat but I can round up some slop to feed the local mutts in town."

The large black wolf had come around several times over the last day or so whining and raising his paw as if to shake and I put together it was Bernard stuck in his transition. I jumped when he let out a vicious bark, causing me to tumble sideways, crushing one of my plants.

"Bernard Howell you better heel!"

The wolf cocked its head and resumed its stance showing teeth and saliva. No matter how many times I had seen a werewolf in person it always unsettled me.

"Sit! Heel! Sit Down!" I screamed several commands but the wolf just paced angrily back and forth in front of me like he was waiting for an opportune moment to attack.

Before the animal could decide to pounce or not, I swiftly reached into my bra and pulled out the vial Shelly had given me a few days prior. I held it out in front of my body and it did its intended work, which was to produce a protective force shield. Instantly the wolf yelped and got low to the ground timidly. The hostile atmosphere had shifted with the vial in plain sight.

"That's right, you mutt! Your ass better sit! That's what I thought!" I stood up and brushed myself off. Boldly I approached the wolf who was now on its side batting its eyes sheepishly and wagging its tail in a manner of defeat. "Now we both know how much power is in this vial, so don't think for one minute that I won't use it to turn your ass into dust or liquid or whatever the hell it does to destroy your kind." I crept closer and kneeled so I could pat its head "While I have this potion, you're going to be my bitch!"

The wolf whined and snorted.

"Oh, I know you're not a female kind of dog, but you're my dog and you will do as I command. Now I want you to sit!"

The wolf hesitated for a brief moment but then sat on its hind legs with its head down as to not make direct eye contact. Proudly, I wagged my head and clucked my tongue.

"Now that's a good bitch."

Standing next to the wolf, we were almost the same height. 5 feet 8 inches. Even while sitting, the beast was mammoth-sized.

"See, I don't know how long it will take for you to turn back to your unpleasant human self, but until then you will serve as my protector. When you turn back, let's not forget our special arrangement."

The wolf made a few puppy like noises indicating agreement and opened its mouth slightly to pant in a peaceful way. I continued tending to my garden all the while bemused at the power I held in the center of my bosom. The small vial containing some of the most potent and powerful witch's brew could transform or destroy any living thing. The only problem was, I had no idea how to use it properly. I needed to take a trip to the bayou to look for an off the grid Magi and then convince him or her to assist.

I continued talking to the wolf, "I wish you could talk so you could help me figure this shit out, Bernard but you had to go and get bibidi babidi boo by Mother Howell." Saying her name in a formal sense still brought on a full body chill and caused goosebumps all over. "I wish you would stand guard overnight to catch those thieving deers from eating my precious salvias."

The wolf didn't respond but whipped its head towards

the driveway. Its ears laid back, flat and poised for an attack. The low growl seemed to rumble even the darkest parts of my heart. I cupped my hand over my eyes to get a better view. A small dust cloud was forming, indicating a car was coming up the driveway.

I'm not expecting company. "Quick, get out of here you mangy mutt before someone sees you!"

The wolf swiveled its head towards me, bared its teeth then took off in one leap. The swift movement of the large beast frightened me and I pressed my alternate hand to my chest to ensure the vial was still in place. I stood with both hands on my hips once the silver Honda came to a stop.

"Dr. Howell, I hope this isn't a bad time?"

"Hello again Mr. Ramirez, what can I do for you?"

He made small talk which caused my brows to furrow but I smiled.

"Well I hope the real reason is for my tea, won't you come inside please ."

He looked around again, as if he was looking for danger and then followed me inside.

"You take yours with lemon and sugar?" I shouted from the kitchen. When he didn't reply I continued, "I take mine with rum on rare occasions or bourbon if I'm being fancy." I carried the tea tray to the sitting area where Mr. Ramirez was admiring the dark ebony-colored wooden clock piece on the wall.

"This is interesting woodwork. Haven't seen anything like this before. Is it valuable?"

I exhaled heavily before answering,

"My husband called it a Tribal gem, I think it's rubbish and belongs in a fire pit or thrift store."

"And yet it still hangs on your walls where your husband left it. Dios bendice la Muerte," he retorted while reaching for the cup of tea.

I tried to stop my eyes from rolling and pointed to the small recliner.

"Please sit and tell me what you need Mr. Ramirez."

He cleared his throat and sounded nervous as he asked if everything okay with Anika and me. The sharp gasp escaped my lips and the tension in the room got thick.

"I'm only asking because when I mentioned you to her she got very upset and practically stopped talking to me."

I chuckled and took a sip of my tea while motioning for Mr. Ramirez to do the same.

"Mr. Ramirez, I hope I'm not hearing what I think I'm hearing. Did you come to my home to question my parenting skills or to gather personal information on my baby, which is highly inappropriate, I might add?"

Mr. Ramirez began to cough indicating liquid entered his airway or he was afraid he had been found out.

"No ma'am Dr. Howell, you're an amazing mother and I'm a happily married man to my beautiful wife Rosita. I'm only concerned because I offered Anika the job and I just want to be sure I'm not coming between you both or inheriting any family drama. I know how upset you were when she chose to be a veterinarian over your choice for her."

To avoid my gaze, he turned the cup up and finished the tea in two large gulps. I could tell he was lying and was happy I chose to spike his tea with the freshly picked poppies from the garden. When his eyes focused again, he blinked several times as he peered at me.

"Mr. Ramirez?"

I held the notes for a few seconds on each vowel. He squinted his eyes before he spoke,

"AniChela? Is that you?"

The infused tea was working quickly causing him to see Anika instead of me. I cooed,

"Yes baby, it's me."

I leaned forward to kiss him. Mr. Ramirez hesitated for a moment, but an urge of euphoria swept over him as he felt my warm tongue explore the inside of his mouth. He leaned back on the small couch. There was no hesitation when I reached for his belt and slid down his trousers. I was pleasantly shocked with the caramel-colored erect appendage fully pulsating with each breath he took.

"AniChela, lo siento, deja que papi te compense," he uttered breathlessly.

I froze, unsure of what he said in his native tongue. When he saw my moment of confusion, he repeated in English "I'm sorry, let Daddy make it up to you." I smirked and awkwardly shimmied out of my gardening pants. I wasn't sure how long the aphrodisiac potion would last and wanted to get inside Mr. Ramirez's head for any information that could be useful. I tried to ease onto his manhood but shrieked when he slammed upward inside of me.

Is my daughter having relations with this man? I contemplated as I tried to catch a rhythm. Mr. Ramirez was swiveling his hips every which way like he was salsa dancing. He uttered all sorts of love languages to "Anika" and apologized for the earlier incidents. He brought up memories of her college days and even spilled the beans about their secret relationship that started in high school. When he appeared to be in a full trance, he slowed his movements and laid perfectly still which allowed me to gain the momentum. It had been a while since I had sex with anyone but even now as a visual imposter of Anika, I reveled in the warmth felt in my loins as his girth slid in and out of my womanhood.

I asked him why was there such interest in me. Mr. Ramirez opened his eyes, smiling, still hallucinating, "I love you." His eyes pierced mine as he confessed. "You were special. I didn't know at first, but once I got closer I knew it had to be you. I didn't plan for this, I had other plans, but I fell in love... with you... I... I..." his body began to stiffen and without notice, he exploded inside of me.

I continued to hover over him and his limp manhood, processing what he said. This was just a fool in love. It disgusted me that he was infatuated with a younger girl for years, my daughter at that. As I got lost in my thoughts, his hands shoved me downward.

"What the hell, Dr. Howell?! Oh my God! What the fuck?!"

He rushed to put on his clothes to hide that his skin was beaming a beet red. With a smug look of satisfaction on my face, I quietly sipped the remainder of my tea while watching him panic.

"Calm down Mr. Ramirez, we were two consenting adults."

He stuttered and tripped over the pant leg he was attempting to put on. "I saw Anika! I thought it was–oh my God!" He was tearing up and seemingly more afraid of Anika finding out than his wife.

"Well, this can be *our* secret Mr. Latin Lover Cradle Robber." I was grinning like a Cheshire cat. "I'm assuming Senora Rosita may be too sick to care, but Anika may not take too kindly to us... sharing." I slapped my knee while belting out a long loud laugh. It gave one the impression of an evil character in a fairytale. Mr. Ramirez shook his head and stormed out of the house. I continued to double over in laughter as he hastily retreated with his car tires spinning out in the yard.

EBONY

MY COUSIN TURNED INTO A DOG. I knew it was her. I knew the pendant and I just could tell it was her. After I passed out and was found by Montel, KB, and Aunt Estelle on the ground, Anika was gone. Just as quickly as she appeared, she was gone. I tried explaining to them but no one wanted to hear me. Montel gently grabbed me and dusted me off before grabbing me by the hand and pulling me inside of Aunt Estelle's home. All three of them asked me questions like what did I see, who was out there, but I couldn't gather the words to tell them.

"Ebony are you okay?" Montel asked. I was able to nod yes but I wanted to get out of Aunt Estelle's house quickly.

"Can I go home?"

Montel nodded and said that he would go pull his truck around the front. I watched KB bite his nails in the corner. Aunt Estelle seemed to not be panicked at all. Just 10 minutes ago when we first pulled up she was losing her mind and showing me affection that I've never seen from her. Now she seemed unbothered and defeated.

"Aunt Estelle, are you going to be okay?"

She looked me up and down and I couldn't tell if it was disdain or if it was pure hatred. What happened to the loving woman just a few minutes ago?

"I'm fine Ebony you just get home to Mama and make sure she's okay," she rushed out. All of this seems so long ago yet only happened less than 24 hours ago. Riding in the truck with Montel on the way back to Atlanta, I didn't know how to feel. I didn't know what my colleagues were thinking of me and where my position stood. I'd seen the video played on *Media-TakeOut* and *YouTube* for the past few weeks but I was able to put it in the back of my mind and not worry about it. Now it's time to confront this hurdle and see where everything stood.

"What you thinking about over there?" Montel asked me. I almost forgot he was there.

"Nothing but everything at once, if that makes sense."

"That makes perfect sense for you, Ebony Gregory."

I playfully punched him in the arm.

"Fuck you, Montel," I chuckled.

He laughed and told me to watch my mouth but in the back of my mind, I'm thinking I bet you do want to watch my mouth.

When I saw the sign say 10 miles until Atlanta my heart started to race. It was time to face the music. I had an appointment to meet with my partners at the firm at 3 and I had two hours to get home to get ready. Montel gave me the gentlest, sweetest kiss on my forehead before leaving me at the front of my penthouse. He turned back to look at me one more time before sticking the key in his own home.

Inside my house, it was just like I left it. I wouldn't call myself a neat freak, but I did need everything to be in its place. I got that from the flightiness of my mom. We weren't dirty and we didn't have a bunch of bugs, but our house was full of junk and things that she hoarded. It was so embarrassing to have people come over. So I promised that whenever I got my own home I would be the total opposite, and I was. Almost to a point where I was anal.

I jumped in the shower and washed my hair for the first time in what seems like weeks. I thought back on all the things that happened to me back home in Ravenwood and couldn't help but chuckle to myself. I felt like I was living in a movie, yet these things were really happening to me. My aunt was trying to kill me, my cousin turned into a werewolf, and I was seeing this beautiful woman and was given instructions on things to do. I had no idea who she was, but I felt compelled to listen to her and do everything that she instructed.

And then there was Montel. Montel more than showed me how much he wanted to be with me and how he cared about me and I can't say that I didn't feel the same. I was just afraid of hurting him. I don't have the best luck when it came to men and I don't want to do anything to lose him.

Montel offered to drive me to meet my partners at the firm but I told him I would drive. When I got to the parking garage my beautiful baby, my Audi Q7 was parked right in its place. I paid good money for this parking, so it better had been. I raised my hand to press the key fob and nothing happened. I tapped it against my thigh and tried again thinking maybe the battery had died and still nothing. I pressed my lips tight in annoyance while pushing the small silver button to release the fold-away key to manually unlock the door. When I turned her over she was completely silent.

I did it again and all it did was click. *Fuck*, I said slamming my fist on the steering wheel.

When I looked in my rearview mirror, I could see my back door slightly ajar. My battery had run dead. So now I did need Montel. I looked around for his truck in the garage but did not see it in its normal space. *Fuck*, I swore again. After looking for his truck a little while longer, I decided to pull my phone out and call an Uber. I did not want to be late for this meeting.

As I sat in the Board Room across from the three partners that had just made me one of their colleagues, I couldn't read their faces to see where this was going. Finally, Mr. Schwartz spoke first.

"Ebony, since joining this firm we can only speak very highly of you. You've been a great addition to our practice and help develop our Diversity Program. We're not exactly sure what's going on with you. We know you lost your mother young and you do have a family in South Carolina."

I held my hand up to stop him.

"Mr. Schwartz, are you firing me?"

He shook his head feverishly. "No, no the opposite actually. We believe that you could use a leave of absence. After looking in your HR file we've seen that you've only taken one vacation in the six years that you've worked for us. So no we don't want you to go anywhere, but we do want you better. The Firm has decided to give you a two-week leave of absence with pay."

I begin to smile this was too good to be true until I saw his face drop.

"However we do require that you have medical clearance before you come back."

Bingo! There it was! They thought I was crazy. I could

feel the rage burning in my stomach, the same place where it had been burning for the past couple weeks. Just as I was about to give him a piece of my mind for even questioning my sanity, I saw the beautiful stranger standing behind him.

"She needs you, you must go home," she said to me telepathically.

I scrunched my eyes and cocked my head to the side. Mr. Howard, the eldest partner, looked at me and asked if I was okay. I wasn't looking not at him but behind him over his shoulder. I quickly compose myself and told him, I was fine and that I understood. I looked at the other partners and they all seem to agree and give a sigh of relief. Surely they didn't think that I was going to be the angry black girl and air this whole room out but who could blame them? I stood to shake their hands and was handed an envelope.

"Before everything happened we weren't able to give you this," Mr. Howard said.

When I opened the envelope I pulled out a check written on our expensive stationery. It was a check written out to me for $20,000.

"It's your signing bonus we weren't able to give it to you after the news conference, but you earned it."

I could hardly contain myself. After extending me well wishes and shaking hands, I exited the boardroom and headed to the elevators. When I got to the first floor, imagine my surprise when I saw Montel waiting for me.

"So how did it go?" he asked me.

I shook my head and smiled. "What are you doing here?"

He shyly looked down at his shoes before speaking. "I knew you were coming to speak to them today so I wanted to know how things went."

"Well, it started badly because my car battery is dead so I

had to take an Uber but my partners have given me a two week vacation paid and I was giving my bonus for becoming a partner. The bad only thing is, I do have to have medical clearance before I come back but I'm not worried about that."

As if he didn't hear anything else I said Montel asks,

"Your battery was dead?"

"Yes my battery was dead, I got to the car and turned it over and it was dead. My back door was cracked ajar so it must have kept the light on."

Montel shook his head in disbelief. "That can't be right."

I looked at him like he was crazy, how does he know what happened to my car?

"When I pulled off from beside you this morning your car was secure. Do you remember that you gave me a key a while back when you wanted me to change your headlight? I hit the alarm to lock it. I've been meaning to give you your key fob back."

I made a mental note to make sure that I got it back from him. He said there's no way that my battery could have been dead because my alarm wouldn't have gone off.

"How did my door open? Did you open it?"

Montel shook his head again "No I didn't. Every time I come down in the morning before I leave I always hit the alarm just to make sure your car is locked, here let me give it to you now."

He passed me the extra key fob to my car and asked if I wanted a ride back home. I gladly took it but this didn't make any sense, why would my car be open? When we pulled back up into our garage I went back over to the car using the key fob again. I wasn't able to open the car door so I stuck the key in and open the back door.

What I saw caused me to let out the loudest scream that

I had ever produced. On the floor of the backseat of my car was a pickaninny doll, but the doll had the features of my Aunt Estelle. What made it even more frightening were the pins. One pushed into her head, a pin in her hands, and a pin in her heart.

ANIKA

GRANDMA LOU and I sat at the kitchen table as Mr. Ramirez slowly slurped up a bowl of homemade chicken soup. He had come unannounced, claiming he was coming to ask me about his job offer when a sickly feeling came over him causing him to vomit. Grandma Lou, always the caregiver rushed him inside and offered him some ginger ale and a bowl of soup she whipped up in record time.

I felt a little more cautious. My instincts were telling me his body language and story was off, but I couldn't pinpoint the truth. I had no reason to distrust him. He had only given me his heart the entire time I knew him so reluctantly I pushed away that gut feeling that screamed danger.

Grandma Lou looked at me and said "I'ne fuh kno you got job now! Gone, Gal! Dat be gud to keep ya mind from wonda."

I almost crushed her spirit by telling her I had left my real job back in D.C. when Mr. Ramirez interrupted.

"Well, she hasn't officially accepted... yet... I came by to offer a more competitive benefits package to help sway her in making the right choice." He emphasized benefits with a wink.

"When Gawd Bless Ya, don't question it jus say Thank Ya! He is still in the blessin' business oh yes he is," she swung both arms in short opposite circles as she began a quick hop to praise her God. She went to wash the dishes and put away the soup items when Josh whispered to me,

"Anika, I need to tell you something."

I looked at him and saw his face still had a pale look. "What are you up to?" I asked suspiciously. "Why did you stop here today?" he reached for my hands but I jerked them back and saw his eyes get teary.

A small alarm went off in my head and I thought maybe a bad thing had happened. *Was it his wife? Did she get sicker or did she die? Was he sick or did we get found out?*

"I just need... can I hug you, please?" he begged with a look so strained in his eyes it made me look away.

Grandma Lou had already moved on to her rocking chair back out front to finish shelling the beans we had started. I stood up and slowly crept towards him. Without taking his eyes off me he touched my hands, then arms and shoulders. His hands caressed my face and my hair like he was afraid I would disappear.

"What the fuck is wrong with you?" I hissed dodging the remaining of his touches.

He breathed a sigh of relief but a new constipated look came across his face. "I need to confess something." Before he could say anything else, my canine ears caught the faintest pitch of a high pierced howl. It was beckoning for me. It sounded like Granny Cary.

"Hey, can you confess this thing to me in the car? I need a ride to my Granny Cary's house. Do you mind?"

I didn't give him a chance to offer before I was out the front door to tell GranLou I would be heading out. I strutted to his silver Honda, the same one I had dissed him in front of recently and opened the passenger door. The seat was torn in some areas and held together by heavy masking tape and there were a few prescription bottles on the floor with the name, *Rosita Ramirez*. A tinge of guilt hit me, but I pushed it away as I heard the howling again. It appeared that neither Josh nor Grandma Lou was aware of the clarion call and I was glad because I didn't have a way to explain that.

Josh got behind the wheel and drove at a steady pace as I gave him directions. When we were on a long stretch of road he said, "I never meant to hurt you. I will never hurt you on purpose."

There was an awkward pause when I didn't reply because I didn't know where this was going.

"I know we haven't talked about seeing other people but Anika I-,"

"Whoa Josh, this is a bit much. Who you fuck besides me is none of my business. Besides you have a wife. I'm not stupid enough to think I was the only one."

Even as the words left my mouth I felt a painful jab in my heart. It was already bad enough I had gotten involved with a married man, but to think he had extra lovers made me sick and somewhat angry. However, I wasn't giving him the satisfaction of knowing that.

"Pull up over here, I can walk the rest of the way."

Mr. Ramirez parked the car over on the side embankment and looked around.

"I haven't been this far in the Ravenwood's forest before. This looks kind of sketchy. Are you sure you're ok?"

I rolled my eyes and pointed in the direction of the house. "Yes. I grew up in this sketchy forest. Granny Cary's house is right there down that path. You can see some of the front porch and chimney from here."

He leaned over and tried to see through the passenger window where I pointed, but shook his head. "All I see are spooky trees. AniChela, I don't like this. Let me drive you to the doorway."

I exhaled and nodded and he put the car in drive. It stalled a bit and then cut off. He restarted the ignition but the car went dead. The lights on the dash all flashed and he hit the steering wheel. We both jumped out of the car and went to the front hood.

"Please let me walk you at least."

I heard the third howl much louder this time and with wide eyes looked at him. He didn't seem phased. I shrugged my shoulders and when we took a few steps he doubled over again and held on to his side. He vomited the little bit of soup and soda he had just ingested less than an hour ago.

"Josh, I got it from here. You need to get home. I can see if my Uncle Bernard has jumper cables or anything to help with your car."

He nodded and stumbled back to the Honda, which was now making clicking and hissing noises.

Instantly a thick fog came rolling in, blocking the view between him and I. The Honda coughed a bit then started up and surprisingly the windshield wipers turned on. I tried to see if he was okay but heard the car slowly take off as I strained my eyes. I could barely make out the faint red color of tail lights as I tried to fan the fog away.

"This area is protected," the voice came.

I screamed and cursed inwardly as I turned to see the beautiful stranger standing beside me.

"Where did you come from?"

She smiled as she answered, "I'm always here. This area is protected. Come, we waited for you." She seemed to hover above the ground into the fog.

I had to speed walk to keep pace with her and felt the need to start a conversation. "Who are you?" I asked curiously.

"I am Khari."

When she said her name a sense of familiarity came over me and I felt safe and secure. I looked ahead and could see the fog dissipating. Lining the dirt driveway on either side were rows of trees that had blue bottles on each small branch. As kids, we always tried to guess what type of soda or beer the glasses contained as they never had a label and the blue was so pretty as it sparkled in the sun.

I could feel the roughness and hear the crunching below my shoes and recognized the broken blue crab hulls and crushed oysters shells imprinted into the dirt. It served as a makeshift paved walkway up the center of the yard to the front porch. I saw the chimney clearly now as dark clouds of smoke billowed from its top, indicating the old wood stove was at work. I smiled and had pleasant childhood thoughts dance in my head as the light blue shutters and painted blue porch ceiling came into view.

As kids, we would lay out on old comforters and pretend we were birds flying in the sky. Once we even tried to stand on each other's shoulders to paint small white clouds onto the open blue canvas. As I continued walking I noticed Khari had silently disappeared without bidding me a farewell and in the screen door stood Granny Cary.

"My child, come."

I could feel her smile welcoming me behind the screen. I hadn't seen her since we changed into wolves under the last full moon so I was anxious to ask her the many questions I had. We hugged each other.

"I heard you call for me, but you're in your Granny form."

"You can't always expect to see the wolf child, you are to be the wolf at heart."

I had no idea what that meant but followed her to the hearth where there was a small fire going and a cast iron pot sitting in the middle. We sat near the fire and talked for what seemed like hours.

Granny Cary told me stories about my dad and his siblings as they grew up and a lot more history on wolves and the Were's. My brain was like a Hoover vacuum and I tried to suck in every bit of information I could. She stopped talking and went to the cast iron pot and stirred the contents. "Venison meat, bone broth, chopped carrots, celery, onion powder, allspice, salt, and pepper," she said before I could ask. It was an old family recipe and a meal that I hadn't had in ages. My salivary glands went into overdrive and my sense of smell, sight, and hearing switched from human to wolf.

"Will my senses always amplify during certain times?" I asked Granny Cary as she picked up a plastic bucket and headed towards the door. I followed her around the front yard as she sprinkled cracked eggshells around the perimeter and reworked the area with table salt.

"You will learn to control all your senses once the change becomes you. Right now everything is on overdrive, *all* your senses," she enlarged her eyes and used her head to motion to my pelvic region.

"Granny!" I yelled quite embarrassed but she laughed and made her way around to the backyard. "Why are you littering your yard with this food waste? We could use these eggshells for a nice vermicompost pile," I said, trying to educate her.

She turned to me, "Crushed shells and salt is designed to ward off evil from the outside. This area is protected."

The way she said that last part made me think of the beautiful stranger, Khari. I quietly followed her as she continued to salt her yard and then came back around to the front porch.

"The blue painted ceilings, shutters, and doors keep evil from entering the safety of the home. It's called *haint blue*, a witchy kind of blue, only when used in moderation," she pointed to the blue bottles on the trees. "The blue bottle trees are used to trap and kill any plat-eyes or evil shape shifting spirits of the dead. It is our way, to protect the land and protect the family."

I soaked up all her knowledge like a sponge as she resumed her heritage lessons about the ways of the ancestors. I felt an ache for my dad. All the time I had lost as a child and adult by not being closer to my Granny Cary. She always seemed so private and shrouded in mystery, but I assumed it was the natural aging process and the fact that America was not her original home.

We went back inside and ate a bowl of Venison stew over rice. I had two servings and gulped down a glass of ice water as my belly sagged over my pants. Granny Cary told me more stories, this time about the Hag, a vampire-like creature that gained sustenance from a person's breath as opposed to their blood. The Hag would find a sleeping victim suitable to *ride* and would spend all night sucking in their breath, rendering them in a trance like state and at times taking their victim's skin like clothing. She explained how important it was to have every room outfitted with a salt shaker and hair-brush or broomstick. Instead, of attacking the hag couldn't resist counting all the bristles and would do so until morning. The sun would trap the hag without skin causing it to suffer and die. The salt would also serve as a barrier to ward off additional evil spirits.

Once we both were full as ticks, I began to nod and enter a dream like state. In my dream, I stood at a doorway at my old school, which was the area between the cafeteria building at the senior trailers, near the forest side. It was evening and the grass was overgrown a bit. There was a chain link fence surrounding the building with barbed wire on top. Entering the doorway represented an "escape experience" that was being hosted by 2 gunmen inside the school building. There was a single file line filled with people I recognized and others I didn't know but felt familiar. Ebony, my father Thad and even her Aunt Leola were also there. This went on for a while until I noticed a secret side door near the bathrooms. I tip toed towards the door and heard the gunmen yell, "HEY STOP!" They pointed their weapons towards me yelling.

I jumped up startled to see Granny Cary over me waving a lavender and peppermint infused sage stick over my head.

"Hey child, hey," she said more soothingly.

I realized I had drifted off into a deep slumber, outside was pitch dark. I grabbed my cell phone and sucked my teeth aware I had no cell reception. I needed to make contact with GranLou so she wouldn't be worried since I didn't make it back yet.

"I will send a message to Louise Gregory, you stay here

and rest child. This area is protected." She left the incense burning in a large shell next to me and went outdoors.

I felt disoriented and decided to walk around. I looked at my cell phone again to check the time and noticed it was half past 11 pm. GranLou would be up watching the *Late Show* and maybe wondering if I was ok. I casually explored around the home letting my eyes adjust to the darkened areas and tried to channel my wolf senses.

I felt so many emotions and feelings in this home, like it was a powerhouse for the magically inclined. I saw old family photos and paintings on the walls and came to a large door towards the back of the house. It was sealed tight and had a special brass lock with strange characters imprinted on the front. I reached out to touch it but heard a stern warning,

"Do not touch if you are not ready."

I turned to see Khari looking at me, shining more radiant than ever.

Ready for what? I mused looking now more closely at the lock.

I decided to take a picture of it so I could send it to Ebony. I hadn't seen much of her since she picked me up from the creek. I knew she needed time and space to process everything. I asked my question again expecting Khari to answer but instead, she smiled and placed one hand on my forehead and placed the second on my midsection.

In a fast paced vision, I saw Ebony smiling and spinning in circles as she recited what sounded like a poem in a strange language. The vision continued to spin and I felt dizzy and caught myself from falling as she removed her hand.

"Do not touch if you are not ready," she said again and let herself out the back door.

I was dumbfounded for a while, wondering why she had shown me Ebony. *What did she have to do with this lock?* This made me make a mental note to revisit my mother, Estelle. I had some questions for her about her family's history and any relations to magic.

ESTELLE

"You were special. I didn't know at first, but once I got closer I knew it had to be you. I didn't plan for this, I had other plans, but I fell in love..."

I REPLAYED the conversation in my head over and over as I stirred my now cold tea. I couldn't stop thinking about the way my body felt when Mr. Ramirez was inside me. Even though I appeared to him as Anika, I could feel every sensation. The warm fuzzy feeling, the physical pleasure and the start of a budding orgasm made me shiver in real time.

I was sad momentarily as I thought of my recently departed husband Thad and our lovemaking. He wasn't nearly as gentle and passionate as Mr. Ramirez but it was energetic and enjoyable. I imagined his thick biceps, broad shoulders and the way he would ravage my neck and breasts with his lips and tongue. An escaped moan parted my lips and I snapped out of my daydream when the loud clink of the spoon hit the side of the saucer.

Damn It.

My nether regions felt moist and was I surprised at the

embarrassment of self shame. I was living alone and a grown ass woman who still had needs. The sex between Thad and me had slowed down considerably before his death and I was never into self pleasing because I wanted to be loved fully by him. The complete connection between Thad and I was disrupted by one major stumbling block, my dead sister Leola.

I furiously shook this memory from my thoughts and got up to pour out my cold tea and wash the dishes. I mused over how ignorantly I missed the taboo love link between my daughter and her mentor, Mr. Ramirez. I needed to be extra vigilant in keeping Mr. Ramirez from being intimate with Anika. My thoughts were interrupted by a series of light tapping on the back door.

"Who is it?" I called out, wondering why someone would come to the back instead of the front.

No one answered. I quietly peeked through the Venetian blinds and gasped.

"Anika baby?" My voice was shaky. I tried to recover by clearing my throat. "You have a key, why didn't you use it, and why are you coming around back? I've told you time and time again, front door."

"Mommy?"

I inhaled sharply and stopped rambling. I was excited and afraid simultaneously to see my daughter standing there. I moved to the side and waved, gesturing to Anika to enter the home. Anika hesitated slightly before walking through the door looking around immediately as she entered. I held my breath as she eased past and caught a glimpse of an object near the wood line. My eyes squinted and as they adjusted, I could see the outline of an elderly looking woman staring back at me.

"Mother Howell?" I asked under my breath.

"What did you say?"

Anika brought my attention inside the house. I eyed her suspiciously and smiled.

"Were you in the woods?"

She stiffened and didn't respond. There passed a moment of tense silence between the two of us. I turned to look out the door again and didn't see anyone. I stepped out onto the small back porch and scanned the entire length of the backyard as far as my eyes could see. I knew in my gut I had seen someone. However, the harder I looked, my brain began to convince the rest of my senses that I imagined it.

Suddenly there was a sharp pain on the left side of my temple. I rubbed my fingers against it while closing my eyes.

"You still have those migraines?" Anika asked with some concern in her voice.

I plastered on a smile before turning to face her, "The stress of it all, right!" I re-entered the house and noticed Anika continued to put distance between the two of us.

"I would ask if you would like a cup of tea but..."

"So you can try to poison me or kill me?!"

It almost sounded like a snarl. I jumped back a little feeling hurt.

"Baby... I would never try to kill or–"

"Mommy stop it! How could you? Why would you?" Anika was now tearing up.

I stumbled going towards her to comfort her but she moved a few more steps now placing the oval dining table between us.

"Anika Emerald, let me explain. Please," I begged while wringing my hands and flexing my cramped fingers. Now was not the time for my arthritis or carpal tunnel to start up.

It made me feel old. It also made me look devious and dishonest.

"Explain what? You can't even admit you tried to kill me and Ebony the last time we were here!" Anika exploded. She faltered a little bit when she said last time because actually, the last time was when she transformed into a wolf and left Ebony passed out next to Montel's truck.

I placed my now stinging hands to my side to show I meant no harm and tried to calm her down.

"Please let me explain."

The fact that the word please was used multiple times didn't go unnoticed to Anika. As her mother, I hardly ever used the word as if it was a curse itself. Anika stood behind one of the high back dining chairs as she gritted her teeth waiting for me to explain myself.

"Sit down. I'll tell you everything."

I pulled out a chair and sat down still keeping eye contact with Anika. I closed both eyes tightly and raised both brows trying to ease the pain that was now slowing throbbing in my head. Under the table I continued to massage the palm of my hands, alternating from left to right while wiggling all 10 fingers.

My eyes stretched wide when the chair scraped across the dining floor as Anika slid it out so she could have a seat. She only did it to annoy me.

"I am your mother. I have only and always wanted what's best for you. Besides as a healthcare professional I..." I hesitated when Anika folded her arms across her chest impatiently. "What I'm trying to say is, when you were born, you had a condition. One that you inherited from your father. A genetic abnormality thing." I went on to explain that for years we spent thousands of dollars seeing the best specialists, even leaving Africa to come back to the states for quality care. "When that didn't work, I learned about some herbal remedies to help keep you and her brothers healthy and safe."

Anika sat stone-faced, I couldn't read her expression. I continued,

"The night you and Ebony came over, I used my tinctures and herbs to place in your teas but accidentally placed too much in. Blame it on my mind and not my heart. I was still grieving losing your father and just wasn't being careful."

For added effect, I used one hand to touch my left temple again and the other was placed on my chest which had now started to sting a bit.

"When you both passed out is when I realized I might've overdone it a bit. I swear Anika, that is the truth!" I stared helplessly hoping my daughter believed this version of my story. Anika looked deep in thought for a moment and asked,

"Did you drag Ebony into the woods?"

At this, my eyes widened as I stuttered, "What... I.... no baby! Sometimes hallucinations are a side effect and I'm sure whatever your cousin told you was just that." My head now throbbed, both palms felt cramped and that stinging pain in my chest made me lose my breath momentarily as I held my gaze with Anika.

Suddenly gripped with fear I watched as Anika nodded her head up and down while licking her lower lip. The room became silent and the only sounds that could be heard were the ticking from the loud wood tribal clock in the front of the house.

"Anika, I love you and only want the best. I've always taken care of you. I send you herbal teas and homemade vitamins to keep you healthy while you're in DC. I've been sending the same to Ebony along with my special mustard sauce she enjoys. See baby, nothing has changed. It's all a big misunderstanding. Just a slip of the hand. That's all." With this, I raised both hands to feign innocence.

The silence that came next made me even more nervous. I kept wanting to close my eyes. I thought maybe the events of the last week had me exhausted. I needed to get the proper rest for the upcoming work week yet I had so many questions to ask Anika but was afraid of pushing her too far.

Did she really come from the woods? Was Mother Howell with her? Did she transform fully into her wolf form? Did she have any memory or idea of what had happened to her? More importantly, why had she come today?

Anika pushed the chair back from the table causing the legs to scrape against the floors, a sound I loathed, but let slide.

"Mommy, does your side of the family practice magic? Maybe you won't lie to me about this."

The question took me by surprise. It shocked me so much I felt as if Anika fired a shot instead of asking a question. I jumped up from my chair placing both hands on my chest as if the proverbial gunshot wound was real. My chest felt like it was on fire. I tried to open my mouth to respond but fell backwards, and hitting my head on the table on the way down. Blackness swirled around me.

"Anika?"

I called out but on the second attempt, I fell silent as the darkness swallowed me. I was still alive but felt like I was in limbo, going in and out of consciousness as Anika made her way to me.

When I first came to, I heard her on the phone

exclaiming her mother just experienced a heart attack. It seemed the anger she had been carrying was immediately replaced emotions of worry and regret as my eyes closed again.

"Help!" Anika screamed, which caused me to open my eyes again.

I weakly reached for her when we both heard a voice behind us.

"Child, let's go."

It was Mother Howell standing in the back doorway.

"Oooohhh Granny please help! I think mommy had a heart attack, we need to get the ambulance here," I could hear Anika plead.

Cary Howell hobbled closer and threw a white powdery mixture that glittered into my pale face. A small puff of smoke appeared when it hit me and instantly I drew in a sharp breath but my vision remained cloudy.

"What the ffff-..." I heard Anika whisper as she backed away, leaving me helpless on the floor.

"Child, let's go," was the last audible sound I heard before the blackness enveloped me again.

What seemed like hours later I opened my eyes, staring at the dining room ceiling. I rolled my head from side to side on the floor looking around. Slowly I remembered my daughter being there. "Anika!" I was met with silence and a cool breeze that washed across my face from the open back door.

EBONY

I WATCHED Grandma Lou dance around the kitchen preparing breakfast like I've seen her do countless times over the years. Only age had slowed her down tremendously. Anika to my surprise was home with her mother. Montel and I had made the drive up overnight and arrived-just in time for breakfast. My grandma made it known that she wanted the day with her girls and that he had to get lost. He chuckled of course at her comment but was very much okay with obliging.

I text Anika to see where she was and how long it would be before she got to the house. I looked up at the old woman who had made a feast as if she was feeding 10,000 people. There were Roger Wood sausages, bacon, eggs, grits, and her homemade biscuits. Montel and I ate like we hadn't eaten before while Grandma sat across from us smiling at our enjoyment.

My hair started to itch, so I did the customary black girl pat to avoid messing up my tracks. Grandma Lou chuckled to herself,

"I never understand y'all churn with these fake hair and beaten' yo'self up in da head."

I laughed at her but then remembered I needed to get my hair done. It had been about a while and I wouldn't be going back to Atlanta anytime soon. "Grandma Lou, who does hair around here?" I asked her. Grandma looked off into the sky like she was deeply thinking.

"Oh, that's right. 'Leek gal do hair. I think her name Teagan."

I looked at her crazy, "Teagan?"

"She means Artesian."

It was Anika, she had snuck into the conversation and the home without us knowing it. I smiled immediately. It felt good to be near her.

"Do you mean that girl from Parker's Ferry that thought she was Beyonce?"

Anika laughed, "The one and only."

Artesian, or as we called her growing up, Tee Tee was this boughetto-country bumpkin who always thought that she was more than what she really was. But I was hardly shocked that Malik made her his woman.

Anika made herself a plate and sat down at the table with the three of us. We ate the rest of breakfast in silence but with her and I shooting daggers across the table, reading each other. When we were done Montel gathered the breakfast plates up and took them to the sink and began to wash dishes. Grandma Lou announced that she was going to her room to get ready for our day out while Anika and I retreated off to my childhood bedroom. I didn't say anything, I waited for her to speak.

My cousin began to ramble and rambled about her paternal family history. She told me that the beautiful stranger I had been seeing was named Khari. I didn't understand everything she was saying about the lineages though.

"Would you like to go with me to my grandmother's house? She can explain everything." At that moment there was a slight knock at the door.

"Come in," we both said in unison.

It was Montel. He walked over and gently kissed me on my cheek, I felt warm all over. He gave Anika a church hug and looked at both of us and smiled.

"So what do you have planned today?"

Montel rumbled through about 20 pamphlets in his hand. "You guys have so much history here I could sightsee for weeks."

Nika grabbed the pamphlets out of his hand and laughed. "Listen all you need to do is follow Highway 17 to the ocean and you'll have the time of your life today. GranLou really said that you can't hang out with us?"

Montel nodded. "That she did. She said that she wanted the day with her girls and I think it's a good idea."

I looked at him strangely but I knew that he could handle himself out here. Montel gave me a quick peck on the cheek before exiting the room and asked me if I needed anything before he left. I smiled and shook my head no. He kissed Grandma Lou on the cheek and gave Anika another quick hug as he grabbed his coat and left the house.

"So what do you have planned for us today?" Anika asked.

Grandma Lou turned from the kitchen sink where she was finishing the dishes. "Well, I wanted to go to the Farmer's Market..."

That statement caused an immediate groan from my cousin and me. We remembered the countless hours spent at the market, where Grandma Lou would promise that we would only be there for a few minutes. After talking to everyone at every booth, taste testing and shopping, 3 to 4 hours would easily pass.

"Oh, y'all hush up. Ya best tah be glad ya still got ya old grandma fuh be 'round."

Anika and I felt immediate guilt. It was clear Grandma Lou was in her last days, but we didn't like to think about it. We knew enough that we needed to cherish these times with her.

"Ok, okay Grandma Lou. Stop talking like that," I lamented. "So what else did you have planned?"

"Well," she started, wiping her hands in her apron. "Then I thought we could have lunch with my bridge club. Dey ask bout you two all the time. Plus we gotta eat."

Anika and I both nodded at that.

Suddenly, I saw a flash of light. I looked around to Anika and Grandma Lou, but they were none the wiser. Then I heard the drums, the same cadence from the night in the woods. Again, I looked at my grandmother and cousin, but this time they were gone. I was back in the middle of the circle, only the beautiful stranger wasn't there. The congregants seemed to be worshipping me. I moved my body to the familiar groove to the beat of the drums and began to speak in the tongue of the crowd. I would say a line and my group would reply. My body tingled, but I had a sense of, this is where I needed to be. I heard my name being called faintly,

"Ebony, Ebony."

It sounded like Anika but all I could see was my congregants and hear the beat of the drums. *SMACK!* Grandma Lou laid a slap across my face bringing me back to reality. I was out of breath like I was running a marathon.

"Ebony, are you ok? Where did you go?" Anika asked concerned. Grandma Lou was putting some ice in a wash-cloth for my face.

"Yea, yea, I'm ok. Yall didn't see them?" I inquired.

"See who chile? We been fuh call yo name and you was staring off into space, like you bun 'sessed" Grandma Lou said, gently placing the cloth on my face.

I didn't understand. One minute I was finishing my breakfast, the next I'm gyrating my body to the beat of the drums.

"Lemme finish getting dressed so we can get out of here," Grandma Lou said.

Anika and I sat silently at the table waiting for her.

The Farmer's Market was a pretty cool place besides Grandma Lou's antics. All the pretty colors of the produce, the different ethnicities of people selling their products. Anika and my's favorite part was taste testing but I didn't get to enjoy the market, because there she was, the beautiful stranger.

Without speaking or summoning me, I knew she wanted me to follow her. Grandma Lou and Anika were deep in conversation, they didn't even notice me walking off. She would appear, then disappear. Each time drawing me to wherever she was leading me. When she completely disap-peared, I looked up and I was at the back of the market. Instincts made me turn my head to the East and that's when I saw it. The sign read; *Monifah: Spiritual Healer.*

Her head was down, preoccupied with the cards in her hands. I walked slowly towards her and as if my presence gave off vibrations, she dropped the cards and jerked her head up.

"You..." she stuttered. She walked around from her table,

grabbed my hand, and pulled me towards her booth. I let her. When she was satisfied with us being alone, she pulled a cord and the curtains closed around her booth. Finally, she spoke again, "You found your way home, I see."

I still couldn't speak. She reached for my hand and traced the palm lines.

"Yes," she said excitedly. "It is you! We've been waiting for you!"

I looked at her puzzled, "Waiting for me? What do you mean?" I was so confused, yet I wasn't afraid of her. Any other person would be hightailing it out of her booth, but to me, she seemed harmless.

"You are the one, it's your time."

"My time?" I repeated.

But before I could get my answer, the curtain of her booth yanked open, revealing Grandma Lou and Anika not too far behind.

"There you go, we bun da look all over for you." Grandma Lou yanked me out of my seat so hard, that if I were a child, I would have thought I was in trouble.

"I'm right here Grandma...."

"I see now. Let's go," she said, cutting me off.

I looked back at Monifah one last time, only for her to cry out again, "It's your time."

Our trio left her sitting there, but not without Grandma Lou shooting an evil glance over her shoulder.

SHELLY

MAMA HADN'T STOPPED TALKING since she settled into the passenger seat of my car.

"Senior? What's got you so hyped today?"

Mama just smiled and squeezed my hand. "I'm just happy to hang out with you today baby. It's been a long time since we've had a girl's day."

Last night after dinner she and I decided that we would be going to the spa and to have lunch today. Money has always been tight since daddy went away, but we never went without or didn't get to do our little girl's day. I remember the days daddy sent us off with $10,000 to shop and enjoy ourselves. Those days were long gone, but Mom and I always found a way to splurge a little.

I pulled into the Roadrunner to get some gas before we started our day. That's when I saw him. At the pump across from me was Montel filling up his truck, but mama saw him before me.

"Why, if it isn't Mr. Montel, as I live and breathe," Mama said out of her window. Montel looked up stunned until he saw who it was.

"Well hello, Miss. Senior," he flashed that million dollar smile. "What are you ladies up to today?" he asked, turning his attention to me.

Showtime, I said to myself. "Well, mama and I are having a girl's day. Nails, hair, you know?"

Looking at mama, Montel said "You ladies look good to me. What more do you need?" Mama blushed, he was laying it on thick.

"What about you? What you got going on?" I asked him.

Montel sighed while replacing the gas nozzle. "I have no idea. Grandma Lou wanted the girls to herself today, so I'm out here fending for myself. Gonna see what all Charleston has to offer." Mama perked up at this comment,

"MJ, why don't you go with him and show him around," she suggested.

Mama had her own ulterior motives, snagging me a husband. Usually, I would object but this was perfect.

"Oh Mama, I'm sure Montel doesn't want me tagging along."

Senior cut her eyes at me, she could see right through my fake coyness.

"Actually, that may be a good idea but I don't want to cut into you guy's girl's day." Mama had already jumped out of the passenger's seat and was behind my wheel. "No imposition at all. We can have a girl's day anytime. You two go ahead and enjoy this beautiful day."

With that, she sped off in my luxury vehicle like it was a sports car. I made a mental note to chastise her about how she was handling my baby. I turned to Montel, who looked nervous.

"Everything ok?" I asked him.

He looked at his surroundings as if he were contemplating changing his mind. He looked at me and smiled. "Everything's great, hop in."

Montel unlocked his truck and I opened the heavy door to jump in. The manly fragrance hit me like a boulder. It was like it was summoning me inside. I heard Marshella Sr. in my ear as I thought about my approach.

Playing the damsel in distress will never go out of style. Men love to play savior. The more helpless, the better. But never, I mean never make them think you need them.

I did a couple hops and grunts attempting to jump into the high sitting pick-up truck. My 5'7" frame could have easily given it one good jump and made it into the truck, but I was gonna play the damsel in distress. After hearing one too many hmmph's from me, Montel dashed around the truck to my side.

"Oh, this is embarrassing," I said dripping with fakeness.

Gently, Montel put one hand on the small of my back, I made sure to deepen my arch to give an added effect. The other hand, I hoped would be used to prop me up on my ass. But to my surprise, he tucked it under my armpit. Like I was some damn child. I rolled my eyes but still used it to my advantage. I giggled and buckled at my waist, making sure my ass was front and center for him to glorify.

"That tickles Montel," I giggled playfully slapping his muscular arm.

He chuckled and watched as I put on my seatbelt before closing my door. Once secure in his seat, he turned to me and said

"Ok, where to?"

I was preoccupied. I was in a staring contest with Anika and Ebony's cousin, the mouth of the south himself, Malik Gregory. I rolled my eyes, releasing our connection, as I thought to myself, he'll ruin everything with his gossiping. I made a mental note to reach out to Miss. 'Stelle to see how she could help me with this.

I noticed the beach towel on the backseat and correctly assumed he was headed to the beach. "You were going to make it a beach day?" Montel nodded.

"There wasn't too much I knew of, and I love the water."

I smiled up into his brown eyes.

"Well, if you swing me back to my house, I'll grab my swimsuit and I'd love to join you."

Montel sat silently for a few seconds too long for me, then said, "Ight, cool."

I grinned and squealed because Marshella Sr. also always said,

Men want their women happy and giddy. Not sad, mean, and miserable. And it worked, Montel laughed before asking for my address.

Once we reached my house, my Benz was parked in its usual spot. When I reached our front door, the deadbolt was locked. That caused me to panic a little bit. Mama and I only put the deadbolt on at night before bed. I slowly and quietly unlocked it and stepped inside.

Immediately, sounds of love making hit my ears. "This heifer," I said under my breath, ascending the stairs to my bedroom. Whoever it was, was putting it on Mama. She was hollering and making all kinds of sounds I had never heard before. Nosiness caused me to pass my room door and make my way to hers. The door was cracked slightly so I could see inside.

He had the sharpest hearing because the door didn't make an audible sound but he heard it. He turned to me and grinned a devilish grin, he didn't stop or try to cover himself, it was almost like he wanted me to see him.

"What the fuck?" Escaped my thoughts and lips, as I covered my mouth.

Mama heard me and instantly jumped up to cover herself. If the shock of seeing them together wasn't enough, when he pulled out of her, his dick kept going and going. He had the longest, thickest dick I'd ever seen in my life. Standing in her doorway with my mouth open still in shock, Mama grabbed my elbow and led me to my bedroom. Once we were there, I yanked my arm away from her.

"Really Senior, Mr. Bernard? How long has this been still going on? Shit, did it ever stop?"

Mama slapped my face, I went too far.

"Let's never forget who's the Sr and who is the Jr. and what Bernard and I do is our business. What are you doing back here?"

I rolled my eyes and sighed. "Montel and I are going to the beach."

"Ohhhh," Mama squealed.

"Woman calm down, and hand me that brown one piece."

Senior shook her head furiously, "Ohhhhh, no ma'am. You will wear this." She held up a hot pink 2 piece that barely covered my private parts and a sheer white cover-up, that barely covered anything. I didn't feel like arguing with Mama, especially after catching her getting dicked down.

"Okay woman, I'll wear this," I said, snatching the swimsuit from her and stuffing it into my sorority beach bag. "Do you wanna check to see if your company is in your room with THE DOOR CLOSED?" I stressed the last 3 words.

Mama laughed, "He's gone already. Trust me."

I reached for my bedroom door, turning back one last time to her for reassurance. Senior nodded.

Once I got outside, Montel was already on my side to help me in the truck. I watched as Mama giddily watched from the bay window. But before I was gently lifted in the truck, I whispered to myself, *damn, that nigga works fast.*

Passing my house, which was not on the way out of the country or anywhere else for that matter, was Grandma Lou, Anika, and Ebony. You intentionally had to pass my house. And Malik gave them intention. Goofily, Montel waved at them. Grandma Lou was the only one to wave back. I was in a duel stare down with the girls. My gaze towards Ebony screamed *game on bitch*!

The beach was hot and muggy as expected. But the cool breeze off of the ocean water did offer a gentle relief. Montel and I shared small talk getting to know each other a little more. He offered nothing more than I could figure out on social media. But what did stand out the most, was how he felt about Ebony. I was so glad that my shades were of a darker tint, so he couldn't see my eyes roll at the sound of her name.

After 5 minutes of constant Ebony talk, I was ready to give him a distraction. Standing, I intentionally slowly pulled my cover up off and tossed it on my beach chair. I did so with my back turned to Montel and when I finally faced him, I got the reaction I was looking for. His mouth was so slack, 10 flies could have gone in and out and he would have been none the wiser. I bent over, displayed the 38DD's that I saved and paid good money for, grabbed him by his muscular thighs, and said, "Come on, let's get wet!"

I took off running and when I looked over my shoulders, he was on my tail. Before my toes touched the water, Montel scooped me up from behind and dunked me into the Atlantic Ocean. I stood up, my hair immediately began to spring into curls and saltwater was nose-diving into mounds of my breast.

"Oh, that's how it is?" I asked, giggling.

Montel smiled and threw his hands up and shrugged.

"OMG!" I screamed, pointing to the water behind us.

Montel whipped himself around prepared to fight off any crab, jellyfish, or shark if he had to. As soon as he did, I jumped on his back, toppling us both into the water. We frolicked and played for about another hour before we returned to our chairs and my oversized sorority beach umbrella.

We were out of breath from the jog back and realized we didn't get any water or snacks.

"I can run up to the gas station we passed and grab us some things."

I waved him back into his chair.

"There are always vendors up and down the beach. Plus, I'm not hungry, just really thirsty. Enjoying yourself so far?"

Montel nodded, "I really am. I almost backed out at the last minute, but I'm glad I didn't."

"Hello, we're with Bishop England High School and we're raising money for our mission trip to Costa Rica. We're selling drinks and snacks. Would you like to purchase some, we take debit too," the blonde Zack Morris looking kid spewed.

"See, what did I tell you?" I winked at him.

Montel pulled out a $10 bill and bought 2 waters and told them to keep the change.

I waved thanks to them and sat back in my beach chair. We watched the boys stop about 10 yards in front of us and count their earnings. Montel handed me the bottle and a bolt of electricity hit my palms. I took it as being dehydrated and needing the cool drink. But when I took the 1st swig, my throat burned like hot lava was slowly traveling down.

I stood trying to catch my breath. I took another sip and felt the fire inside again. My coughs got the attention of Montel, who was fervently patting my back. "Do we need to get help Mister?" The high school salesman asked. *Zack Morris* was frightened and stood off to the back. "I don't know Tanner. Maybe we should." I waved and shook my head no, I didn't want to make a scene. "Are you sure? Mr. B said that his donations were good and we should use them today at the beach and we would sell out. Let's go ask him."

Grasping at my neck I followed the boys with my eyes. Under a black umbrella, in an almost too small speedo that brought back flashbacks of the horrid earlier event, was Mr. Bernard. He met my eyes, smiled that slick grin of his, and nodded a salutation to me. It hit me what was going on and what I needed.

"Cccaaalll...." I fought to get my words out.

"What, what are you saying?" Montel asked me.

I pointed to my bag and put my pinky and thumb to my ear like a phone. Montel fumbled through my things until he reached my iPhone. It was getting worse and I was starting to get dizzy. I knew I was gonna lose consciousness soon. I got my password in after 3 attempts. I went to the notepad section and before I drifted into that dark place of nonexistence, I typed, *Ms Stell.*

ANIKA

MY SHINS BURNED and I yelped from the hard kick under the table. All the older ladies from GranLou's bridge club turned to look at me suspiciously. I recovered quickly by taking a sip of red punch then glared at Ebony who had delivered the blow whilst sitting across from me. Ebony had not eaten one morsel of food and had been texting me from across the table ever since we arrived.

Both of us received a group text from Malik which read, *some shady shit going on* and then there was the gut-punch of when we saw Montel and Shelly together. Ebony was trying her best to remain calm mostly out of respect for GranLou and I was trying my best to keep her calm by texting her.

Ebony: I'm so fucking ready to go
Anika: We can't leave GranLou, calm down
Ebony: That nigga tryin to play me
Anika: With HER skanky ass...we need a plan
Ebony: Oh I have one, WHUP HER ASS!!!

Anika: Eat something, blend in, GranLou and her posse' is staring

WE BOTH JERKED our heads up when GranLou called out,

"Dunnah is on da table, gon' eat ya belly full now."

She eagerly turned her attention back to her card playing while Ebony and I used our plastic forks and played around in the potato salad, green beans and rice with gravy.

I knew Ebony and Montel weren't official but seeing him with another woman shook us both up. I needed some fresh air and decided to walk out front to check out the surroundings. The meeting place for GranLou's bridge club was in a small shopping plaza that had connecting food and clothing stores. Ebony wandered by me and headed straight for the Red Dot.

"I need a fuckin drink," she said still steaming from earlier.

I started to follow her but my eyes went across the street to the sign that read, *Ravenwood Veterinary Clinic*. I didn't hesitate when I stepped off the curb and ran across the street to avoid oncoming traffic. I saw the silver Honda parked alongside the building and knew Mr. Ramirez was inside.

A small smile escaped my lips as I heard the various chorus of animal sounds and it reminded me of my job back in DC. I missed working with animals and maybe being here would give me a new purpose and a positive outlook. I was leaned over peering into a large saltwater tank when a young woman with a Spanish accent interrupted,

"Hola, you look to buy pescado o no?"

I turned to face her sitting behind the counter area and looked at her chubby cheeks and straight black hair.

"No, is Mr. Ramirez available?"

She looked at me strangely as if she wasn't sure of how to respond but tried to communicate with me, "You buy pescado. It good fish, pet si."

I approached the desk, "I need to hable' Señor Ramirez, por trabajo... me doctora." I cringed at my Spanish. I had taken over 5 years in school and still couldn't string together a decent sentence but the chubby-cheeked looking receptionist smiled and pressed a button that allowed the door to open to the back. She didn't bother to give me any additional instructions so I made my way down the hallway peering into rooms hoping to find Mr. Ramirez.

After I came to the 3rd door on the right, I saw him at his desk engrossed in work. On it, he had a few framed pictures of him and his wife Rosita. A decorative glass display case with a curved serrated silver knife, a grim reaper bobblehead that doubled as a paper weight and a green folder labeled R.E.D. took up residence on one side of his desk.

He was staring intensely at the printed document. He scribbled a few notes with his ink pen with his left hand and then used his right to peck a few letters on his MacBook. I admired him from the doorway for a few minutes and chided myself for giving him a hard time a few weeks ago. This man really had genuine feelings for me, despite having a wife.

I cleared my throat before my thoughts turned lustful. He jumped causing the folder to fall and the papers to flitter across the room.

"I didn't take you for the scary type," I giggled as I helped to pick up the papers.

He came to me quickly and I thought he was happy to

see me and was reaching for a hug but instead snatched the papers from my hand.

"These are important documents... why didn't you call before coming... how did you get back here... who sent you?" He was rambling like he almost didn't recognize me.

"Well damn Jay, excuse me! I didn't realize you worked for the C.I.A. I came cause you were almost begging me to come to this clinic!" I turned on my heels now pissed off again for the second time that day and started to march towards the front of the animal clinic.

Mr. Ramirez ran behind me and caught me by the arm.

"Anika I'm sorry! You just caught me off guard and usually the front desk buzzes me when I have a visitor and then I was caught up in my work and-"

"Well, those must be some important ass papers cause you almost took my damn head off."

I shot back, now with one hand on my hip. His hand was still on my other wrist and he pulled me in close and placed his lips on mine. I heard the papers flutter as they cascaded back to the floor. I started to give in but the sounds of aggressive barking from the room across the hall caused me to reassess my surroundings.

"Wait, I didn't come here for this."

I exhaled out a deep breath, trying to control my own urges.

"I came because I wanted to formally accept your job offer."

Mr. Ramirez looked at me and gave me a bear hug. I felt myself lift off the ground and got a little dizzy when he twirled me in the air.

"Yes! Yes! Thank You! You have no idea how much help we need around here. When can you start?" he asked excitedly. Once my feet hit the ground, I smoothed out my hair and widened my eyes. I told him I needed to contact the Licensing Board to see if they would issue me a temporary 60-day license before I could start. The looks he was giving me were of relief and passion. I knew only the animals had eyes on us right now but even that made me feel weirded out. I was rescued by the buzz in my shirt pocket, indicating I had a new text message.

I glanced at my iPhone and saw Ebony's name flash across with *Where did you go? I got alcohol and chips.* I one handed typed *ok, otw.* I looked back up at Mr. Ramirez who was now staring at me with his head cocked to the side.

"You ok? You seem a little off today."

He nodded his head and reached out his hand to shake mine, "Yes, let me formally welcome you to The Clinic. Now it's not as fancy as what you're used to up north, but we stay busy and the people here mostly want fleas and ticks gone. No major issues unless it's with livestock."

I furrowed my brows, "You treat cows and horses too, what issues do they have out here?"

We began a slow walk back towards the front desk. He began describing that something had been attacking at night, leaving gashes and injuring some of the larger animals.

"It could be local kids out here doing shit for kicks or it could be something else." He sounded cryptic when he said, "something else."

I looked at him, while my animalistic senses started to tingle. He started to share more but hesitated.

"Josh don't tell me we got Big Foot living out here," I said jokingly, wondering why he was so tense.

He laughed, helping break the ice.

"We just might, but I'm even more excited that we have Dr. Anika E. Howell living back here for now."

Instantly the mood shifted from heavy and tense to seductive and flirty. It had been a while since I'd worked with him so I just chalked up this behavior as his work mode. I did need to set clear work boundaries with him if we were going to be in close proximity.

He grabbed me and wrestled me into the supply closet and locked the door. I was terrified. He had a devilish grin on his face while coming at me so fast I couldn't even scream. I waited for him to attack but instead, I felt him turn me around quickly with one motion pulling my yoga pants to my knees while bending me over.

The initial entry of his dick was swift and erotically deadly as I gasped for air. The next series of pumps caused a fire to burn within my core that sent electric popping sensations across my skin. Mr. Ramirez was fucking me so good from behind that I didn't realize my nails were turning into claws as I held on to the wooden shelf. I was stuck between throwing it back and stopping for fear he saw. The wolf side of me was over powering my human side.

My phone fell out of my pocket, lighting up with Ebony and her picture. "Oh shiiiiiit," I moaned as feelings of passion swept over my core. Mr. Ramirez had a tight grip on my waist as he continued to pound into me. I tried my hardest to concentrate on retracting my wolf claws and hoped the animals who were now in a frenzy throughout the entire clinic would mask our impromptu lovemaking. What caused me to freak out was my reflection on my iPhone screen which was now dark. My eyes were yellow and glowing.

I stood fully erect and had to stop Mr. Ramirez from

recognizing these changes in me. "Jay wait," I said while trying to catch my breath. I kept my eyes closed tightly just in case they were still glowing.

"Lo siento, I forgot to ask for your permission, please forgive me AniChela."

I looked down again at my phone to check my eyes, with my eyes back to normal I sent a quick text. I turned to look at Josh who was also breathing heavily and wore a look of concern on his face.

"It's ok... thanks for the job... for putting in work... and I'm sure I'll enjoy all the fringe benefits," I said sexily while hurriedly fixing myself up to head out. I squeezed his dick as I slipped past him out of the closet and ran into the receptionist. She furrowed her brows and said something in Spanish while pointing down the hall to Josh's office. Embarrassed, I walked towards his office trying to plan my escape.

Once inside I decided to pick up the papers that were scattered and casually began to read a document:

There is proof that high levels of lycanthropic patterns are present here in Ravenwood. There are identified suspects causing this problem. They are genetically listed: XX, XY, and XY. The latter has been officially identified and executed per standard operating procedures by this senior officer. Waiting on final confirmation to continue extermination. Addendum: New suspect with close ties recently located. Will complete a thorough background review to determine if more members of the Anubis Order are presently active. Report provided by Ramirez Enterprising Dynasty

I made a mental note to ask Mr. Ramirez if this dynasty included plans on expanding the veterinary clinic or if he was getting into animal research. I didn't understand the content of the letter but before I could process any of it the receptionist entered the room, scolding me again in Spanish.

She raised her brows as she took the document from my hand and communicated in her best English that Mr. Ramirez was out of the building. She then led me by the hand towards the back emergency exit and pushed me outside, slamming the door quickly to silence the alarm.

I tiptoed through the high grass and weeds and headed back across the street to a staring Ebony.

"Okay bitch.... you lucky I covered for your ass cause Grandma Lou been asking for you."

She wore a smirk. Then she gave me a quick once over as I straightened my clothes and then the duck lips. All I could do was clear my throat and reapply my lip gloss as we both laughed and headed towards the car.

MY CURLS DANCED FREELY in the wind as the convertible's drop top peeled back. I glanced at myself in the rearview and saw my reflection with my *Dolce & Gabbana* designer sunglasses and signature Ruby Woo red lipstick. I was a beautiful woman despite my age. I leaned in closer to inspect, I thought there was a wrinkle near my forehead. Suddenly the music lowered as my car announced I had a call. I slowed down to put in my earpiece when the display read, Shelly. My breath caught in my throat when an unexpecting male voice came on the line,

"Mrs. Estelle?"

The voice seemed unsure.

"Yes, who is this?"

The car was now going even slower and my hair wasn't blowing as much from the wind.

"Uh yes, this is Montel, we uhh met briefly at Grandma Lou's. Well, I'm on the way to the Emergency Department with Shelly-"

I cut him off abruptly,

"What did you do to her? Where is she?!"

A small panic rose in my belly. I wondered what Shelly had gotten herself into.

"No ma'am it's not that at all. We spent the day at the beach and while we were talking she started to have some sort of reaction. Almost like an asthma attack."

I could hear a hint of concern in his voice.

"Monroe I want you to tell me exactly what happened!"

I had now pulled the car over so I could go in the trunk to search through the briefcase.

"It's Montel ma'am. We played in the water, came back to relax. We bought bottled water from some high school kids and then she started having an attack like she couldn't catch her breath or talk. She was able to type out a message for me to call before she passed out. Her skin started to look pale and so I grabbed her and started on my way to the ER. She is still breathing, but she is convulsing and foaming at the mouth a bit. She doesn't look good ma'am."

I found my stash of syringes containing the antiserum and got back into the convertible.

"Listen to me Maurice, I want you to bring her to my office. Do not take her to the ER. Trust that I know how to handle Shelly and her... medical needs."

There was a long pause and I knew that Montel was contemplating ignoring my request. I continued,

"Listen, I've been taking care of Marshella Jr since she was a wee child, I am a medical professional and her boss. I have her medicine with me and I could meet you and get this thing settled in no time. I need you to trust me. Bring her to my West Ashley office."

I rattled off the address and heard him sigh heavily. I then made an illegal U-turn and headed back down the highway towards my office. When I arrived, his large truck was haphazardly parked out front taking up two parking spaces. He was already at the passenger side, I could hear him talking to Shelly.

"Shelly! Hey, are you ok? Shelly!"

She was in bad shape. Her nails had turned into those ugly crusted yellow claws and her skin was an ashen color. I shoved past him and injected Shelly with the anti-serum while dodging her claws. I quickly turned to him to inspect for any damage. I knew she couldn't have turned him into anything as though she wasn't a full-blooded Were, but any scratches or bites would leave a very nasty wound or infection.

As I patted his strong muscular arms, chest and back I was relieved to know he didn't have any damage.

"What the hell?" he asked, exacerbated as I did one more once over on him. "I'm ok, it's Shelly that is in trouble. What did you give her? What is going on with her?" he fired questions rapidly.

"Excuse me, Mr. Maxwell, you better be glad I got to her in time," I said with an icy voice while using my index finger to jab at his chest. "What were you doing with her anyways? Aren't you supposedly with my niece, Ebony?"

It wasn't lost on him the way I sneered when I said niece. He took a step back before calmly responding.

"For the record, my name is Montel, ma'am. I'm just concerned about Shelly, that's all. Yes, I'm here visiting with your niece, Ebony whom I also care about."

The last part of his statement hit me like a ton of bricks. I would deal with that later. As I took one step closer to him I hissed,

"Well, let the record clearly show that I'm here now and the only person you should be concerned about is yourself. If you knew what I knew you would take that midnight train back to Georgia and leave well enough alone!"

He looked at me and raised one eyebrow wondering what I meant.

I turned back to Shelly who was now stirring in the passenger seat, moaning. Her skin was gaining its luster and her nails had reverted back to normal. Gingerly I lifted her lips to check her teeth and all seemed normal except her gums looking dry.

"What happened to her though?"

Came the booming masculine voice from behind.

"Shelly has a uhh... a condition that affects her endocrine and nervous systems. It's sort of like having a mixture of diabetes, sickle cell anemia and Parkinson's."

I was rattling off a series of medical diagnoses hoping it sounded scary and too advanced enough for Montel to follow or ask follow-up questions. The detective nature in him only pressed in.

"So what did you give her? Will it help?"

I rolled my eyes and turned to face him with a fake smile plastered on my face. "I never heard you say the two of you ate food, only took sips of water. Mr. Montel sir, a person with a low glycemic diet has nutritional needs and to have Shelly out all day and in the sun and saltwater has definitely done a number on her body. I gave her a prescription that is suitable for her needs. You have heard of HIPAA? That means I can't divulge any more information regarding her or what I give her for treatment as her primary care physician."

He gritted his teeth and looked over at Shelly who was now opening her eyes,

"Miss. 'Stelle... Montel... what's going on?"

I led them both into my extra suite in the back of the office building which had a mini-fridge stocked with snacks, fruit and drinks. It also had a small twin futon that doubled as a sitting area and some house plants scattered about. I contemplated locking them both down there but thought against it. I looked Shelly in her eyes as Montel went to fix her a small snack to eat.

"Miss. 'Stelle, it was Mr. Bernard. I saw him, I saw him!" Her voice rose in panic.

I shushed her and rubbed her hand. "Shelly, listen to me carefully. I need you to stay put. Stay here if you have to and keep this man here with you." I nodded at Montel who was walking back to us. "Do what you have to do to keep him here. I'll deal with Bernard." I stood and faced Montel.

"I'm going to leave her in your care. Feel free to stay here as long as you want. I don't recommend you moving her as motion can cause her symptoms to reappear," I lied. "I have a very important meeting out of town and I will check back in upon my arrival. Everything here is on an automated system so no need to worry about locking up. But I trust you will follow doctor's orders?"

Before he could respond, I pressed the button on a small remote that turned on soft pink LED lights, a humidifier with cinnamon infused essential oil, and a mini speaker that started playing smooth jazz. I took one last look at Shelly and winked seductively before going back to the car. *That damn Bernard! What is he up to?* I peeled out of the parking lot and made my way back to the interstate while navigating over my thoughts about his scheming.

SHELLY

HE WAS FIRING questions at me so fast I couldn't keep up, nor come up with lies quick enough. So in true Marshella Sr. fashion, I feigned exhaustion and said I would rather not talk right now. Montel, as I expected, gave in. After freshening my glass of water from the water cooler, he sat at the end of the couch and just looked at me. His expression was one of sorrow and pity. I didn't want or need his pity. I wanted him.

"Don't look at me like that, Montel. I'm not dying."

His expression didn't change.

"I just don't understand. Ravenwood is like a whole other dimension than what I'm used to. I don't know what was going on with you. Are you sure we shouldn't go to the hospital?" he asked genuinely.

I shook my head no.

"Miss. 'Stelle will take care of everything. What I do know is my feet are killing me" I answered, kicking off my Miu Miu sandals.

Instinctively, Montel picked up my left foot in his

masculine hands. The warmth of them traveled up my body. A moan escaped my mouth, I didn't stop it.

"Marshella," he used my real name. "I need you to tell me what's going on."

Too tired to fight, I began.

"A long time ago, I fell in love. Now that I think about it, it's the only time I ever have been. My love died, and on the night he died he had a terrible fight with his twin that ended with both of them dying. My love was Miss. 'Stelle's son. I tried to break up their fight, and while trying, I was hurt. Scratched, to be exact."

Montel listened without speaking, still massaging my foot.

"I didn't know until recently, and this you have to believe, that scratch would change my life. I never understood why Miss. 'Stelle took an interest in me until recently as well. She was my mother's sorority sister and my father had recently gone to prison, so I chalked it up to being a good sister to Senior. She would always have sweets of some kind or one of her homemade brewed teas for me. They were tasty, I was a child. Why would I turn her away? She took me in her home when my mother was away in rehab."

I looked up to see if he would react. He didn't, he picked up my other foot to massage it.

"She saw me off to college being sure to visit me once a month. I never paid attention to the timing. Anika and I were never the same after her brothers died. And we didn't go to the same college. Yet Miss.'Stelle made her way to me monthly. And I was grateful. It wasn't until the night of the crab crack that I knew something was wrong. I felt my body changing, I felt... felt off."

"You did disappear that night. Where did you go?" he spoke up.

I watched him gently pull each of my toes, then slide his masculine hands slowly down to my ankles.

"Miss. 'Stelle came and got me. I was changing."

I waited because I knew it was coming.

"Changing?"

He stopped massaging at this point.

"The Howells come from a long line of beasts. When my love scratched me, he transferred some of it to me. I was changing into a werewolf. Today, at the beach, the last of the full-blooded Were-men was there. Anika's uncle Bernard. He knows I'm afflicted and I don't know what he wants to do to me, but he used those boys today to get to me. Had you not gotten me to Miss. 'Stelle in enough time, I would have changed or worse died."

Montel stood up and ran his hands down his bald head.

"Are you fucking with me right now, Shelly? I've heard a lot of bullshit in my line of business, but this... this takes the cake."

I stood and grabbed his hands.

"I wouldn't lie. Especially not to you. I don't like or want this as much as you. I don't know what my life would be like without Miss. 'Stelle. She knew all along and went to great lengths to make sure that I had as normal of a life as I could. And for that, I'm forever indebted to her."

Montel looked at me with pity again.

"Do the girls know?"

I shook my head, "Not that I know of and not that it matters. Anika hates me because she thinks I'm the reason for her brother's deaths. And Ebony, she's loyal to Anika, so..."

Montel put my hands to his soft lips and kissed them.

"Damn girl. I don't know what to say."

I gave him a weak smile.

"That means Anika"

I cut him off.

"Yes, she too is a Were. But her powers far surpass mine."

"And Ebony?"

"As far as I know, she's fine," I lied.

There was no need to speak on what I didn't know or fully understand. All I know, my orders were to keep him away from her. I took Montel's arms and wrapped them around my waist.

"I didn't even get to thank you for today. Thank you for listening to me and calling Miss. 'Stelle. You can't imagine what the hospital would have done had I fully changed."

I put my lips to his, they were just as soft as I thought they were. Montel drew me in and his tongue escaped his lips and entered mine. He tasted just as sweet as I thought. We kissed softly and passionately for what seemed like forever.

Montel lowered me back on the couch and placed soft kisses on my shoulder blades. I ran my hands down his muscular back and did my best to catch my breath. He pulled my cover up over my head and kissed my lips once more. Montel pulled the string to my halter bikini top down, but before my twins could spill out we heard the voice of the unexpected.

"I KNNNNNOOOOWWW YOU FUCKING LYING!!"

Staring behind him, taking in the whole scene was Anika and Ebony.

EBONY

MY FEET WERE STUCK to the ground. And my mouth was sealed. In my head, I was screaming right along with Anika beside me at Shelly and Montel, but mentally I was elsewhere. After leaving brunch with Grandma Lou and her bridge club, we turned onto her dirt paved road, the car began to make a funny sound. The only reason Grand Lou's 1977 Pink Cadillac stayed in showroom condition is because when there was any small sound or jerk that didn't feel familiar, she was taking it in to be checked out.

"GranLou, you probably ran over something," Anika lamented.

She shook her head. "Uh, uh. I knows my cah. Sumpin wrong. Imma take em to Jiffy Wube fuh get look at. Steve always gets me right."

When we pulled into the yard, Malik and Tee Tee were sitting on the porch. I laughed to myself as I watch Malik rush to put out a blunt and Tee Tee fan the air. Malik ran to Grand Lou when we exited and gave her a big hug. I may have grown up in her house, but Malik made sure all us cousins knew he was her favorite.

"There's my sweet baby boy. Always on time, er' week fuh see his gamma!" Grand Lou exclaimed.

He stuck his tongue out at the two of us. We both stick our middle finger up at him.

"Heeeeeyyy Nika and Eb!" Tee Tee yelled, reminding us that she was there.

Anika walked to her a gave her a polite *hey girl* and hug. I followed suit.

"Oh, uh uh, you need to come see me and see me quick like," Tee Tee said, running her fingers through my tracks.

I rolled my eyes, laughed, and let the comment roll off my back. "You're right. When is your next availability?"

"Guuurlll for you, just let me know when you're ready. These hoes, I mean, I'm sorry Miss. Louise, these girls around here can wait."

Grandma Lou just sucked her teeth as she led us inside.

Malik agreed with Grandma Lou that she should have the Caddy looked at. Nika offered to drive behind her to make sure she got there safely, plus she wanted to take me to a new herbal shop that had opened not too far from her mother's West Ashley practice.

On the way, tailing Grandma Lou, Nika teased me.

"I knnnooowwww you didn't let Tee Tee talk about your weave like that. This chic has green hair, really?" Nika joked.

"Then she said hoes in front of Grandma Lou," I added, doubled over laughing.

"But that's Malik gal. Can't tell them they ain't the Jay Z and Beyonce of Ravenwood, chile!"

We watched our grandmother slowly pull into the Jiffy Lube and sure enough, Mr. Steve came waddling out to look under her hood.

"Bet Mr. Steve been looking under Gran' Lou's hood for years. How many times in our lives has she dragged us to this same Jiffy Lube?" Nika laughed.

"Girl you are sttttuuuupppiiddd!! Ew, you think her and Mr. Steve... well... you know?" I asked her.

She put her Camaro in park. "Is the word you're looking for, fuck? Are you serious? Pop Pop been dead before we were born. Your grown ass think all this time GranLou ain't popped it for a real nigga?"

I rolled my eyes at her and chuckled.

"Yo ass can be so crass sometimes, you know that?"

Grand Lou and Mr. Steve slowly walked towards us, we got out to meet them.

"Ohhhh, looka my lil gals. When ya grewed up on me like dis ya?" Mr. Steve asked. Same thing he said whenever he saw us together.

"Yet you stay so young," I replied, kissing him on the cheek.

"Looks like I need a new ah'tanatuh. Steve here said he can be in and out my girl in no time."

Nika stifled her laugh as I elbowed her to get it together.

"Okay, GranLou. Just call us when you're done, we'll still follow you home just in case," Anika reassured, as she gave our grandmother a quick hug.

"See you later," I said, as I gave her a quick peck on the cheek.

Nika thought the herbal shop would be a nice distraction to everything going on. It was a cute, boutique-ish, black-owned shop. We ordered 2 cups of Elderberry Tea while we browsed.

When the young waitress brought them, we sat at one of the tables.

"So now is as good of a time to tell you, but looks like I'll be staying around Ravenwood. I took a job at the animal clinic with Mr. Ramirez," my cousin admitted.

"Oh, that's what you were doing over there at the clinic," I teased her.

Anika tossed a napkin in my face.

"Shut up girl, but you're not all wrong. You know I had to get some while I was there. But when we were doing it I started to change."

"What do you mean change?" I asked.

"Like how you saw me that night. I saw my eyes and my reflection and they were getting yellow. And my nails started to curl," Nika explained.

"All of this happened? All while you were fucking?" I asked her.

My cousin nodded her head.

"What the fuck Nika? Can you control this at all?"

"That's why I'm going to see my grandma this afternoon. And you've got to come with me."

Of course, I was going to go with her, I'd go anywhere she asked me to. Anika was more than my cousin, she was my only real friend. I don't think she even realizes how much I value our relationship, but even more, her.

"Well, would you look at that," I exclaimed, rising from my seat.

Behind Nika's head on a plush purple pillow, was a bloodstone ring. It was like it was calling me towards it, because, for a moment in time, I saw nothing else but it. I lifted it from its home and slipped it on the middle finger of my left hand. It felt like a part of me. Nika, who had followed me, gasped when she saw it.

"Is that what I think it is?" she impatiently inquired.

"Is it glowing, Nika or is it just me?"

We looked at each other and headed to the register without answering. After we got back to the Camaro, our tongues were finally released.

"I always say the universe puts you in certain places, at certain times for a reason. I've been wanting to visit that shop since I got to town. But I needed you with me. Needed you to find your bloodstone." Nika surmised as she squeezed my hand.

My heart knew what she meant, the stirring in my soul knew what she meant but what did it mean?

Grandma Lou hadn't called us yet so we decided to ride around. Nika had it on *Sirius Channel* 47, the throwback channel, so every song that came on, we belted our lungs out.

"Ahhhhh shit!" I said turning up the volume. It was Adina Howard's *Freak Like Me*. We both sung in unison,

Let me lay it on the line
I got a little freakiness inside
and you know that a man has got to get with it

I had my eyes closed as I traveled back to '95 with my Cross Colors and Echo Jeans.

I don't care what they say
I'm not about to pay nobody's way...

I was singing alone. When I opened my eyes, I saw what silenced my cousin. Parked outside my Aunt Estelle's practice was Montel's truck.

"What's Montel doing with mama?" Nika said, turning into the parking space near the truck.

When I reached to pull the door open, it was locked.

"What in the hell?" Nika cursed. She looked around the corner where her mom usually parked, but the space was empty. She pulled out her keys and put her finger to her lips in the *shhh* motion. Nika unlocked the door, and the keypad of the silent alarm started flashing. She punched in a series of numbers and it disarmed. "Mama is so predictable. It's my birthday," she whispered.

All the lights were out, except for the light in Aunt Estelle's private lounge area. We heard voices but weren't close enough to hear what they were saying. As we slid down the wall, each of us on either side, we walked as softly as we could. I was on the wall that had the doorway, Nika opposite.

"I KNNNNOOOWWW YOU FUCKING LYING!!" My cousin yelled.

I stepped from where I stood next to her and saw what caused her uproar. Laid on the satin futon in a bikini was Shelly, kneeling, damn near with one of her titties in his mouth was Montel.

Nika entered the room and went off, I slowly walked behind her.

"Wait, wait I can explain," Shelly pleaded, trying her hardest to get her cover up back on.

"I ain't waiting for shit! Your ass been asking for this ass cutting since my brothers died and bitch you're about to get it! What are you doing in my mama's office anyway, fucking tramp?"

Nika lunged at her, but Montel scooped her up before any damage could be done. What did he do that for? Nika wailed into Montel with all her might, fighting and kicking. His muscular frame absorbed each blow.

"How could you do this to Ebony, you fuck boi, how could you hurt her like this?" Shelly, now cowered in the corner, as I blocked had the doorway. I couldn't move. My feet were magnetically stuck to the ground. And that same power took away my speech. All I could do was cover my mouth.

"Hurt her? HURT HER? I have done nothing but showed your cousin how much I love her!" Montel boomed.

"Love her?" Shelly finally spoke.

"Love me?" I could finally speak.

"Yes, love you but, all you did was push me away. I've loved you since I saw you moving into our building. But I'm a man, Ebony. All you did was play with me."

I couldn't answer. One, my hand had gone back to my mouth in shock. Two, Nika was back at it again.

"You're a fucking liar! I know this bitch, she's been a nasty whore since we were children. Just like her nasty mother!"

This caused Shelly to throw caution to the wind and barge Nika. The two women began to do the *Jerry Springer* hair pulling tussle. I noticed the hands of both women began to change. Their nails grew and curled. Their canines began to elongate and their eyes turned yellow. The "Ouch's and uggh's" turned to sneers and growls. I stepped in to try to stop the girls, but Montel tried to hold me back.

"Are you crazy? Do you see what is happening?" he pleaded.

I shrugged him away and proceeded towards the girls. Nika had Shelly pinned on her back and was prepared to sink her teeth into her. Her bloodstone pendant swung from her neck. But when I touched her to stop her, Shelly was lifted from the ground and was slammed hard into the wall behind Montel.

All 4 of us stood in silence, unbelieving, what just happened. Montel stepped forward but was stopped by some sort of invisible force field. He stepped forward again, but this time was pushed to the ground, defeated. Shelly let out a blood-curdling scream and pointed towards Nika and I.

"Look, look!" She screamed.

Montel looked up and was equally afraid as he backed into the wall.

Nika and I looked at each other and gasped. Around her neck, bloodstone was illuminated and a prism-like light aimed at the ceiling. The bloodstone on my finger was doing the same, with the same prism light. Only Montel and Shelly only saw the illumination of our stones. The prism light was for her and I alone. Our eyes traveled up to the sky and we both collectively gasped at the same time. At the end of her prism was a hologram Grandma Cary, at the end of mine was the beautiful stranger.

Night had crept up on the four of us inside of the building. We didn't hear Grandma Lou's call that she was ready. Didn't hear Shelly's phone ring when Estelle called to check on her. But who did hear everything, sitting inside the small silver Honda with high-tech listening devices, was none other than R.E.D aka Mr. Ramirez.

ANIKA

I HAD uneasy bubble guts as I made my way towards Raven-wood. I was occupied by my thoughts and about the events that had transpired. I barely heard Ebony telling GranLou that we were okay and we would be home for dinner. The entire drive was a blur. It was as if the bloodstone pendants had communicated with each other throwing us both into a state of shock, panic and causing all 5 senses to escalate into a frenzy. Despite all of this, I never noticed the silver Honda tailing me the entire drive.

It took Ebony punching my arm to gain my full attention.

"What?!" I shrieked as the pain sensors registered in my brain from the blow.

"Bitch if you don't calm yo ass down! And slow this damn car down! I'm fucking pissed too but I don't wanna die! Especially not before I get to talk to Montel and defi-nitely not before I kick Shelly's scheming manipulating bootleg werewolf ass!" Ebony huffed.

I looked down at the speedometer and noted I was going over 80 mph. I slowed the car down to a steady 65.

"I mean what the fuck just happened back there? Did you see that light and the Beautiful Stranger like at the end of a tunnel? I hope this isn't a premonition of the angel of death or some shit," Ebony continued.

I didn't reply because at the end of my tunnel stood Granny Cary and the feeling of dread scared me and made me want to get to her even faster.

"I mean the way you're driving right now I might be right. Damn girl, you are in SC, not DC!"

Ebony braced herself in the passenger seat as I sped through the 2nd red light.

"I don't know Eb. I do know my Granny Cary can explain. I didn't think your ring would activate with my necklace."

I was thoughtful as I checked my speed again, and looking in all my mirrors for signs of state troopers. The Honda had placed 1 car between us as not to be as obvious.

"Wait did you say activate? Like we Captain Planet or some shit?" Ebony started to laugh as she stared at her new ring with awe.

I exhaled loudly not being able to erase the feeling that had still overcome me. I couldn't believe the nerve of Shelly and Montel. Good thing we got there when we did. It brought back so many memories from years past when I had caught Shelly sucking the dick of one of my twin brothers while being fucked doggy style by the other. There seemed to be a lot happening based on the look on all their faces. It showed different versions of the same story but being the protective big sister, I felt betrayed by my once long time childhood friend.

"How do you feel now? Is your ring doing anything? Lighting up? Vibrating?"

I stole a minor glance as I tried to keep my eyes on the road. Ebony held her hand up and rotated her wrist, expecting the ring to project light or anything magical.

"Nope! It's just like a regular piece of jewelry, but it's so beautiful."

We turned down the lonely stretch of road heading to Granny Cary's and parked the car by the mailbox. We jumped out and held hands as the thick fog that had just appeared engulfed us. Slowly we moved, but this time with confidence towards the house. Just minutes later, I didn't see Mr. Ramirez slowly park behind my Camaro and get out to survey the area.

We sauntered up to the front porch and noticed how quiet everything was. There was no fire burning, no wind blowing, no wolf howling, absolutely nothing. I touched my pendant for reassurance and noticed it was cold and uneventful. I looked over to Ebony who seemed to be looking around in all directions possibly for the Beautiful Stranger.

I opened the door and called out, "Granny Cary?" We both were met with silence. The house felt empty which was odd because this place always made me feel warm and welcomed. We finally let go of each other's hands and closed the door. At that moment, we felt a jolt of electricity and our pendants shined a bright light towards the back of the house to the large door with the brass lock. We looked at each other, both recognizing the lock from a picture I had sent her via text messages weeks ago. We were being summoned by both Granny Cary and the Beautiful Stranger.

We ran towards the back and the large door was unlocked and inside we saw both Granny Cary and The Beautiful stranger sitting side by side on what looked like an altar of various incenses, oils, flowers and stones.

"Granny Cary.... Khari?" I asked as I looked at the two women side by side.

Ebony gasped as she took in the sight. She opened her mouth to speak but nothing came out. So she stood in the doorway staring at the scene.

I could see some resemblances between my Granny Cary and Khari. They both had flawless skin, except Granny Cary had scattered beauty marks due to aging. Both had high cheekbones, but it was the eyes that were exact. Only today it seemed the eyes were glowing a golden hue.

"Granny, what's going on?" I asked wanting to step closer but it seems my feet were stuck to the ground the same as Ebony's. Simultaneously both women spoke,

"I am she and she is me. I am Cary and I am Khari."

I didn't understand. The duality of voices seemed to overlap in a beautiful melody and it made both pendants vibrate and reproduce the bright light. It shone on the altar where both women sat and it was then we noticed a beautiful assortment of stones, all red. Again they spoke in unison,

"I am she and she is me. I am Cary and I am Khari."

I turned to look at Ebony who swallowed a lump that had formed in her throat. It appeared her ability to speak was granted.

"Wait so are we seeing the same thing? Am I seeing your Granny and the Beautiful Stranger who is Khari?"

Without hesitation, we saw the two women stand on top of the altar and they seemed to be like mirror images. Whatever one woman did the other did. Instantly they both merged into one being. They looked like a 3D hologram figure so we could still see them just as clearly as separate women. Again they spoke,

"I am Khari Howler, I am Cary Howell. We are one and now we are none."

Soon after the beautiful stranger disappeared and Granny Cary plopped awkwardly onto the altar bed. I shrieked. Ebony and I ran frantically towards her.

"Oh my God! Is she ok? Should we call 9-1-1?" Ebony asked with panic and fear in her voice.

I checked her for a pulse and found one. I could also see she was breathing but it was labored.

"Granny! Pleeeeease Granny stay with me! You have to help me! Help us!" I cried remembering Ebony was next to me.

She didn't open her eyes but she pointed her finger and we followed the direction to the collection of red stones.

"Does she want us to grab one?" Ebony asked still with her phone in hand ready to call for help.

I squinted my eyes, took baby steps towards the foot of the altar and touched the collection of stones.

"Oh shit! Anika! Look!"

With my hands still on the stones, I turned to look back at Granny Cary and she was now levitating above the altar. My eyes widened and I heard Ebony scream and then hit the floor when we both saw Khari lift into a sitting position from Granny Cary's floating body.

"Young Wolf, you will spend this moment getting your final set of instructions. It is your time."

She vanished into thin air. In the corner of my eyes, I could see Ebony sprawled out on the floor after she had fainted. I put my eyes back on the collection of stones. I felt a strange urge to sort through them until I came across two that were identical and lifted them from the pile. When I did, I heard Granny Cary's voice and saw that she was now lying supine and straight on the altar with her eyes open and her smile bright and wide.

"My Child! You have done well in this short time. The ancestors are proud. This area is protected and you are protected as long as you have your bloodstone."

She reached her hands for me and I rushed to hug her as she lay.

"Granny, what is happening to you? Are you... dying?"

She smiled and replied, "I am willingly passing my mantle. The Bloodstone will protect you but the Red Jasper stone will give you creative power."

She took my hand that held the two matching red jasper stones. I felt hot tears collecting behind my eyelids.

"What do you mean to pass the mantle? Granny please don't talk like that! I have so many questions! Things I don't understand!"

I was shushed and felt a warmth around me in the room. I noticed that every candle was now lit and the aroma became pleasant as the incense and palo santo wood was also lit and burning slowly.

"There are people who might say, the Families of Power are cursed, as cursed as the Kingdom of Were's, but I say together they create a legacy and a bond that must never be broken. The grimoire must stay with the family. It will be where you are. Only the Bloodline of the Enchanted can summon it." Granny Cary continued as she closed her eyes and I jumped when I heard a sea of voices chant like a mass choir,

I am one... from moon to sun... the blood will run... until it is done.

I looked around the room and saw the faces of many who were beautiful and had features that reminded me of Khari. I spotted Khari as she stood near Ebony's body which was still laid out across the floor and seemed to be in the way for someone to trip over. I tore my eyes back to Granny Cary and on her bosom was the grimoire. It was sealed shut and 6 of the 7 stones were placed on top. I remembered that when I placed my bloodstone pendant in the center the book opened. However, when I reached for the necklace I heard Khari next to me,

"It is time."

Instantly the stones sunk into the grimoire like it was in quicksand and the entire leather bound book vanished as the entire altar now became engulfed in flames.

"Nooooo!" I screamed as I looked around for water or a blanket to put out the fire but I couldn't move.

Everyone in the room slowly started to dissipate into the smoke that was filling the room. The smoke was not toxic smelling but had the sweet jasmine, vanilla and lilac fragrance that brought about a peace I had felt before. The last face I saw was Khari who recited

"Only the Bloodline of the Enchanted can summon it."

Just like a vapor, she was gone suddenly.

The blood curdling yell mixed with a howl escaped my inner being as I now stared at the altar that contained only ashes of what used to be Granny Cary. In the midst of my screaming Ebony rose from the ground and groggily asked,

"Who sprayed lavender lilac?"

I was now crouched at the altar in disbelief. My hands sifted through the ashes which were surprisingly cold to the touch. Everything from the incense, the wood, and even the stones were all turned to blackened soot.

"Oh my God! Anika, what happened?"

Ebony came next to me and whispered with a tone of

disbelief. Just then a cool breeze entered the room followed by a menacing growl,

"What y'all doing in here?"

It came from Uncle Bernard. He stood looming behind us like a large shadow ready to tear us to bits. He took one step forward and sniffed the air. Instantly his eyes darted between the two of us and then went to the altar. He rushed past me so fast that he knocked me into Ebony and we both fell to the ground.

"Mother! Mother! Mother!!!!! Aaaaaooooooo!!"

The sound of his howl was so sorrowful and painful that it pricked my heart. Suddenly he turned to us, eyes yellow and fangs protruding.

"What did you do?"

He lunged for us and at the same time both Ebony and I placed up our hands defensively to brace against the attack when we heard a large canine yelp and a heavy thud. We opened our eyes and saw that the light from our pendants was shining directly on him and it was causing him to writhe in pain. It seemed to have a paralyzing effect also so we both looked at one another and yelled "RUN!"

We sprinted as if we both were on the track team in high school and made it to the car in record time. We hauled off so fast that we didn't even see Mr. Ramirez sitting in his vehicle in the brush, nor his drone with wide lens camera flying overhead recording everything.

As we hightailed it off the back road, Uncle Bernard was seen in the rearview mirror chasing us in his werewolf form. He didn't recognize Mr. Ramirez either and without checking his surroundings he morphed back into his human self once realizing he wasn't going to catch up with us. He took one look around and sniffed the air again and disappeared back into the fog leading to the house as our car sped away.

As we rode down the road, I screamed like a banshee while Ebony tried to console me. I should've let her drive but I was too worked up to listen to reason. By an act of God, we safely made it to GranLou's house where we saw her sitting out front with Mr. Steve standing on the porch steps talking to her.

I came out of the car still screaming and Mr. Steve came running to me as best he could, given his bad knee. He caught me just in time before I ran smack into GranLou.

"Grandma she's gone! Miss. Cary is gone! It was horrible, there was a fire and ohhh Grandma!"

I could hear Ebony wail and GranLou hugged her. I felt my insides swirling and darkness approaching as I heard Mr. Steve grunting to carry me to the front porch. I vaguely remember hearing GranLou.

"Lawd I need to call 'Stelle. This chile gon need huh mammy."

The sound of a solitary howl was carried by the wind in the distance and everything went black.

EPILOGUE

THE CRUSHING FEELING NEVER SEEMED to leave my chest. The death of Granny Cary hit me hard, even harder than when my father had died. I sat at the head of the tombstone and draped my arms across while talking softly,

"Granny Cary, I don't understand. I've done everything exactly how you said and I can't find it or I can't do it."

The *it*, I was referencing was the grimoire. On her deathbed, Granny Cary told me that only the bloodline of the enchanted could cause the grimoire *to be where you are.* I had recited the incantation chant over a thousand times and had even tried it in various languages. Still, nothing appeared and nothing happened.

Uncle Bernard had already gathered all the crystals from the room besides the bloodstone and red jasper, but they didn't seem to do anything independent of the grimoire. I remembered going over there not too long after the public memorial service to inquire about the stones and the grimoire but was met with hostility and threats from my Uncle. Little did I know that in the wake of Granny Cary's death and for weeks after, Bernard and my mother spent countless hours scouring over every square inch of the house for the book. Estelle even tried bewitching the remaining stones but it was no use. I was unsure whether Bernard knew there was a chant that was supposedly the key to finding the grimoire. He had taken the stones believing they would lead him to the secret location of the grimoire.

One time I snuck into Granny Cary's house and tried chanting the incantation but was met with silence and dust bunnies. I also tried re-entering the room with the large door and brass locks but it was once again sealed shut.

I blew out a long breath and looked at the tombstone. "*Granny Cary, what am I doing wrong?* I stood up, dusting off my pants. I lightly gripped my bloodstone pendant and recited the chant once more, *I am one... from moon to sun... the blood will run... until it is done.* Nothing happened except the continual chirping of insects and the sound of birds singing songs to each other across the trees. Again, I repeated but with a little more force, *I am one... from moon to sun... the blood will run... until it is done.* Still nothing. Even the bloodstone pendant felt ice-cold to the touch.

"So what? Your ass a rapper or lyricist now?" came the slick response from Ebony as she arrived with a bouquet of flowers in her hand.

"Hey cuz! You scared me, girl!"

I greeted Ebony with a hug.

"What the hell are you doing out here anyways Nika, talking to yourself and all?" she looked concerned and nodded her head when her eyes saw the tombstone. "May she Rest In Power. Your Granny Cary was such a beautiful soul. I know you miss her dearly," Ebony stated matter of factly. "I came out here to clean off mama's grave and to leave her some fresh flowers. She would have a fit knowing her resting place looked dusty and deserted," she divulged as she looked towards the end of the plot where her mother, Leola Gregory laid. "What was that you were saying anyway, sounded like a poem?"

I shoved my hands in my pockets and shyly hid my face.

"Well not really... it's a chant."

Over the last couple of months, Ebony and I had grown close enough for her to know that I had lycanthropy genes and I knew she was able to see spirits and do a little Geechee infused magic. We didn't have any more joint instances of our stones interacting, however.

"Oh, you mean like a spell?" she said amused. "Anika Emerald Howell, let me find out you trying to do magic like your little cuzzo!" She punched my arm playfully and dodged me when I swatted back. "Okay say it again, let me check you out, see if I can pinpoint where you're going wrong."

I told her everything Granny Cary had told me about summoning the grimoire and what resonated most was that familial magic of some sort could make the grimoire appear. I didn't know the answer to that riddle and had tried the spell in various locations. I figured being at the graveyard where Granny Cary was buried may be the missing link.

After reciting the chant several times I cussed, "Damn it!" Ebony paced around looking for clues and thinking out loud.

"Okay, the chant sounds a little elementary, no pizazz, no mystery.... I don't know cuz... you think it's a code for something else?"

We both sat down in the grass and just looked around at the family graves.

"Okay you know I love riddles and this thing is eating at

me.... let me try to figure this out," Ebony said again before waiting for me to respond. I shrugged my shoulders and laid back to stare at the sky, while Ebony cleared her throat before chanting,

"*I am one... from moon to sun... the blood will run... until it is done.*"

Instantly swift hurricane force winds came from all directions and bore down on us. The heavy jasmine, vanilla and lavender scented fog encircled us like a thick winter coat and we both shrieked and grabbed onto each other. "What the fuck?!" Ebony yelled over the boisterous sounds of the howling winds.

I released my grip on her and noticed the leather bound grimoire appear out of thin air and float right in front of her.

"Oh my God! You did it! You cast the spell!" *But how?* I questioned.

We looked at the grimoire and noticed the small indentations on the front, the 2 brass locks and the large indentation where my bloodstone pendant went.

"What do we do? Is this wind dangerous? It's like a category 5 hurricane around us!" Ebony screamed at me.

We both took turns trying to open the book but it wouldn't unlatch. Even after placing the pendant in the middle, the book did not open.

"What now Nika?" Ebony started to tremble.

I grabbed both her hands tightly.

"When Granny Cary did this, she spoke calmly and it seemed to make everything less hectic."

I told her the words and Ebony looked at me for a minute, closed her eyes and recited

"Lape'... Lape'... Lape'."

Instantly the winds died down peacefully and the fog

cleared but still left little puffs swirling around us like ringlet curls. Once I removed the bloodstone pendant, the book vanished into thin air.

"Okay, what the fuck?" Ebony demanded with a little tremor in her voice. "Maybe you should try it, I mean it's your family legacy right?" Her eyes appeared huge.

I repeated the chant more than once and nothing happened. I looked at Ebony,

"You do it.... maybe because you know some magic, maybe that's why it worked." She hesitated.

"Anika you *are* magic, I mean it's the same spell. It should work for you especially. I don't know shit about this!"

I pleaded with my eyes and she let out a long breath.

"I am one... from moon to sun... the blood will run... until it is done."

The hurricane force winds started up again along with the thick sweet smelling fog. My eyes enlarged as I stared at her as recognition crossed her face.

"Anika..." she started slowly. "I thought you said only the Bloodline of the Enchanted could... but how? Am I directly related to Miss. Cary Howell too?"

Made in the USA
Middletown, DE
21 August 2022

71923723R00149